In the Grip of God

Journey into Corinth

Rob,
Stay in the Grip of God
George Cargill

A Novel

By

George Cargill

IN THE GRIP OF GOD BY GEORGE CARGILL
Published by Brimstone Fiction
1440 W. Taylor St. Ste #449
Chicago, IL 60607

ISBN: 978-1-946758-19-4

Brought to you by the creative team at Brimstone Fiction:
Rowena Kuo and Meaghan Burnett.

Library of Congress Cataloging-in-Publication Data
Cargill, George.
In the Grip of God / George Cargill 1st ed.

Printed in the United States of America

This book is dedicated to two men, my father and grandfather, preachers who never let age or retirement negate their call from God to minister the gospel of Jesus Christ.

George O. Cargill, Sr.
Porter T. Cargill

ACKNOWLEDGEMENTS

Writing *In the Grip of God* has been a blessed agony for me. I have heard of authors who could write thirty thousand words in a weekend. Not me. Days when I can finish a thousand words are sterling. After writing an outline and the first chapter, I laid the work down for a year. Then, each day began with the Spirit saying, "Write the book, write the book, write the book!" My faith being weak, I took the first chapter to Michael Ross, an author friend, and asked him to read the first chapter and tell me if I had been wasting my time. Michael continually encouraged me and eventually coached me on writing a proposal for publishing. As I continued, my wife, Jo, became a reader whose honest and faithful advice about readability kept me out of the weeds. Lisa Calhoun, the wife of a pastor friend, volunteered to edit the manuscript for grammar, helping with my difficulty with commas and the inevitable problems of consistency. At a writer's conference, Rowena Kuo of Brimstone Fiction listened patiently to my stumbling pitch and saw something worthwhile in what I wrote. I owe all these people a debt of gratitude. But I owe the most to God, Who must get all the glory.

TABLE OF CONTENTS

CHAPTER 1

ALONE

"I was with you in weakness and in fear and in much trembling."

–Paul

Dark clouds of fear and worry began to roll across the mind of Saul of Tarsus, known as Paul, the Apostle of Jesus Christ. Sometimes a squall line of anxiety would come over him for no apparent reason, sweeping out of a clear blue sky of calm to agitate his spirit. But this particular black cloud that hung around his mind had a source. Paul had been left alone.

Alone! The word itself sounded terrible in any of the several languages he could speak fluently. Aloneness depressed Paul, giving him a sense of impending danger. Paul could not live for long in a condition of loneliness. Infants die from loneliness, perishing from the lack of a caring touch.

Whenever Paul stressed over the cares of living, he sometimes thought that he would like to be a recluse, until the time came when he faced true isolation. Then, in panic, he would rush back to hear the comforting noise of people and to be near the troublesome selfishness of another human being. Lonely people live with a dark hole that they cannot fill. Paul had the comforting nearness of Jesus. But he needed a human in the flesh. He longed for his companions and someone to talk to so that he would not feel so alone.

Paul headed into Corinth on a mission that he could not accomplish by himself. As he walked down the Lechaion Road to the city, he grew evermore aware of the enormous challenge of bringing the gospel to that pagan metropolis. Truly, the entire world passed through Corinth. A colony of Rome, the city bustled with various kinds of people, citizens and subjects of the Empire. With all of that, it still retained its Greek flavor. The city boasted many warehouses that were transfer points for freight being hauled across the Isthmus of Corinth. Visitors from every part of the Empire traveled through Corinth to mix with the native population. Corinth had established itself as a cosmopolitan city like few others in the Roman sphere.

How could anyone here ever understand the cross of Jesus? Would they embrace the resurrection of Jesus Christ, or would they scoff at him as the elite thinkers did at the Areopagus in Athens? The whole life of the population succumbed to the flesh. Men, and many women, fulfilled their religious obligation by engaging prostitutes at the temple. Who could convince them to lust for holiness? The common people were completely in the grip of idolatry. The gods of metal, wood, and stone were something that they could see, touch and kiss. In every household, rich and poor, there were shrines to these gods. Sometimes it was just a shelf before which they could stand and burn some incense as they muttered a prayer to something that never changed expression or answered them. In the homes of the prosperous there might be an entire room dedicated to their gods. Who could convince them of the truth? He reassured himself that someday every knee would bow to the Lord Jesus Christ. Now, however, he remained alone, and the knee of Corinth was unbending.

Paul muttered words of supplication as he walked along the road into Corinth. He cared not that anyone heard him. Besides, he very much appeared the Jew with his Hebrew *chiton*, mantle distinctively marked with the gamma pattern, a rolled-up pallet of straw for a bed, a great bottle-shaped basket slung over his back in which he carried provisions, and the curls that dropped down over his ears. A headpiece protected his balding head from the Mediterranean sun. A curly, untrimmed, graying beard flowed down over his chest. Jewish travelers were conspicuous and often ridiculed. If someone noticed and laughed that he talked to himself, Paul ignored their sidelong glances knowing that his countrymen often suffered in the same way.

Paul had just passed through the great wall that surrounded Corinth. The six-mile course of that wall was only interrupted by a great mass of rock called Acrocorinth which dominated the landscape. Topping this mountain stood the temple of Aphrodite, goddess of love, the patron god of Corinth. From this temple, a thousand prostitutes served their god. The wall of Corinth reminded Paul of the low wall that surrounded the Courts of the Hebrews at the Temple of Jerusalem. At those unguarded openings in the wall were inscribed warnings that proscribed death to any Gentile who wanted to worship the God of Abraham but profaned the holy ground by passing through that waist high wall of hostility. No such warnings were inscribed, or penalty provided at Corinth, the city of immorality. Any who wished were welcomed to enter the gate and join flesh with a priest or priestess of love.

"The blood of Jesus has abolished the wall of hostility between us and the Gentiles. All may enter into the holy presence of God and receive grace. Hallelujah!" Paul spoke this through his teeth in Aramaic, increasingly conscious of others on the road.

Traffic increased as he neared the city proper. Buildings that housed markets, brothels, homes, bath houses, and shops lined the road. Carts, horses, chariots, litters, and many pedestrians filled the wide rock pavement. The sidewalks held groups of people conversing. Paul saw sailors, tradesmen, soldiers, farmers, prostitutes, and laborers, many slaves of various occupations, people from every part of the Empire. He saw one of the rich ladies of Corinth walking along with a female slave holding a sunshade over her head. Words and sounds of a multitude of languages intermixed with the common Greek language of the eastern Mediterranean. The noise of this great Achaean city was indescribable.

As beautiful and prosperous as this Gentile city appeared, it persisted as a sewer of depravity. Paul had difficulty understanding the powerful grip that idolatry had on the common folks. It was easier to understand the attitude of some of the elite classes who acknowledged the Pantheon but did not believe a bit of it. He fully understood those who ruled and used religion to control the masses. But it was obvious that all people of Corinth were under the grip of the flesh. And never was the bondage so great and the grip of the flesh so tight as in this city that Paul hoped to evangelize.

He kept on the lookout for any other Jews. If he spotted them first he might be able to guard himself against being assaulted by any who may have followed him from Macedonia. As a natural Roman citizen, he had the protection of the courts. But the streets were a different story. Almost all his fellow Jews had treated him with respect. But there were a few ...

Sosthenes, among those who persecuted him, was the worst and leader of them all. He had pursued Paul from Galatia to Macedonia with the same fervor with which Paul pursed the followers of Jesus before he was struck down on the road as he neared Damascus. He wondered if Sosthenes had obtained a warrant for his arrest from the religious authorities in Jerusalem similar to the ones Paul had carried for the Christians at Damascus.

As Paul thought of these things, the basket over his back seemed to chafe against the scars of the beatings he had suffered at the instigation of former persecutors. He wanted to avoid contact with other Jews as much as possible until he could enter the synagogue where the ruler would be anxious to avoid any trouble or disturbance. A Jewish man had rights there. In the synagogue, on the Sabbath, he would be safe, but, in public he was vulnerable.

As Paul approached the center of the city, the temple of Apollo on his right loomed over the other nearby structures. He passed by the *macella,* the meat market, crowded with vendors, priests, butchers, shoppers, and the intermixed smells of blood and decaying meat. All cities have their smells, but to become accustomed to the odor of Corinth would take some time. He entered the Peribolos of Apollo, a vast colonnaded pavilion that served as a shelter from the sun and rain showers. Although an assault on the nose, Corinth equally offered a feast for the eyes with its grand architecture and majestic Roman look. The Romans had destroyed the city during the Achaean league rebellion, and the city had lain in ruins for one hundred years. Then, Julius Caesar had rebuilt the city as a colony one hundred years prior to the time that Paul stood in the Peribolos, where it reclaimed its reputation of being one of the most immoral and decadent cities since Sodom. Corinth allured the favor of Emperors who delighted in perversion.

Paul paused before the statue of Apollo and looked up at the cold marble visage. *"Praise be to the living God, Jehovah, the God of Abraham, Isaac, Jacob, Joseph, Moses, and the prophets."* Paul's prayer went up silently. *"And to the Son, Jesus, who gives me eternal life. How did it come about that mankind thought that they could trade the glory of the invisible God for things that their hands made? Worshiping created things instead of the Creator? What fools!"*

He turned and continued through the Peribolos and descended into an adjacent courtyard where a lovely fountain flowed, called the *Fountain of Peirene.* A spring housed by a marble structure fed the large open well area through six arched openings. An inscription read:

"Drink here where Pegasus slaked his thirst. Give thanks to his father Poseidon the god of water and his mother Medusa the Gorgon."

Paul felt no rumbling of conscience as he took a cup out of his basket and dipped into what some would call consecrated water. He washed his hands in the customary Jewish way and then dipped his cup again and took a long drink. It was the best water that he had tasted in a long time. He splashed some on his face, and it trickled in little rivulets down his beard and sprinkled a few drops on his dusty sandaled toes. It reminded him that he had no place to wash his feet and lodge. He looked forward to finding a good bath house. Plenty of time remained in the day, though, and if he had to, he could stay in the basilica. His dwindling purse told him, however, that he must find some employment and inexpensive lodgings soon. He took another long drink of the cool spring water.

"Nothing like it," Paul muttered as he took a breath between gulps. "Living water."

I am the water of life, he could almost hear the sonorous voice of Messiah as they had communed in the arid desert of Arabia. Paul's lips had been cracking and his tongue was parched with thirst. He had pleaded with the Master for some cool spring water, living water. *Saul,* Jesus had said to him, *if you will drink of me, out of your insides will come an everlasting spring that will supply all the living water you will ever need.*

"I thank the living God for this living water." Paul turned from the fountain, patted his lips and beard dry with the edge of his chiton and walked out of the courtyard into the open Agora. As he exited, he looked straight across the forum at the Bema, the judgment seat of the court. He could see that the tribunal was in session. He strode briskly over the pavement toward the placards that held public notices and the docket. He read that Gallio the proconsul was presiding.

Paul continued to the area of the market vendors. As he walked away from the Bema, the Lectors began carrying out the sentence of the court by beating some miscreant. The man had been stripped of his clothing and danced over the pavement with every blow. The surrounding crowd hooted and yelled their approval. The man screamed in high pitched little yelps as the officers of the court flailed him with wooden rods. Paul paused with the rest of the crowd to watch. The man flopped on the forum floor and curled up in a fetal position while trying to protect his genitals with his hands. Paul felt his stomach knot up as he remembered the blows and the humiliation of being stripped and beaten in the Agora in Philippi.

"Please, Lord, no more beatings, I am afraid that I can bear no more."

It was not the first time that Paul had prayed like this. The prayer had barely gone up when a vision of an angelic face came to Paul's mind. Immediately stones smashed away the face of Stephen. On that awful day in Jerusalem, he had helped murder an innocent man by carrying out the unjust sentence of an illegal court with mob action. That face floated through his thoughts in the day and flooded his dreams at night. Paul was shaken out of these thoughts by the man on the pavement who cried and urinated uncontrollably. The crowd imitated his sobs and laughed maniacally. Paul turned away from the spectacle, trembling with disgust and fear.

He kept walking until he was among the various vendors that were set up in the Agora, completely distracted by what he had witnessed. He walked aimlessly among the booths containing products of every description. Paul ignored the noisy hawking of the merchants. Business seemed to be very good. The Agora was crowded, and people moved about like ants in a heap, causing the casual observer to wonder what all these people could be doing. He began looking around for something that he could eat. Fresh vegetables, bread, cooked foods, clothing, perfumes, furnishings, jewelry, wine, herbal medicines, pottery of all kinds, footwear, doves, and other small livestock were melded together in Paul's senses with colors, smells and a cacophony of huckstering. The sellers of idols, pagan trinkets, and other superstitious objects were numerous. Then there were the traders in human flesh, selling the slaves that kept the Empire working. Prostitution was evident everywhere. Procurers for brothels walked through the market like fishermen trolling the waters, hoping to catch some fool before he spent his money on something useful. The merchants of human misery were also present, the herbalists posing as "sorcerers." Paul was always grieved by those *pharmaceoi*, the devils who peddled their mind-bending drugs and love potions.

He was heartened, however, by observing that those few of his fellow Jews whom he happened to see in the Agora completely ignored him, not seeming to be on the alert for strangers.

"Friend! *Friend!* I have something good for you."

Paul realized that one of the procurers had approached near with a woman in tow and had broken into Paul's trance-like thoughts.

"What...?" Paul's mouth held itself open in mid-sentence.

"What, what, what, indeed! I have a delicacy for you, that is what." The man flashed a cloth hinged book in front of Paul's face. A painting of a nude woman in an obscene posture filled Paul's eyes.

"*Unthinkable*, "Paul sputtered, caught off guard by the man's boldness.

"Not at all, think of *your* beard on *her* breasts!" The man kept up a constant banter while flipping through the book flashing one scene after another. Paul stared at page after page, unable to tear his eyes away. Finally, he pushed the book away.

"No, no, it is God's will for me to be sanctified, I must not fornicate!" Paul regained his poise. Some of the people of the Agora took notice and began laughing.

"No! No! It is the will of the gods that you delight in the thighs of lovely Lilia!" He tried the book again, but Paul would have none of it. "Give the Jew a look, Lilia." Lilia pulled her himation back so that Paul had the full view. She moved close to Paul and began searching his clothing with her hands.

Paul flinched back. "Do *NOT* touch me!" More laughter and ridicule came from onlookers.

"Touch you, indeed? You are filthy! And you smell worse!" The scene drew more onlookers who joined in the laughter.

Lilia drew her clothing back in place and turned to the procurer. "I'm not touching him until he has a bath. And look at his face, he would not last a *moment*!"

"There you go," exclaimed the procurer, "a bath and a romp with Lilia! And I *guarantee* you that she will make it last longer than a moment! Come now, you have the coin! You Jews *always* have the money."

"How could I do such a thing and sin against God?" Howls of laughter came from more onlookers.

"Sir, I will take you just a short way from here and Lilia will show you how!"

"To Hades with you and your iniquity! Get away from my face!" Paul pushed past the man, who reeked of perfume and fornication.

"I know, you want a little girl, or perhaps a boy!"

Paul did not even look back as he hurried down the way.

"I could even get a foreskin sewn on you," the man screamed at Paul, following him at a short distance. "You … *Jew*!" The man hurled obscenities and insults at Paul's back as those in earshot were laughing and shouting similar insults.

Paul's face flushed hot as he walked off through the market. But it was not the procurer, or the woman, or the crowd that was the object of his fury. That man did not know, nor could he know, the extent of his depravity and the evil of his hatred of Jews. In fact, Paul made a mental note that sometime later he would have to find an appropriate and safe way to tell the man the good news about Jesus. Paul was not angry with the man. Paul was angry with Paul. His eyes had been fixed on the pornographic book. And he could hardly take his eyes off Lilia. He had felt an involuntary reaction in his body as the images passed before him and she searched out his clothing. *Fifty years of age and I am burning with passion as though I were fifteen.* He had never fornicated in the flesh, but he had struggled all his life in the spirit.

"Lord, I have had this thorn in my flesh long enough! *Please take it from me!* Have I not resisted temptation? Have I not kept my integrity? Have I not subjected my body to the strictest discipline? Have I not made myself as one who has forsaken the passions of the flesh? Lord, sometimes I think that all I have done to build your kingdom, my joy and crown, could be lost! Like Esau who sold his birthright in a moment of weakness! After I have preached the gospel to others, will I be shipwrecked in the end?" Paul prayed aloud in Aramaic as he moved through a myriad of people. He must have looked quite the sight as the crowds parted before him like the Red Sea before Moses.

At once, Paul seemed to grow deaf. The noise of the Agora, the shouted obscenities of the procurer, and the laughter of the onlookers decreased and receded like the tide. He saw that people's lips were moving, but no sound came to Paul. Then, in the completeness of that surreal silence, he heard the sweet voice of Jesus.

My grace is enough for you, Paul. In the weakness that you call a thorn I find an opportunity to be perfect in you. Trust in me. I was tempted in just the same way as you have been and who is it that can convict me of sin? To you, my beloved brother and friend, I give both of my wisdom and my strength. Flee from fornication. Resist Satan, and he will flee from you.

"Lord," Paul prayed, "Give me rest at this moment, please. I need you to calm my spirit and quench my burning."

Peace, be still.

Calmness flooded Paul's spirit even as the tide of sound flooded back into his consciousness. But he could not hear the noisy crowd or haggling merchants or the annoying procurer trolling the Agora with his bait. Paul stood before an open door. He scarcely knew where he was or how he arrived at the threshold of this place of business. He looked up at the sign over the doorway.

GAIUS TITIUS JUSTUS

Publishing, Scribal Services, Supplies

Latin, Greek and other Languages

Expert writing, careful work

Paul stood before the door and thought of the providence of God. Sometimes the only thing that he sensed from God was a check to his spirit and a blockade of his carefully crafted plans. But, how many times had the Lord let him wander around through desolate places filled with danger, scourging, beatings, hunger, thirst, shipwreck and all kinds of adventures? Suddenly, with all the misgivings and pleading in prayer, with all the wandering and thinking about the will of God, Paul would find himself before an "open door," both figuratively and literally. It was an "open door" that no one could shut. When he walked through these "open doors," he had learned that there was nothing that could stand in his way. No one, and *nothing,* could keep him from accomplishing the work that God had ordained for him.

Go into this place and ask for work. The Spirit's voice had remained with him.

"Yes, Lord," Paul said, as he stepped confidently through the open door.

CHAPTER 2

TITIUS JUSTUS

Remember, brothers, our labor and hardship, how working night and day so as not to be a burden to any of you, we proclaimed to you the gospel of God.

-Paul

Paul stepped into a courtyard occupied by rows of tables lining each side of the enclosure. Scribes were sitting on varicolored cushions along a stone bench with their backs to the courtyard wall. Some of them worked sitting with their feet on the floor while others sat cross-legged on the stone bench. Leather tubes containing scrolls of parchment and papyri stood on end beside and in front of the tables. A man walked along the rows of tables inspecting and supervising their work. Wide awnings shaded the work area. Beyond the tables, the courtyard opened through an iron gate into a spacious and beautiful atrium where other workers at tables were busy with shelves and bins of various merchandise. A few customers were inspecting parchments and calamus reed pens. The building had a second floor with balconies overlooking the atrium. From the furnishings, paintings, and statuary, Paul surmised that the second floor served as a residence for a very prosperous family. Looking on through the atrium, he could see part of a well-kept Roman style garden. From somewhere, Paul heard the pleasant hushed tones of a flute.

The man who was supervising looked up at Paul and walked over to greet him. He had a himation wrapped around his body and neatly draped over his arm. The scribes sitting on the stone bench were dressed only in tunics.

"Welcome, sir. May I be of service to you?" The man spoke Greek with the pure accent of a native.

"My name is Saul of Tarsus. I am also known as Paul. I would like to speak with the proprietor." Paul was aware of his road-worn clothing and dusty feet.

The man ran a cool eye over Paul before he answered. "May I tell him what your business will be?" The man's politeness was perfect.

"I have recently come from Athens to Corinth, and I am looking for work."

"You are a scribe?"

"Not by trade. But I can write in Greek and several other languages, and I can read others." Paul wondered why the Lord sent him into this place. He anticipated the next question and continued, "I am a tent maker by trade, I work with cloth, skins, and leather."

Paul was surprised when the man, without changing expression, said, "Come, follow me, please." He followed as the man turned and led him back into the atrium.

The Lord has gone before me to give me favor, praise the name of Jesus, Paul thought as he walked past the tables and through the iron gate. The man took him to a stone bench topped with a cushion. Everywhere, Paul saw luxury and the finest quality of art, rugs, and furnishings. Parchments and papyri were displayed in wide offset shelves. All sorts of leather storage tubes, scrolls, wax tablets, wood panels, inks, quills, and styli were displayed. He saw something new, *codices,* books of wood, parchment or papyrus bound with leather or cloth. Paul felt his ears turn red when he saw a stack of small books identical to the one that the man had forced in front of his face in the Agora. Instruments of blessing or of cursing, depending on what is written or painted on them. He noted that there were also products for artists: pigments, brushes, and tools for sculptors. A man who was helping a customer glanced at Paul and then returned his attention to the sale of merchandise.

"Please sit here, and you can see my master. It may be just a while. May I offer you some wine or water?"

The man's eyebrow rose slightly when Paul replied, "Yes, a cup of water would be refreshing." There was a time when Paul would have died of thirst rather than take a cup of water from the hand of a Gentile. The man had to be surprised that Paul would acknowledge his worth as a human being. But, Jesus had declared that no human being should be considered unclean. And, after all, the world of the Gentiles was the harvest field given to him by the Lord to gather in the fruit of the gospel of Jesus Christ. He had learned to work, eat, lodge, and become friends with Gentiles. Most importantly, his respect for them increased as his association with them enlarged, and he had grown to love the Gentiles in the church as his own soul. He had even learned to value women, talking to them and praying with them, recognizing their importance in the church that Christ was building through him. *Because there is neither freeman nor slave, male nor female, Jew nor Gentile, but we are all one in Messiah Jesus.* Paul eased the basket from his back and sat down on the cushioned bench.

The man returned with a large, silver cup, and as he handed it to Paul, he bowed slightly with an expression that said, "From one human being to another, I greet you." The free man and the slave, the Jew and the Gentile, were reconciled by a cup of water.

Paul looked steadily in the man's eyes, took the cup, and acknowledged the man's bow with a smile and a nod of his head. The man retreated into the courtyard. The flute player began a pleasant tune. Paul loved to compose extemporaneous psalms to any music he heard. So, while he waited, he put lyrics to the tune, slipped into the spirit, and whispered the song.

>Jesus Lord in our hearts,
>Lamb of God all the redeemed worship you,
>Son of God glorious in heaven,
>Only-begotten all the angels worship you,
>Son of Man revealed on earth,
>Second Adam all the creatures worship you.

"Lord God, Father in heaven," Paul began praying in the Spirit, *"May Your will be done in my life. Fill me with the knowledge of Your will. I sanctify myself right now unto death that I may be sanctified by You. Make me holy today, Lord, clean and pure, clothed with Christ, and pleasing to You. Forgive me, Lord I pray in the name of Jesus, where I fell short of your glory in the Agora today. I said, 'To Hades with you,' to a man who tempted me in the market place. I am sorry for those words, Lord, for I would never curse a sinner to the grave. And I pray that You would not hold it against him for his offense against me. For the curses and insults, I forgive him in Your sight, O Lord. Give me an occasion that I may speak to that man about salvation. I plead earnestly for his soul. Increase my love for all the people of this city. And for the weakness of my flesh when fixing my eyes on the iniquities in that book and on that woman. I beg Your forgiveness. Please put a guardian before my eyes so that—"*

"Kurios ... sir... *sir!"* Paul was brought out of his thoughts by the soprano voice of a servant boy. "Master will see you now. Follow me, please, sir." Paul rose and followed the boy across the hall to a room where a door opened into another atrium which, in turn, opened into a spacious garden. The boy led Paul through the garden, stopped at a door, and with a wave of his hand said, "In here, sir."

A man Paul estimated to be about thirty years of age approached, dressed in a Roman citizen's style tunic which showed a body that proved many hours in the gymnasium.

"Greetings." Clean-shaven and a full head of black hair cut short, he looked every part the Roman with a Greek body.

"Greetings to you, *kai shalom*. My name is Saul of Tarsus also known as Paul. I have recently come to Corinth from Athens, and I am looking for employment."

"Gaius Titius Justus," he replied with a slight nod of the head. "What are your skills, Paul?"

"I am a tent maker by trade, and I am skilled in working with both cloth and skins."

"Why do you not go to one of your Jewish countrymen?" Titius said with his palms outward.

"My God directed me toward your door." The truth was always the best. "I follow the voice of the Spirit of my God in all things great and small."

"Perhaps you missed the great will of the God of Abraham by a small distance." Titius' face held a quizzical smile.

Paul was lost for an answer.

"You know, the synagogue?" Titius almost cracked into an outright laugh at Paul's befuddlement. "Do you realize that the synagogue of the Jews is next door to my house?"

"Next door?"

"Yes, next door." Titius waved at a wall of the room. "I share this wall with the synagogue. And I do much business with several men of the synagogue—I have learned to trust their honest trading. But mostly I *love* your religion. In truth, I am what you Jews call a God-fearer. I like your God, the God of Abraham, and I admire His commands. My wife, Olivia, shares my enthusiasm for the books of Moses. And the prophets! What prophesies!"

"I hardly know how I came to your door. God told me to ask you for work." Paul was just coming even with the conversation. "You are a God-fearer?"

"Yes, truly! I could never be a proselyte, though. *Circumcision!*" Titius shuddered.

Now it was Paul's turn to smile. "I said that I was good with skins!" They both laughed.

"I have been told that you accepted water from my servant?" Justus asked.

"Yes, truly, it was refreshing."

"No Jew has ever shared bread or drink with me in my home. What kind of a Jew are you?"

"I am a Pharisee, a son of Pharisees." Paul looked steadily at him and pointed upward. "Who has found new knowledge about Gentiles." As he spoke, Paul heard the Spirit, *This man belongs to Me and will obey the gospel when you share bread and salt with him.*

"Being a Pharisee," Titius answered, "I assume that you are an educated man. How were you educated?"

"My father was a tent maker, but also a Pharisee, a Jew of the tribe of Benjamin, who was born of a freedman of Tarsus, also a Pharisee. My early education was from my father and from a pedagogue who was his servant. From an early age, I learned my family's business of tent making. But I was also strictly trained in the ways of the Pharisees, the separated ones. My native language is Tarsi, but I am also fluent and literate in ancient Hebrew, Aramaic, the Common Greek tongue, and the Romantic language. When I came of age, I was sent to Jerusalem to study under Gamaliel, the greatest of all the Rabbis of the Jews. There, I was immersed in the Torah, the Books of Moses, also the Prophets, as well as the wisdom and poetry of the Jews, and the history of Israel. I was also trained in the traditions of the Jews which is a vast body of interpretation of the law by the rabbis and the scribes, which we call *The Law*." As Paul went on with this resume, he wondered how this would ever help him with a Gentile like Titius, who might be looking to hire a scribe.

"You can read *and* write the *Koine Hellenisti*, the common Greek language?" As Titius asked this, Paul nodded his affirmation.

Titius continued, "You speak Greek expertly, almost without an accent, but can you read and write it as well? It is the language in which we all must be fluent and literate if we wish to engage in the commerce of the Empire."

"Yes, truly," answered Paul, "It has become like a native language to me."

"Well, then, my dusty Pharisaic friend," Titius said, smiling broadly, "you may be just the person for whom I have been looking for a *long* time. Come with me, I want to show you something!"

Paul followed Titius out of the room and across the garden to a large set of ornate oak doors hung with bronze hinges. Titius opened the door and tiptoed into what appeared to be a library. As he followed, Paul grew more mystified by the moment at the turn of events that had occurred in less than an hour's time. Open cabinets lined the walls with scrolls of parchment housed in leather containers. A stream of sunlight entered through an oculus in the ceiling and was suffused softly throughout the entire room by means of its beautiful architecture. Scribal tables stood in the center of the room where men concentrated on copying script from one parchment to another. Other men, artists, painted and decorated the scrolls with all kinds of designs and figures. The man who had been supervising the scribes in the courtyard now walked around the room, looking over the shoulders of these scribes and artists. He glanced briefly at Paul and bowed his head slightly. A reverent atmosphere permeated throughout the room, broken only by the clicking of the calamus pens being dipped into the ink wells, the faint scratching of the quills, or the sound of scribes sharpening them.

"Alexander," Titius' voice broke into the spell that seemed to be on the room. "When the scribes come to a convenient place in their work, have them take a rest. I wish to talk to Paul about the work we are doing here."

"My lord," Alexander acknowledged the command with a bow of the head. He returned his attention to the men at work. Titius and Paul watched silently as Alexander moved among the scribes and artists and touched one after another on the shoulder and spoke to them. One by one they covered their ink wells and wiped their pens clean before getting up from the table and leaving the room. When the last left the room, Alexander started to follow them out of the door.

"I want you to stay, Alexander." Titius caught his arm as he walked toward the door. "I want you to listen to what we have to say about this project. I want to impress upon you again the importance of what we are doing here."

Paul walked over to the table of one of the scribes and looked at what was being written. "This is a *Psalm*!" He looked at Titius and then at Alexander and then back at the parchment with amazement. "This is from the Septuagint, the Greek translation of the Scriptures, commissioned by King Ptolemy and Cleopatra for the great library at Alexandria!"

"Read it to me," Titius said, "please, sir." He moved into position to look at the parchment as if to see that Paul followed the text exactly.

"This is a Psalm of David," Paul spoke, "the most famous of the ancient Kings of Israel and a prophet. This Psalm is prophecy. It is meant to be sung. The original music is not known but I can sing it as it is sung in these days."

"Very well, sing it," answered Titius. "But keep to the text exactly, please."

"To be sure," Paul began to sing the Psalm as he had sung it many times. The ancient language of the Hebrews had been lost to all but the scholars. The Septuagint was the Greek translation of the Scriptures read in many of the synagogues, especially among the Hellenistic Jews. As Paul read and sang, he could have done it all from memory. Paul's voice was deep and sonorous as it reverberated in the room.

Why do the heathen rage?
And the nations of the earth imagine vain things?
The kings of the earth stood up,
And the rulers gathered themselves together,
Against the Lord,

And against His Christ,

Saying Let us break through their bonds,

And cast away their yoke from us,

He that dwells in the heavens shall laugh them to scorn,

And the Lord shall mock them,

Then shall He speak to them in His anger,

And trouble them in His fury,

But I have been made King by Him on Zion His holy mountain,

Declaring the ordinance of the Lord,

The Lord said to me, "You are my Son,

Today have I begotten thee,

Ask of Me, and I will give thee the heathen for thine inheritance,

And the ends of the earth for thy possession,

Thou shall rule them with a rod of iron,

You shall dash them in pieces as a potter's vessel,"

Now understand ye kings,

Be instructed all ye that judge the earth,

Serve the Lord with fear,

And rejoice in Him with trembling,

Accept correction lest at any time the Lord be angry,

And ye should perish from the righteous way,

Whenever His wrath shall be suddenly kindled,

Blessed are all they that trust in Him.

"Beautiful!" Titius and Alexander were both clapping their hands. "The lines that have the same sequence of syllables have the same tune! It is sung that way in the synagogue. Can you dance the way that they do also?" Titius was enthusiastic in his praise of Paul.

"*How,*" asked Paul, ignoring the request to dance, "in the name of Heaven do you happen to have a personal copy of the Septuagint Scriptures? Outside of the synagogues of the Jews and the library of Alexandria, I know of none!"

"I became enamored of the scriptures," Titius waved his hand at the many scrolls encased around the room, "as my wife and I attended the synagogue and listened to the teaching on the Sabbath. I especially love the Friday evening Sabbath service which is a study of the Scriptures by the learned men of the congregation. What stories! What commands! What prophecies! I requested that I might come to the synagogue during the week and read. Crispus, the synagogue leader, arranged it. As a Gentile I was not allowed to touch anything. But Crispus spent hours reading the scrolls from the synagogue floor so that I could listen from the God-fearers' gallery. Eventually, he arranged to manipulate scrolls for me so that I could read for myself."

Paul interrupted, "I am surprised that he allowed you to even look at the synagogue scroll."

"Well, my Pharisee friend," Titius said, shrugging his shoulders and holding his hands out with palms up. "Much can be accomplished by a generous donation of money. And I have continued to be generous in order to continue with religious instruction. I have plenty of denarii!" Titius smiled at Paul.

Paul rolled his eyes in resignation. "You are correct about that."

Paul was often accused of having ulterior motives about preaching the gospel of Jesus, one of them being money. He had seen how money had an undue influence in the church, and he had seen preachers pierced through with many sorrows because of their love of money. So that no one could accuse him of avarice, he never took any kind of salary or honorarium for preaching or teaching. Although he had no condemnation for those who did take remuneration, he kept a strict discipline for himself in this matter. He was determined to work with the skill of his own hands for his living, the result being that he lived at various times both in plenty and want.

"I determined to have a copy of the Scriptures for myself," Titius continued, "and so, I sent a group of scribes to Alexandria to the great library there, and they copied under the eyes of the librarians. They brought the entire Scripture back with them."

"That must have cost a fortune!" exclaimed Paul.

"You must understand, Paul, that I am a businessman, publishing being one of my enterprises. I have great interest in the Scriptures, but I look to profit as well. It was an investment in what has turned into a profitable effort. Besides, the expenses were not that great. All of my scribes are servants. They have a good life with me. The few coppers that I give them for spending satisfy them. They are loyal to a fault. What cost the most was transportation, a fee to the library, and a few bribes."

Titius led Paul out of the scriptorium back across the atrium into the room that served as the office. Paul was increasingly conscious of his hunger and weakness. Muscle and bone ached. He desperately needed to rest.

Titius talked as they walked through the establishment. "I have contracted to sell, and have delivered, the Septuagint to a number of synagogues throughout Achaia and Rome. The one that we are working on now is for a prominent synagogue in Rome. I am so happy that the ban that Claudius imposed on the Jews in Rome was lifted last year. Many Jews are streaming back to Rome and their money with them. Since I am a Gentile and so are my scribes, all of the production of the scrolls must be approved by an appropriate Jewish supervisor. Crispus, the synagogue leader, inspects and makes sure that all of the ink and the pens and parchments are made of the appropriate materials. Then the scrolls, which have been handled by my scribes, are blessed in some way by him, and he carries them and provides for them to be delivered. All for a substantial fee, of course, which I pass on to the buyer."

"So," asked Paul, "why am I *just the man you are looking for?*"

"Good question! Crispus seems reluctant to answer some of my questions. For instance, the Psalm you just sang so wonderfully speaks of the *'Christos'* of God, the 'Anointed One.' This 'Christ' is also spoken of in the scroll of Daniel. That prophet predicted the revealing of the Christ and the year of His appearance and that He would be cut off. I calculated the years myself, and it came to the sixteenth year of the rule of Tiberius. Since that appointed time passed some years ago, I asked Crispus if he knew anything about it, and he said, 'I do not know!' This sounded strange to me since all of Daniel's other prophesies were so accurate. Tell me, Paul, do you know of this 'Christ'? You studied in Jerusalem, surely you must know!"

"I do know of the Christ. He lived as Jesus of Nazareth in the province of Galilee. I am His servant, and He has taught me many things. He is the Son of God, born of a virgin. He lived a perfect life and performed many signs and miracles to show His divine nature. He was crucified by Pontius Pilate and was buried. But God raised Him from the dead, and He appeared afterwards to many witnesses, even five hundred at one time. Last of all, He appeared to me, and I have followed Him in all things, even to the threshold of your door."

"Crucified?" Titius blinked. "Raised from the dead? That seems an ugly history for someone who is a king!"

"It is true, none the less."

"Tell me everything," Titius insisted.

Paul heard the Spirit, *First, ask to share bread and salt with him.*

"I will tell you all, I promise. But I must immediately look to employment and get settled in Corinth. I do not have the skills that you require, but I am a tentmaker by trade. Can you recommend me to someone? Later, I would like to dine with you in your house, and I will tell you everything."

"Paul, I will pay you for instruction!"

"I live with a hard and fast rule," answered Paul, "I never take money for teaching that for which Christ charged me nothing."

"That is evident, my friend," Titius said softly.

Paul looked down at his worn and dirty clothing and wondered how he looked with his unruly beard and dusty feet, and even more, how he must smell.

"I will tell you everything, truly." Paul extended his hand, and Titius took it warmly.

"Excellent," Titius said with conviction. "I will truly call you friend if you will come and dine with my family." He picked up a square of papyrus from his writing table, sat down, and dipped a calamus pen into a stone jar of ink. "But first, my Pharisee friend, we must find you some work. I know a man who will need your skills. He makes parchments that I sell. He also made the awning and tents in my courtyard and, oh yes, all of the scroll cases I sell. He is building his business quickly and hiring skilled workers and buying many servants." He began making careful Greek letters on the papyrus.

"Plato!" Titius did not look up as the servant boy came immediately into the room. "I want you to take Paul to the workshops of Aquila, the tentmaker. Then scurry on back here because Alexander will need you."

"Yes, master."

"Paul." Titius stood up and waved the papyrus in the air to dry the ink. "My only fee is that I want your promise that tomorrow at supper time you will join my family in our triclinium. Will you be there?"

"Yes, I will," Paul answered with emphasis. "Thank you for your help. And I have enjoyed our conversation. I have much to talk to you about."

"You will find Aquila to be a just man. He is not only one of your countrymen but also a respected Roman." Titius handed the papyrus to Paul, holding it between his index finger and his forefinger.

Paul caught his breath when he realized that he was going to seek employment with a fellow Jew. He felt the need to stay clear of all contact with the Jewish community until he could understand how he stood with them. *Do not be afraid to go with the boy.* The Spirit's voice was so strong that Paul almost answered out loud.

"Thank you," Paul said as he slipped the papyrus from Justus' fingers. "Until tomorrow, farewell." The men shook hands again with warmth.

"Farewell, friend."

As Paul and Plato left, Paul retrieved his basket that he had left by the stone bench. He followed Plato through the atrium out into the courtyard and onto the street. It seemed that all eyes were on Paul as he walked through the establishment. He noted with satisfaction that he saw no household god in Titius' house.

CHAPTER 3

PRISCILLA AND AQUILA

"Greet Priscilla and Aquila, my fellow workers in Christ
Jesus, who for my benefit, offered their own necks."

-Paul to Corinth

Plenty of traffic filled the streets as they wound their way
through the city. It was becoming a sweltering day, and soon
it would be time for the mid-day nap that was the custom in
Corinth. Upper-class women were not often seen in public.
The others walked about with their himation wrapped around
them as loosely as possible according to the heat of the day.

Sometimes they did not even cover the essential parts of
their anatomy. It seemed as though Paul's eyes would land
where they shouldn't no matter which direction he tried to
look. There were either a lot of them out on the street or he
was noticing every one of them. *Perhaps I will become a black*

and blue Pharisee! That was the nickname that people gave to Pharisees who kept running into things because they tried to walk down the street without looking at a woman. The sights that Paul could not possibly avoid seeing in Corinth were a feast for lustful thoughts. Trash for his soul. He continued to do what he always did with every lustful thought or sight that came to his eyes. He consciously made every one of these thoughts and sights captive to the Spirit of Jesus. *Jesus was a man made of flesh,* Paul thought, *He knows what I am going through with this. Thank you, Jesus.*

Plato finally brought Paul to a triangular-shaped building with several adjacent open work areas when he could see people doing the familiar work of tentmaking. The servant boy turned to Paul at the door and said, "This is the workshop of Aquila, sir. I must return to school with Alexander. He is my pedagogue."

Paul almost laughed at the grief in the boy's voice. "Your master wants you to be educated so that you can be a tutor or a steward and not a slave in the quarries, or walk the water wheel, or worse, end up in the arena. Run along and be thankful! When I see you again I will tell you some stories." He smiled at Plato as he ran off down the street.

As Paul turned to walk into the door of Aquila's workshop, he paused and took a breath. *Go in, little-faith!* He stepped through the opening and let his eyes get adjusted to the light. The large colonnaded room was a bee hive of activity. Workers attended to canvasses stretched over large frames and did not look up at Paul as they cut and stitched. Other workers involved themselves in elaborate and beautiful embroidery.

Piles of fabric and other materials lined the walls. Although confronted by a mass of confusion, Paul recognized materials being made into tents, awnings, flags, banners, and coverings of several types. Off to the side of the main shop floor, rooms showed people working with leather and other types of skins making assorted items. Paul caught the attention of a man who worked on what looked like a canopy made of strips of colored fabric. "Aquila?"

The man motioned with his head toward the back of the shop floor. Paul walked back to a room that looked somewhat like an office. The opposite side of the room opened into another work floor. One of the largest men Paul had ever seen stood up from a worktable and walked over to Paul. He was tall, with powerful arms and huge shoulders. A short black beard and curly hair encircled a broad round face. The man immediately smiled, showing a mouth full of shiny white teeth. He enthusiastically took Paul's hand and said, "Shalom! Brother!" His voice matched his bear-like frame. One Jewish man could always expect a warm welcome from another Jew out in the dispersion. The man's hand swallowed up Paul's.

"Shalom, brother," Paul returned the greeting, hoping that this man would remain friendly when he learned his identity and Paul's passion for Messiah Jesus. The Spirit had counseled Paul not to fear, but he felt far from safe. "Are you Aquila?"

"Indeed I am. What is your name and what brings you to my workshop?"

"I am Saul of Tarsus, known as Paul. I have recently come from Athens, and I am looking for work. I have been referred to you by Titius Justus." Paul held out the note which Aquila took and read. "I am skilled in working with—"

Aquila eyes went large as he cut Paul's sentence short by grasping Paul's hand. He started pulling Paul toward the back of the shop. Paul felt like a little boy being pulled along by his father.

"Priscilla! *Priscilla! PRISCILLA!*" Aquila's voice pierced through the noise of the workshop. "PRISCILLA!"

Through the back part of the workshop, a woman rushed as though she was moving toward a child that had been injured. She was a smallish woman, so small in relation to the man who gripped his hand, that Paul couldn't keep the image of David and Goliath out of his mind. He would have laughed if he hadn't been so frightened.

"Priscilla!" Aquila was now holding Paul's hand with both of his, and he was looking directly into Paul's eyes and bowing out of respect. "Priscilla, meet Saul of Tarsus, also known as Paul."

"Hallelujah!" Priscilla threw both hands in the air and raised her eyes to the beams in the ceiling, "HALLELUJAH!" Some people rejoice because the Psalms tell them to. Some feel an inclination that shouting and dancing is the proper way to worship God. Priscilla began a truly hilarious, spontaneous, un-choreographed, hands-in-the air dance. She sang, danced, and moved around the room with her arms raised, shaking her hands, singing, "Hallelujah, Hallelujah, HALLELUJAH!"

Aquila released Paul's hand and laughed hysterically, slapping his hands on his thighs. Several people had stopped working and came to the door of the room to observe the commotion. Paul realized that his mouth was open as he watched the two celebrating ... what? He could not help laughing at these two who seemed to have gone insane with joy. Soon, sympathetic tears were coming to *his* eyes.

"Brother Paul ..." Aquila gasped for a breath to speak, "... brother Paul." Aquila slapped him on the back with a blow that nearly expelled the air from Paul's lungs.

Brother? Paul felt that he was joining these two in losing his senses.

"Brother Paul, God is great, and He hears us when we call out to Him!" Aquila wiped the tears from his eyes with the back of a massive hand.

"Yes, indeed, He is ... and He does ... do you know me?"

"By the grace of the Lord Jesus Christ," Priscilla spoke, "we DO know you! We heard of your work among of the people of Asia and that you recently had come preaching The Way in Macedonia. We have prayed that the Lord would bring you to us here in Corinth. And, praise God, He brought you to our door!"

For a second time in the day, Paul struggled to orient himself to reality. *Lord, am I walking through a dream or a vision? How can a person endure so many extreme emotions in so short a period? I have only been in Corinth for a few hours, and I am spent!*

Likely seeing that Paul was completely nonplussed, Priscilla said, "Husband, we have overwhelmed this man." She too wiped the tears from her eyes. "Let's go into the house and explain how we came here to Corinth, and Brother Paul will tell us how he came to our door!"

Aquila looked around at the people gathered around the doors watching. "Well, the theater is finished, back to work!"

"It's mid-day," said a man standing in the doorway.

"Oh, yes, yes, as you say, take your nap. But then back to work!"

Aquila led the way with Paul and Priscilla both following respectfully. Paul suspected that the woman had more influence over her husband than it would appear by her submissive behavior.

"Have you had anything to eat today?" asked Aquila as he led them out of the workshop area to their residence, a spacious home in the Greek style with a large and pleasant atrium.

"No, I have not." Paul did not mention that it had been almost two days since he had eaten anything. He had learned to eat well when food was available and to tighten his belt when resources were scarce. Be content in all things, whether there is plenty ... or not.

A servant appeared when Priscilla clapped her hands. "We need something to eat, and we have a guest. Be sure to bring us some figs and some fresh bread."

"Brother Paul, you look as though you could use a good meal. Bring us a large meal. I'm hungry as a lion! Clitus ... *Clitus!*" Aquila summoned another servant, a boy. "Go find Severus, Agricola, and Barbatus. You know them and where they live?"

The boy nodded.

"Tell them to come to my house immediately and bring their family and any servants who are believers in The Way."

The boy ran out of the house on the errand.

As he was led into the dining area, Paul marveled at his circumstances. *How has the Good News come to Corinth?*

Aquila and Priscilla reclined in the Eastern custom at a beautiful low table with ornately carved legs, and Paul settled onto one of the cushions. A servant appeared with a towel and a basin of water, loosed Paul's sandals and washed his feet. Food was set upon the table. There was a meat dish, bread to sop it up, with vegetables and figs. There was water offered, but no wine. Paul wondered if they were under a vow.

"Blessed art Thou, O King of the Universe, Who gives us food. Blessed be His Son Jesus Who gives us life!" Aquila pronounced the blessing, "Let us eat!"

Breaking a two day fast was a delicate thing, so Paul ate slowly and resisted the urge to gorge. Aquila had no such moderation and began consuming the contents of the table at a prodigious rate. Paul could hear the noisy chatter of children coming from an adjoining room where he assumed the children were being fed.

"Let me tell you about how we came to Corinth and why we are so overjoyed to see you come to our door." Aquila continued, "On my mother's side, I am the grandson of a Jewish freed man who was emancipated under the edict of Augustus. His daughter, my mother, was a devout Jewess and raised me in the traditions of the Jews. I was circumcised on the eighth day. She died soon after I reached majority. My father is a God-fearing Roman, and I am a Roman citizen by birth. I was educated in the Torah at synagogue school and tutored in the Roman style by a pedagogue in my father's house. I learned this business," Aquila waved his hand toward the shop, "from my father and have been blessed exceedingly by the Lord."

"How did you happen to become believers?" Paul interrupted, anxious to know how this unexpected result came about.

"It was that Pentecost after the Lord went up!" Priscilla finally spoke. "The men on pilgrimage came back to us in Rome ..."

"FILLED!" Aquila's voice seemed to have gone up to an octave.

"With the Holy Spirit!" Priscilla sat up on her cushion with her hands stretched to heaven. "It was like they were set on fire by the Lord!"

"You know about the Holy Spirit?" Paul felt like he had not quite caught up with reality since he walked into Corinth.

"Yes, yes!" Aquila brought his voice down. "They told us about how they heard the Good News in Jerusalem in our own language of Rome. In fact, *everyone* heard in their own native language. Some of them had seen the Lord and listened to him during Passover. But it was Pentecost that brought them to faith! They were baptized into Jesus by the Apostles. Then, the Apostles laid hands on them, and they were *filled*! Hallelujah! They spent some time there in Jerusalem and then they came back to Rome. Priscilla was among the first in Rome to believe and I not long after." Aquila's voice dropped down to a soft tone. He continued, "The trouble began when we took the message into the synagogue. So many believed that the rulers of the synagogues pronounced an anathema on us. We refused to leave, and they kicked us out."

"We continued to talk to every Jew who would listen to us in Rome. Many believed, Paul, many. It was amazing what the Lord did!" Tears were coming down Priscilla's face. "My husband began speaking to those Romans and Greeks that he knew in business. Many of them received Jesus with enthusiasm having never even heard of Jesus or the resurrection. Even members of Caesar's house, Junia and others, believed. We had fellowships meeting in many homes…"

"Then came Sosthenes," said Aquila darkly, spitting the name out, "and all Hades with him."

"We had to leave Rome because of me." Priscilla interrupted.

"It was not because of you, but of Sosthenes! He, reportedly, is a Hellenistic Jew from somewhere, and a Pharisee. All I know about him is that he showed up with letters from the High Priest in Jerusalem to the synagogues in Rome authorizing them to bring charges against any who followed The Way."

"I know Sosthenes, and I know how it is done," Paul said.

Thoughts and memories came rushing back to torture Paul's conscience. Painful thoughts flooded his mind bringing with them agonizing regrets. The face of Stephen appeared in Paul's consciousness. *Stephen, oh Stephen, how your face shines like the face of an angel. I held their coats while they rained stones down on you! You looked at me and prayed to God for my forgiveness. Jesus, have mercy on me, the greatest of sinners.*

"As you know, Augustus' decree of emancipation gave us, as Jews, a lot of room to manage our own affairs … are you well, Brother Paul?" Both were looking at Paul with concern.

"No, continue, brother. I was just thinking of how I persecuted the church before the Lord appeared to me. Perhaps you have heard of my story?"

"Brother Paul, we have only heard that you who persecuted the church now preach the Good News throughout Syria and Asia in Macedonia and Achaia—and now in Corinth!"

"I'll relate the whole of my story presently," Paul said, "But you, continue, please."

"Sosthenes began summoning people into the courts and charging the believers with promoting an unauthorized religion. He said that The Way is not a sect of Judaism but a new 'mystery cult.' That didn't have much weight with the courts, and they threw all of that out. But the court gave Sosthenes authority to arrest the Jewish believers who were not Roman citizens and try them in Jerusalem. Brother Paul, that is when the whole church, Jewish believers, Romans, Greeks, slaves, *everyone* stood up and resisted. I must admit that there were radicals on *both* sides who began fighting and soon there was a huge riot. It continued for weeks. Caesar lost patience and ordered all Jews out of Rome and dispatched the Praetorian Guard to enforce the edict. It was merciful that no one was crucified."

Priscilla said, "We might have stayed in Rome because of my family connections, but we didn't really trust the mind of Caesar…"

Aquila spoke, "The situation was too uncertain. We considered it too dangerous to test the edict. My father concurred and set us up here in Corinth. God has blessed us overwhelmingly, and we have prospered beyond all my expectations." Aquila paused. "We have been reluctant to speak out in the synagogue. But the *ecclesia*, the church, has grown in our homes."

"We know God causes all things to work together for the good for those who are the called according to his purpose." Paul spoke one of the most encouraging thoughts to have come to his mind from the Holy Spirit, "What can we say? If God is for us, who is against us?"

Aquila nodded his agreement with Paul. "We are grateful to the Lord for all His protection and loving care. What about you, brother? Forgive me, but you do not look well! Tell us how God brought you to our home and of your needs. The Lord certainly guided you here for a purpose."

Paul said, "The shorter story is necessary. I left Antioch with a brother named Silas looking to revisit the all the churches that Barnabas and I had planted on my first trip as an Apostle. From Antioch, we went through Syria and Cilicia to the region of Galatia then on to Pisidian Antioch. To that point, our trip was very successful. We were able to encourage and build up the work to even greater growth than they had experienced. A young Jew named Timothy joined us at Lystra. Like you, Aquila, his father is a Roman and his mother a Jewess. From Pisidian Antioch, we proceeded through Asia. I must tell you both, the time we spent there in Asia was the most discouraging part of my walk in The Way since Jesus struck me down on the Damascus Road. But I learned to trust God even more. Throughout all my journey across Asia, all I heard or sensed from the Lord was, 'Don't go there' or 'Turn away from that city.' I wanted to go to Thyatira, but I was forbidden in a vision by Jesus. We wandered into Troas very confused and weary. We stayed there for a number of days, not knowing what to do next."

Paul sat up cross-legged, leaned toward the table, and began emphasizing every word with a tap of his hand on the table. As he spoke, he thought of the great providence of God that had taken him through every trial, every obstacle, every danger, and every beating that he had received. He and Barnabas had started out into the unknown going wherever the Spirit led them. Often in danger, experiencing severe hunger and deprivation, Paul never wavered because he had an unwavering call of God to be His apostle. In all the chaos of his life, Paul was thankful that his work for the Lord was fruitful. Wherever he went, the Lord blessed him with converts. But if Paul ever had a doubt about the providence of God, it was erased by the hand of the Almighty at places like Damascus, Jerusalem, Antioch, Cyprus, Pisidian Antioch, Derbe, Lystra, Iconium, Troas, Philippi, Thessalonica, Berea, Athens, and now in Corinth. Paul had entered the city literally without a thought about what to do, but God had provided in advance for his every need, both material and emotional. "We must trust the unseen hand of God working to accomplish His will in us! Never doubt His providence or His love for us."

"Amen! Amen! Yes! Yes!"

"One night," Paul paused to take a sip of water, "I was trying to sleep. It was a restless night full of needless worry. During the night, I saw in a vision a man from Macedonia standing by my bed. He was beckoning me and saying, with tears, 'Come over to Macedonia and help us!' I felt as though I had an answer to my prayers! We left straight away and took passage across the Aegean to Samothrace. We made our way southward down the coast to the colony of Philippi. There I found why Jesus would not let me go to Thyatira. Since there was no synagogue in Philippi, and I knew there was a Jewish community in the city, I made my way on the Sabbath to the river where I knew there would be a gathering place for prayer. We really don't comprehend God's way. He would not let me go to Thyatira to work but sent Thyatira to me at Philippi! At the place of prayer in Philippi, I encountered the person from Thyatira that God wanted me to meet so that I would be a witness about Jesus Christ and the gospel would come to Thyatira with power. She was a Jewess, a merchant, a dealer in purple cloth, Lydia of Thyatira—"

"We know Lydia!" Priscilla exclaimed.

"Yes, yes," chimed in Aquila. "She was here in Corinth not two or three months ago. I purchased a lot of purple cloth from her. I even shipped some to my father's shop in Rome. She has beautiful merchandise ... and she's a beautiful woman."

"You would notice." Priscilla feigned a jealous tone.

"I have eyes. What else can I do with them but see?" Aquila evaded a fig playfully thrown by Priscilla.

Beautiful, indeed. Even now, Paul could see her standing at the place of prayer in Philippi, praying to God, as beautiful a woman as any man could dream. And there had been an immediate rush of emotion when their eyes met. She had looked at him frankly and directly as respectable women were not wont to do to a man, inviting him, not in a lustful way but in a respectful way to a better acquaintance. Paul had given up on marriage after his wife in Tarsus had divorced him because of his stubborn allegiance to Jesus Christ. *Divorced.* Since that rupture, no woman had caught his attention like ... Lydia. And there had been an embrace, a private moment of embarrassment but not of guilt. She was available and eligible for marriage according to custom and desire. But Paul was not available, and *that* was according to the Spirit of Jesus. Lydia had been willing to leave her business and follow Paul as he followed Christ. Paul was sure that she loved him, and he had to admit that he loved and desired Lydia. But their union could not be ...

"Brother Paul, hello, you do not seem to be well." At Aquila's concerned look, Paul realized he must have been staring into space for several moments.

"Perhaps the thought of Lydia ..." Priscilla raised her eyebrows in a knowing way.

"Nonsense!" Paul could feel his face warming. "I must remain as I am." There was no way that he could drag a woman around the Empire and expose her to the dangers and hardships that he faced. Besides, the Lord had said *No*. He prayed that the Lord would keep the image and dreams of Lydia out of his consciousness. But Lydia was following him everywhere, interrupting his thoughts and sleep. "I have to please the Lord and not a wife!"

Aquila and Priscilla stared at him, but relief flooded him when the conversation turned back to the subject of Paul's journey to Corinth. "Go on with your story, Brother Paul. What happened in Philippi?" Priscilla's voice had a softness and compassion that seemed to say, *I understand your difficulties in this matter.*

"Say, brother," Aquila interrupted, "let us save the rest of your story for the group that will be here after a while. That would be a good point to resume. We need to talk about your accommodations here at Corinth. Titius Justus said in his message that you are a tentmaker, a worker in skins and cloth. You will work for us. We will pay you ..." Aquila cast an eye at Priscilla, "... thirty denarii per week ...?" Priscilla nodded, retuning Aquila's glance.

"That's too much!" Paul exclaimed. "That is four times what my labor is worth. It is important to me to work for all the money I receive and to preach the gospel freely!"

"It is important to us to support your work, Brother Paul, please let us! Have not we a right to pay our workers whatever we want? And to set their hours and where they will work? We are determined to build the Kingdom of Heaven here in Corinth and our wealth, which is considerable, is for God. We want you to work here, start at an early hour and have the remainder for ministry after the mid-day ... please allow us to do that!"

Accept their offer, they are my chosen people. The Spirit seemed to infuse Paul with an even greater confidence in the providence of God.

"Very well, I accept your offer." Paul smiled at them. "Grace and peace to you in the name of the Lord Jesus Christ."

Paul's body began to sag even as his spirits were lifted by the encouragement of the conversation and food. He was weary and worn from the events of the day.

"Friends, I need rest. I can only with difficulty keep my eyes open!" Paul spoke truly as he had an overwhelming desire to just lie down and sleep wherever he happened to be.

"Certainly!" said Aquila. "We have been preparing even as we reclined at table."

He called for a servant. "Show Brother Paul his quarters and help him with a bath." Everyone had to be acutely aware of Paul's need of a bath.

The room that Paul was led into was spacious and comfortable, tapestries gracing the walls and carpets for the feet. The home had a private bath, and the servant attended to every need, seeming to anticipate everything that Paul wanted. Fresh water, warmed by the servants, embraced him.

The slave was a man younger than Paul but not young. By the way he attended to every detail of comfort, Paul thought that he might be Aquila's personal servant. Paul had never kept a servant and enjoyed every moment of attention.

As Paul began to scrape, brush, wipe, and wash the grime from his body, the servant said, "Sir, may I attend to your back?"

"Yes, indeed." Paul suddenly thought of his back, scarred from many beatings and still tender from the humiliating treatment he received in Philippi. It looked like the back of an obstinate slave. "What is your name?"

"*Doulos*," he answered, speaking the Greek word for "slave." He carefully washed Paul's back.

"What is your *given* name?"

"Castor."

"You are a twin? And your brother's name is Pollex?" Paul chuckled. "Castor, according to myth, was the mortal son of a Spartan king. The demigod Pollex supposedly was from the seed of the gods, twins of the same womb."

"Yes, we were born slaves of my mother and her master. I do not know where she and my brother are. I do not know if they are alive or dead."

"I am a slave also. My master is Jesus of Nazareth of Galilee, the Messiah, the Anointed One of the Jews. He is the same one that Aquila and Priscilla serve. Do you know about Jesus?"

"Yes, Master told me."

"The word of salvation is in your mouth. If you declare with your lips that Jesus is Lord and believe in your heart that God raised him from the dead, you will be saved!"

Tears began to flow down Castor's face. "Sir, Master has told me all. Repent, confess, believe, receive Jesus! I know that is what I should do and what I want to do. But if I do … I am afraid that if I am baptized I will lose my place in this house. If I were emancipated I would just have to sell myself to someone else to have a living."

"Castor, look at my back. Those scars are nothing compared to being saved by Jesus! I am a man who was raised with money and privilege, but I consider all that to be trash so that

I can know Christ and to be found in him and to have the eternal life that he gives. Surrender to Jesus! He will bring you through every trial!" Paul began toweling himself and wrapping himself in the himation that Castor held out to him. "Besides, Aquila is a just man and generous. In Christ, he will call you brother! I don't think that you have anything to fear from him."

Paul put one arm around Castor and raised the other to heaven and began praying for salvation. Castor wilted under the arm of Paul, nodding affirmation and crying out for mercy from God.

I never get weary of seeing people step over from death to life.

"Castor, I want you to go to Aquila and tell him you want to be baptized. Just show me where I can lie down for a bit of rest." He realized that his eyes were very heavy. "Go on, don't worry. Trust in God!"

Paul had hardly touched the comfortable bed until he was asleep, forgetting about the people who were coming to assemble with Aquila and Priscilla. He had no thought of his promise to return for supper with Titius Justus. He forgot to pray. At the last of wakefulness, Paul heard the Spirit, "*Well done, good and faithful slave!*"

CHAPTER 4

DESIRE AND DUTY

"Have I not a right to take along a wife, who is a sister in the Lord, even as the rest of the apostles and the brothers of the Lord and Peter?"

—*Paul, to the Corinthians*

Thoughts are like crows. One cannot keep them from landing on the field. But they can be chased away or left alone to do their damage. A man like Paul may exert self-control over many thoughts. If they are good thoughts, he will cherish them. If they are evil, he will reject them and pray for forgiveness and deliverance. Even a person with the purest heart must learn to deal with the crows. But no one has authority over their dreams. Paul's recurring dream of stones raining down on the face of Stephen was joined lately by another dream. Paul dreamed of Lydia.

The first time that he saw her, he felt a spark of attraction that lit a fire in his soul. It was not just a demon of lust that aroused a reaction from his body. It was that attraction that stirred his soul *and* his body and made a man think of taking a wife.

On the Sabbath, Paul and his companions went to where they supposed there was a place of prayer and found a group of Jewish women. There, he first saw Lydia, and Lydia first saw Paul.

Paul was struck down. *Foolishness.* But he immediately knew that she was struck the same way with the same foolishness. *"Lord, how could I be trapped this way with these feelings—with this fervent desire in my flesh and soul for a woman? Please take this thorn from my flesh!"*

Then, invariably, came the image of the wife he used to have. After she left him, Paul had erased Sarah from his conscious thoughts like a farmer chasing away the crows. But after she died, she visited his dreams frequently. And lately, she was invading his dreams of Lydia.

At this point, Paul tossed back and forth and threw off whatever he had wrapped about him for warmth. It seemed to be the same whether he was camped out along the road or under some hospitable roof. He often embarrassed himself by waking others up among his companions and alarming any who were keeping watch.

"Kurios! Sir!" Castor stood by the bed with a cup in his hand. "Are you well, sir?" The late afternoon sun still illuminated the room where Paul had fallen asleep.

He shook his head out of sleep. "Yes, I just had a dream. Sorry to trouble you."

"No trouble, sir. Would you care for some wine? It will help settle your mind." Castor held out the cup.

"Yes, but could I trouble you to dilute it with some water?" Not only would it help him return to sleep but help with the horrible taste in his mouth.

"Sir, it is already diluted by three parts water. It is the custom of Aquila's house."

"Of course." It was the Jewish custom to dilute wine. Paul took the cup and drank it sitting up on his bed. He remembered that Aquila did not serve wine at the meal, diluted or otherwise. "I did not think that there was wine in this house."

"Sir, he keeps some as medicine, and they use it in some kind of ceremony among their group that follows The Way."

"Of course," Paul repeated himself. Many followers of The Way drank no wine, like those who had taken the Nazarite vow. Undiluted wine had always been frowned upon by Jewish society, while liquors and mixed hard drinks were strictly taboo. Paul generally followed abstinence but took diluted wine occasionally to settle his stomach or, in the current case, to get back to sleep. He never refused the hospitality of the offering of wine. He only asked that it be diluted. Like Aquila and Priscilla, he followed the custom of wine at the Lord's table.

"Castor, when I was talking in my sleep, did I say anything intelligible?" It was an awkward question to ask of a slave.

Castor was immediately cautious. "Not much, sir. I think it was a woman's name, sir."

"Lydia?" Paul hated that his secret was out.

"No, sir, it was 'Sarah.'"

Paul was alarmed by the thought that not only was he talking in his sleep, but he was saying the name of the one that hurt him so much. The one whose name he would never consciously utter. After a pause, for some reason, he felt compelled to explain a word spoken in sleep to a slave. By dawn, every slave in the house would know about it no matter what Paul could say to rescue the moment.

"That's the name of my dead wife." *That's true.* "I miss her." *True enough.*

"I am sorry that she died, sir."

"I am praying that the Lord will help me overcome my thoughts of her." Paul gave the cup to Castor. "I want to be completely honest with you, Castor. I did dream of my dead wife, God bless her soul. But I also dreamed of another I love, a woman I met in Philippi. She loved me also. I had not thought about marriage for quite some time until I met her. Lydia is her name. I dreamed that I embraced her and felt the warmth and comfort of a wife."

"That does not seem to be a bad dream, sir." Castor stood by expressionless and attentive.

"Castor, are you wondering why I have told you this?"

"Indeed, sir."

"You have become a follower of Jesus, Castor. I now count you as my friend and brother. I have trusted you with something that I have not entrusted to any other person, save Lydia. I want you to know you can trust me in the same way."

Castor's voice broke, "I ... I will, sir ... now ... I ... I would suggest that you lie down and finish your sleep." He turned and walked quickly out of the room.

Paul lay back and covered himself with the thin bed covers. He knew the dream would continue. The dream always continued. He fell asleep before he could pray or think any more about the dream.

When Paul awoke, light was streaming into the room and the warmth of the day was beginning to work its way into the house. Paul stretched as he lay upon the bed. He sat up and stretched again. He was surprised at how refreshed he felt even after the dream that had troubled him during the previous afternoon and night.

Castor was right by his side with some water and a chamber pot for which Paul was exceedingly grateful. "Sir, I have some fresh clothing for you and some sandals for your feet. Your other clothes ... well, sir, may I dispose of them? They are quite worn and soiled. Your basket, satchel, and belt are over there."

"Thank you, Castor," said Paul, "I am really grateful for all of your kindness."

"My lord." Castor bowed his head and did not look at Paul. "May I speak to you about something?"

"Yes, indeed," Paul had just put on the new chiton and was admiring the quality of the garment. It was one piece, seamless, similar to the Lord's. He looked up at Castor, noted his humble appearance, and sensed that there was a significant moment at hand.

"Look at me, Castor. Speak your mind." Paul touched his forehead. "And your heart." Paul placed his hand over his chest. "Everything you say will stay with me and with the Lord."

"Sir, I have been thinking about your God, and Jesus, and about how we prayed. I am of two minds about it. Most of what you say makes sense to me. In my heart, I know that it is true. But if I truly 'receive Jesus,' as you say, and ask Aquila to baptize me, he will feel obligated to give me my freedom. I can't lose my place here, sir, please. Aquila is so good to me, and Priscilla is the most wonderful person and kind to everyone. My former master was cruel, and I could never please him. Begging you pardon, sir, but my back is like yours. Could you speak to Aquila for me please, sir, so that I will not be put out? I want to be baptized."

"Castor," Paul said, smiling, "you have nothing to fear. Let me ask you a question. Have other slaves in this household received Jesus in faith and been baptized?"

"Yes, some have."

"And how are they treated? Have they been put out?"

"Well, no, sir. But I have this fear in my mind. Aquila and Priscilla have been established in Rome. Aquila's family is there. The edict of expulsion has ended, and I believe that they will soon return. I fear that when they go, they will sell this business and the slaves and liberate those who have received Jesus. I will have nothing and no support. My only hope would be to indenture myself into another position."

"I can see your concerns, but I think that they may be unfounded. I don't think that you understand how Jesus and the power of his cross changes situations by changing people. I will speak to Aquila on your behalf and about his servants.

"Castor," Paul continued, "I desire with all of my heart that slavery would end. But the fact of the matter is, that there is no way to end it. The economy of the Empire is based on the practice and any efforts to change it would be met with extreme violence. As you fear being liberated, so Rome fears it *more*. This is why crucifixion is the fate of rebellious slaves. And there is no help and no possible refuge for those who would seek to escape. That does not mean that we as followers of Jesus Christ cannot do anything about the situation."

As he was speaking, Paul sat on the edge of the bed and began to put on the new sandals that Aquila had given him. When he attempted to tie the straps of his sandals, Castor interrupted him, "Please, sir, let me help you with those, it is my task."

"No, Castor, I can put on and take off my own shoes, and I can dress myself. I have some other kinds of things I want you to do for me. First, can you properly trim a man's beard and cut hair?"

"Why, yes, sir." Castor answered, "I will go get a razor."

"Not right now. I want to finish our conversation. You can cut my beard and hair after we have talked." Paul motioned with his hand. "Come here and sit beside me." Paul patted the bed beside him.

Castor hesitated for a second. He sat very uncomfortably next to Paul, careful not to touch him.

"Brother Castor, I want to encourage you in your new-found faith. You are worried about being homeless, without substance or support."

"Yes, sir, I am."

"Jesus loves you, Castor. He has promised never to forsake any who follow Him."

"How can He help me? No one ever cared about me except Aquila and Priscilla."

"I want to assure you that Jesus will supply your needs. I truly believe that He has sent me here for your sake. But it would be wrong to tell you that when you receive Jesus, nothing bad will happen to you; that you will never be in need. When I received Jesus, I lost *everything;* all I had gained to that point in my life. Fortune, position, influence, family, friends, all gone in a moment! But in that moment, I gained *everything* that sustains me in Christ! Trust Jesus to take care of you, Castor! When I am in want, the Lord provides; when in danger, He carries me through; when I suffer, He helps me endure; when I lost friends, He gave me the most wonderful brothers and sisters. I have never had children. But I have many sons and daughters in the Lord. Even though I will die, I trust Him to carry me through this life into the next. Just as God raised Jesus from the dead, so will all those be raised who trust in Him. You can trust Jesus in the same way, Castor."

"I want to believe that..."

"It is even more! Through the love of Jesus, I have found peace in my heart because I found forgiveness!"

Castor looked at Paul, "Forgiveness? Why do *you* need forgiveness? Everyone says that you are a holy man."

Paul, taken aback, blinked several times. "Castor, we have been friends just since yesterday. You will learn that I have needed forgiveness in many things, great and small. Receiving forgiveness helped me to gain the greatest benefit of all— power to forgive those who have harmed me. If there is that virtue, or any virtue in my life, it is because of my relationship with Jesus Christ. That relationship with Him is yours, also."

Tears welled up in the eyes of Castor. "I want that, I do, with all of my heart."

"The word is in your mouth, Castor! If you confess that Jesus is Lord and believe in your heart that God raised Him from the dead, you will be given eternal life!"

This time when Paul prayed with Castor, there was no doubt of the result. Castor's face glowed with happiness. What a joy to see someone receive a sense of a divine presence and the knowledge of being touched by infinite love.

"Castor, I can see that God has touched you!"

"Yes," Castor spoke through tears. "Yes, I know that Jesus is real! I want to shout what Priscilla shouts when she is happy, 'Hallelujah!' But I really do not know what that means, and I never had the courage to ask her. What does 'hallelujah' mean?"

Paul laughed out loud at the question and the indescribable look on Castor's face. Paul lifted his hands and face to the ceiling. "*Hallelujah* means ... *praise the LORD!*"

Castor stood up and began walking around the room, "*Hallelujah, hallelujah, hallelujah!*" Paul laughed, clapped his hands, and repeated every "hallelujah."

The noise of this celebration attracted the attention of the household. Priscilla looked cautiously into the room to see what was going on. When she saw what was transpiring, she began a joyful dance, clapping her hands and joining in with the "hallelujahs." Three of the servant women came to the doorway and were smiling and clapping their hands to the praise.

"Castor has been born anew!" Paul waved them into the room. "Castor is about to tell everyone what God had done for him this morning while he cuts my hair and trims this monstrous beard. All of you, come in."

One of the women turned to leave. "We have to get back to preparing the midday meal for everyone—"

Priscilla interrupted the servant woman, "We have time to listen to Castor. We will be able to finish preparations. What Castor has to say to us is more important than food."

Castor left the room and returned with a comb and razor. He also had a sheet which he wrapped around Paul to catch the clippings. He carefully honed the razor with a piece of leather and tested the edge by shaving a bit of his forearm.

"Do not cut my beard short, like the Greeks. But trim it back considerably. Leave my hair long on the sides, like Jewish men do." Paul thought that he probably looked like some prophet who had been living too long in the desert.

"I know exactly how to do it, sir!" Hair rained down Paul's back and chest as Castor began to transform Paul from a desert prophet into a respectable-looking Jewish gentleman.

"So, *Brother* Castor, tell everyone what has happened to you. How do you feel?"

"It is the strangest thing, sir..."

"Call me Brother Paul. I am your friend, not your master."

"...Yes, sir... uh ... *Brother* Paul ... it is just that ... somehow ... I feel *free*. I know that I am still in bond service to Aquila, but I truly do feel *free*!"

Paul tried unsuccessfully to keep his head still while he talked. He motioned for Castor to stop cutting for a moment. "Jesus said, 'If the Son of God sets you free, you are truly free!' But you have received a greater emancipation! By your faith in the natural Son of God, you have been adopted into the family of God as His very own son; the brother of Jesus; and the brother of everyone who has ever received Him in trusting faith. This means you are a co-heir with Jesus with an inheritance waiting for you in heaven!"

"Does this mean that we *truly are* brothers?"

"Yes, Castor." Paul smiled. "That is precisely what it means."

"But, but..." Castor glanced at Priscilla as he held the razor and comb in front of Paul's partially trimmed beard. "I mean ..."

Paul finished for him, "You are saying that Aquila is your master and a free man. How does that work?"

"Yes ... Brother Paul ... how *can* that work?"

Paul spoke slowly, choosing his words, "Aquila is a believer and a brother. In love, he is to care for his servants and hired workers. According to the word of the Lord, he must pay fair wages and provide all that his bond servants need in the way of food, shelter, clothing, and anything else they need. He is not to abuse anyone. If you wish to work for wages rather than be a bond servant, I am sure he will accommodate you. You, in love for Aquila, must work faithfully for him, doing all that you do for him as unto the Lord Himself. When Aquila hears of your faith, he will call you 'brother.' I am going to remind all the church of these principles. In the church, there is no slave, no free; no Jew, no Greek; no male, no female; we are all one in Christ Jesus."

Castor continued cutting. He carefully took the sheet away and looked at Paul. "I want to be baptized."

"Excellent! Aquila will baptize you."

Castor's face reflected the glory of God. He knelt at the feet of Paul. "Thank you! I have never felt this way before. I have found God, and I have found a family. I know that God will help with my situation."

"Truly!" Paul placed his hand on Castor's shoulder and stood up. "Get on your feet, Castor, thank the Lord and worship Him! I am only a preacher."

Paul motioned for all to come closer. "I want us to join hands, and I want to lead us in prayer." All of them, Jew and Gentile, male and female, slave and free did something that was destined to change the world forever. They clasped hands, and in love, lifted their prayers to God in the name of Jesus Christ.

"Father in Heaven, it is in the name of the Lord Jesus Christ that I thank you for your grace that has been poured out on us. I thank you for Castor, who at this hour has been given a home in heaven. I pray that You would be very near to him and let him know that You love him very much. I pray that You would keep him from immorality and evil of every kind. I pray that you would produce in him love, joy, peace, patience, kindness, goodness, faithfulness, gentleness, and self-control. Establish him in holiness and keep him until the day of Your coming. Amen!"

"Amen! Amen!"

"Now," Paul rubbed his hands together and laughed, "I am hungry! Everyone back to work."

As they were leaving, Priscilla took Paul's hand in a handshake and said softly, "Hallelujah, Brother Paul."

"Hallelujah, Sister Priscilla!"

CHAPTER 5

THE CHURCH

"I am with you, and no one will come upon you to harm you, for many are Mine in this city."

-Jesus to Paul

It was hard for Paul to believe that it was only about twenty-four hours since he had entered Corinth. Circumstances had dictated that he would encounter the Gentiles first. The confrontation with the procurer in the Agora had led to him meeting Titius Justus. His meeting with Titius Justus had led to Aquila and Priscilla. Castor, a slave in Aquila's house, was his first convert in Corinth. Now, he would have the attention of the fellowship. Things were moving swiftly, and Paul would have to adapt. But he had learned to be adaptable.

All the church had been invited to the home of Aquila and Priscilla for a midday meal which they called their "love feast."

Paul had slept well into the morning and was now fresh with a new haircut and new clothes. He had pushed the memory of his dreams into the background of his consciousness. His face felt as though it was shining from the strength of the Holy Spirit. He was ready to meet the church and lay out the strategy of evangelizing Corinth.

Aquila and Priscilla introduced the people of the church in Corinth as they gathered in the spacious atrium of their home. Paul was impressed by the number of people who came to the gathering, thirty or forty at least, along with their children. Everyone had brought food and drink which was received by the servants of Aquila. All the ones who had come appeared by their dress and their manners to be Jews. Paul closely observed how Priscilla spoke to each person and the respect with which she was received by them. He was reminded of Deborah, one of the greatest and most effective Judges of ancient Israel. Priscilla and Aquila seemed to operate as partners in ministry. *Perhaps this is the way that women will come into equality in the church. May the Holy Spirit rule!* Paul took note of another couple that stood out as leaders, Andronicus and Junia.

Aquila moved to the side of Paul and spoke up, "Brothers and sisters, I want to thank you for coming to our home for a love feast. This is a special day, because we have a special guest with us, Apostle Paul."

"Amen, Amen, Amen!" Everyone clapped and smiled at Paul with genuine appreciation.

"Yesterday," Aquila continued, "we gathered at my insistence to greet Paul. But he needed rest more than he needed to talk to us!"

There was laughter and clapping at the statement of Aquila. *Everyone must have been told the sorry state of my appearance yesterday.* Paul smiled and nodded his head to acknowledge the truth of Aquila's statement.

"Paul will speak to us after we share a meal." Aquila looked at Paul. "To begin, Brother Paul, would you pray a prayer of thanksgiving for the food?"

Paul raised his eyes to the ceiling and stretched his hands outward with palms up, after the manner of Jews, and prayed:

> *Father in heaven, blessed are You and blessed be Jesus Your Son,*
> *Who creates the fruit of the vine and food for us,*
> *We thank You for the nourishment that sustains our life,*
> *And we thank You for the food that sustains our souls,*
> *Unto everlasting blessedness,*
> *And eternal life. Amen.*

"AMEN," was spoken from the whole assembly.

"Let us begin eating, and remember to love one another." Aquila moved toward the food while he was speaking. Several of the women went into an adjoining room to check on the children. Everyone began eating, talking, and enjoying each other's company. Paul could not remember a meal that he enjoyed more. He remembered to eat lightly as he still had to go to the home of Titius Justus for supper that afternoon. When they finished, the servants began cleaning up the tables and taking the leftover food to the kitchen where they would eat. Paul watched as Castor was helping with the chore of getting the room ready for a meeting. Catching Castor's attention, Paul motioned for Castor to come to him.

"I want you to stay for the meeting and sit here next to me." Paul patted the couch next to him so that everyone could see that Castor had been invited to be next to Paul. "You can eat later. It is more important that you be here." Castor looked anxiously at Aquila and was answered by a nod. He sat down next to Paul looking very unsure of himself.

"Thank you all for coming to the love feast." Aquila stood before the group. "About this time yesterday, a man came to my shop looking for work. When he gave his name, Saul of Tarsus, better known as Paul, I guess that I frightened him by my reaction. I grabbed his hand and dragged him through the shop shouting for Priscilla. When she learned who he was, she broke out into her happy hallelujah dance!" The room broke out in laughter. Some of the young people started imitating her dance with hands waving in the air.

"That would frighten anyone," Priscilla said as she laughed along with them.

"It was quite an introduction to the church in Corinth!" Paul was smiling broadly.

"Well, I want to introduce him to you now," Aquila continued. "We had heard of one who formerly persecuted the church but is now building the church. We heard of how Paul was doing great work and bringing the gospel with power to Asia and Macedonia and now to Achaia. We heard of one who was chosen of Jesus to be an Apostle. This is how I receive him, as one who has authority. I receive him as one sent to us from the Lord. Brother Paul, we welcome you."

There was a great deal of applause as Paul rose to the front of the group to speak. *I wonder if they will like me so much when I tell them what I am going to do!*

"I am an Apostle of the Lord Jesus Christ." Paul looked around the room and saw that he had the attention of everyone. "Although I was not of the original twelve, I received everything that I have directly from Jesus. All that I received from Jesus I confirmed with the other Apostles. I am now working as an ambassador for Jesus Christ to preach the glorious gospel to the Jews *and* the Gentiles. I am a Pharisee, the son of Pharisees. I have been educated in Jerusalem in the traditions of my ancestors at the feet of Gamaliel, going far beyond many of my countrymen in knowledge and practice of the traditions of Judaism. I was zealous beyond measure."

Paul paused and looked around the room as his words sank in. "How many of you have heard of Sosthenes?" From their faces, one might think that he had mentioned the name of Satan. "I can see that you know him. I was just like him! Like him, I persecuted the church. I threw the saints, both men and women, into prison ... and I voted for their death. I was going to Damascus with warrants for the arrest of saints in that city, when the Lord struck me down to the ground in a flash of light. Blinded, I was led by the hand into Damascus where the Lord guided me to a wonderful brother named Ananias. He laid hands on me and prayed for me to regain my sight and receive the Holy Spirit. From that moment, I have lived as a slave of the Lord Jesus Christ and a steward of the mysteries of salvation in Christ Jesus. It is by the mercy of God and His grace that I stand before you today to testify that Jesus came to save sinners, of whom I am the worst. I have much more to say about my conversion that I will share with you in the coming days. But I want to speak to you now about my mission in coming to Corinth and how I believe the Lord will give us success."

Paul motioned to Castor to come up and stand with him. "Already, the grace of God has been with me. Castor has, this morning, received Christ. God has given him to us as the first fruit of my labor here in Corinth from among the slaves."

The faces of the people changed in a moment from expressions of joy and happiness to expressing no emotion whatsoever. Paul was presenting them with something that they could not think about.

"How many of your servants have, by seeing your faith, expressed their faith in Jesus Christ?" A couple of hands went up. "Where are they?" There was complete silence and no movement in the room in reply to this question from the Apostle.

"The Lord Jesus said something to me that was repeated later to me by another Pharisee, by the name of Nicodemus. 'Thus, for the love that He had for the world, God gave His one and only Son that *all* ...'" Paul paused for the effect of the word and repeated it, "'... *all* who believe in Him should not be destroyed but have eternal life.' This means that God loves Castor as he loves each one of us and has received him into the family of God. We must receive him into the church, the assembly of Jesus. I am asking Aquila to baptize him this afternoon. Castor is our brother and our equal in the church."

Paul moved Castor back to his seat. "I know, brothers and sisters, that we cannot presume to change the system of slavery in the Empire. It is not legal, and it is too dangerous to everyone, slave and free alike, to begin freeing slaves. But I propose a new way of doing the master-servant relationship. Outside of the church, the slave must serve obediently and faithfully as unto the Lord. The master must treat the servant with dignity and respect supplying all of his or her needs. But, inside the church, at our worship on the first day of the week, and at our love feasts, all are equal before God."

"But who will serve?" The voice came from somewhere in the room.

"All will serve!" Paul replied. "I will serve you," he waved his arm outward toward the group and then placed his hand over his heart, "and you will serve me. We will be brothers and sisters who are servants together in the love of Jesus."

"There is a valuable saying that comes from the Lord. It is in a song which I will teach you." Paul began to sing.

> *In My house, in my temple, in my church,*
> *There is no Jew, there is no Greek.*
> *In My house, in my temple, in my church,*
> *There is no male, there is no female.*
> *In My house, in my temple, in my church,*
> *There is no free, there is no slave.*
> *In My house, in my temple, in my church,*
> *We are all together, one in Christ!*

"Come, sing with me." As the room joined Paul in the simple melody and lyrics, Aquila moved to the side of Castor. He extended a hand, and Castor grasped it.

"Brother!" Aquila greeted Castor.

"Please don't put me out of your service. It would be the end of me!" Castor spoke through tears.

"Have no fear, but trust in God. See, the whole church comes to you." One by one the people came to greet Castor and call him "brother" just as they would do with any new convert.

"I never heard," said Castor, "of a slave with this much happiness!"

After a time, the crowd began to break up, and the noise of conversation and chatter of the children began to lessen. Paul found himself in conversation with Aquila and Priscilla together with another couple, Andronicus and Junia. They were talking about what had transpired and what they might do to change the servant-master relationship. The master was as much in bondage to the system as the servant. But everyone knew that because of Jesus the situation must change. Paul suddenly changed the course of the conversation.

"I must go and declare the good news about Jesus Christ in the synagogue of the Jews." Paul saw genuine worry cloud their faces.

"That will mean trouble!" Andronicus exclaimed. The others nodded in agreement.

"We came to this city from Rome," said Aquila, "because of the riots caused by the preaching of followers of The Way in the synagogue. That is why Caesar expelled all of the Jews from the city!"

Andronicus spoke up, "We have been careful to speak about Jesus only outside of the synagogue and in private. Crispus, the synagogue leader, and the other elders know nothing of our faith," he exclaimed with increasing volume. "Everyone we have convinced in private is striving to keep it that way!"

"It will all fall on me!" Paul spoke softly, "On me alone."

I have taught you how much you must suffer for My sake, but not in this city.

"I am an Apostle of Jesus Christ. That means that I am one who is sent to proclaim the good news about Jesus Christ. Jesus Himself taught me how to go about this. In every city, I am to go to the synagogue first, because salvation comes to the world through the Jews. Then, to the Gentiles, both free and slave, man and woman. I do this so that all will be saved. For there is no distinction with God. Just as in the song that we sang, in Christ there is no Jew, Gentile, slave or free, man or woman. We all become one in Christ Jesus. I have been commissioned by the Lord to bring this message to every human being in the world, from the lowliest servant to Caesar himself. By the power of God, my words spoken and written will endure to the end of the age so that the gospel will be known in every nation on the face of the earth. For this purpose, I must be obedient to suffer every hardship and danger. But, I know that I can do all things through Christ, who strengthens me."

The group remained in silence for a moment until Andronicus spoke, "I have great fear in this course of action. I am against it!"

"Don't worry, no one will have to stand with me. The Lord will protect me and all the believers in Corinth. But I have to move quickly in this before my enemies, the enemies of Jesus, find me. I am a Pharisee from the school of Gamaliel. I will be given an opportunity to speak for a while. But there are those who have pursued me all over Asia and Macedonia. I think that they have been thrown off their pursuit because I came into Achaia through Athens. But, they will eventually find me. There is one you know, Sosthenes, who pursues with authority from Jerusalem. When he comes, things will change. It is fitting that just as I pursued the church to Damascus with warrants from the Chief Priest, so Sosthenes pursues me with the same fervor with writs from the Temple."

Into the muted moment that followed, Priscilla spoke, "We must listen to Brother Paul. We had heard some things about him, incomplete stories, really. We heard of a man of courage who was filled with the Holy Spirit. He was building and strengthening the churches of Jesus Christ. It was told that a Jew named Paul, a Pharisee, who formerly persecuted believers, now has a love for Jesus greater than his former hatred." Priscilla paused, looking toward Paul. "We prayed to God in the name of Jesus to bring that man to us, and our prayers were heard! Praise God that they were heard! Now that the Lord has brought him to us, we must do as he directs us, because the Lord is with him."

All eyes of the group turned to Aquila as if he was to give the final judgment in their course of action. Aquila bit on his lip as he thought for a moment. "Yes, I think that what Priscilla has said is right. We will do as you propose, Brother Paul. God has protected us from the trouble in Rome and brought us here to Corinth. He has prospered us both in the Spirit and in possessions and wealth. We must keep our courage. I believe that God has placed us here for a purpose. I also believe that you are an Apostle of Jesus Christ. We will follow you as you follow Christ."

Paul nodded his acknowledgement of Aquila's judgment. "Who are the leaders, the most influential people of the synagogue?"

"There is the ruler of the synagogue, Crispus, of course," answered Aquila. "Among the Gentile Godfearers would be Titius Justus, whom you have met. Among the women would be Priscilla."

"Don't forget yourself, Aquila," chimed in Andronicus, accompanied by a murmur of agreement.

"I perceive the unseen hand of God at work to prepare the way for me to bring the gospel to all the people of Corinth," said Paul, as if to himself. "I have been invited to dine this evening with Titius in his triclinium. I think that I will eventually take up lodging there, right next door to the synagogue." Paul laughed softly. "God is good!"

Paul was following a tried and true method of bringing the good news to a community. Go to the synagogue first, if there was one, and seek out the people of influence among the Jews and god-fearing Gentiles who attend the synagogue. Then he would seek out the people of influence in the community, sometimes by getting arrested. The Lord had promised Paul that he would testify to the Emperor himself about Jesus Christ. Paul suspected that it would only come about by a trial for his life. He fully anticipated that he would eventually be poured out like a drink offering on the altar of this world. But not in Corinth, not in Corinth.

"I have to be going," Paul said, "I think that Titius Justus will be a marvelous addition to the Church at Corinth!"

By the time that Paul arrived at the shop and home of Titius, twilight was approaching. Business had been concluded for the day, and Paul was received with enthusiasm by Titius himself rather than by a servant. "Welcome, my Pharisee friend!" Speaking in common Greek, Titius clasped Paul's hand firmly. "Come into my home. We have so much to talk about!"

The triclinium was a dining area in Roman style furnished with a low table and lounging couches arranged around the table so that diners could recline and eat in a comfortable condition. Titius' wife, Olivia, was in the room and greeted Paul warmly with a friendly smile and a soft voice. Paul seated himself at a couch and looked out of the second-floor window opening. He observed the late afternoon light and the long shadows draped across a thriving metropolis. He could see it spread out on a gently sloping vista upward to the Acrocorinth, that huge mountain of rock on which the Temple of Aphrodite stood. It dominated not only the view, but the life and culture of the city.

Servants began bringing food and drink to the table. Paul was hungry, and the food was excellent. Considerate of Paul's Jewishness to a point, Titius offered wine diluted with water and no swine meat that Paul could detect. But otherwise the meal was composed of foods that would not be considered "kosher" by any Jewish person that Titius knew. Paul sensed that Titius watched him closely for any signs of distaste or disgust on his face. There was no danger of that as Paul had trained his mind and his sense of taste to eat whatever had been offered to him in good faith. His only request had been to dilute the wine.

"I am anxious to talk to you," said Titius. "You have not been in Corinth two days, and you are already a famous person."

"How so?" Paul raised his eyebrows.

"Well, for the first part, you were accosted by the most famous of procurers in the city. Reports are that he has the best prostitutes in all of Achaia."

"How do you know that, my *husband*?" Olivia interrupted, with the emphasis on "husband." Paul, who was following the conversation with a mouth full of food, was amazed that this intervention did not result in an eruption of anger from Titius.

"*Reports* are, my dear," Titius answered. "You must know, Paul, that I have not practiced worship at the temple or consorted with any prostitutes for years. I've have been following the commands of God that I found in the Book of Scripture concerning these things."

Paul, mouth still holding an un-chewed morsel, looked at Olivia. She returned his gaze with a direct look and a slight smile. He realized that she was judging his reaction as much as he was judging hers. Paul finished chewing, swallowed, and washed it down with some wine.

"Where was I?" Titius looked at Olivia.

"Stephanas."

"Yes, Stephanas. Well, he has become very wealthy and the priests have complained—"

"What did you say his name is?" Paul could feel his face flush with blood.

"Stephanas … Stephen."

"I can still see his face," Paul mumbled, sitting upright.

"Paul, are you well?" The concerned voice of Olivia interrupted Paul's thoughts.

"Yes," answered Paul quietly, "yes, but I was just thinking that I must go to that man and give him the good news about Jesus Christ."

"Well, you are too late for that!" Titius laughed softly.

"Why, what are you talking about?"

"That's what I have been trying to tell everyone!" Titius continued, "When you were confronted by that man, Stephanas, the whole market place was talking about it! What he said and how you cursed him! But within moments, he was overcome by a vicious fever, and his lungs began to fill with water. The news spread like fire through the city that you had cursed him and, well, you have become *famous*! The last word that came to us is that his physician says he will not last until the first watch. It must be that he truly *is* headed for Hades, just as you said!"

"NO!" Paul exclaimed, springing to his feet. "I must go to him!" The Spirit was shouting to Paul's spirit, "*Go! Go! Go!*"

"It's too late, my friend," answered Titius. "Besides, night is coming, and it is too dangerous to be out in the streets, particularly in that neighborhood. His friends and servants hate you and will be ready to fight."

"I'm going!" said Paul as he began walking away. "Will you guide me to Stephanas, or not? If not, the One Spirit who brought me to your door will take me to his door!"

"Wait! Please, friend, just one moment!" Titius began collecting his thoughts as one facing a sudden emergency. He arose from his couch and began moving toward his office in the shop. "Come with me, Paul, we will take you there directly, but we need some help."

"We haven't a moment to lose!" cried Paul. *I cursed him! He has done much less than the evil I have done! Lord, please forgive me, help me to put right this evil I have done!*

"Plato!" Titius bellowed out. The boy appeared as Titius and Paul entered the office. "Plato, take this message to Aquila the tentmaker." Titius scribbled a message on a piece of papyrus, folded it in half, and handed it to Plato. "Listen, Plato, this is the message, 'Aquila, get several of your servants who can handle a sword, arm yourself, and meet Titius and Paul in front of the Olympia Taverna immediately.' Repeat the message." Plato repeated the message perfectly. "Now,

Plato, run like Hades is after you! Get the note to Aquila. If you hurry you can be back before dark!"

Titius called out, "Alexander!"

"There's really no need for swords," Paul said as Plato ran out of the building into the long shadows of the street.

"Do you want me to guide you or not?" Titius asked, as Alexander appeared. "What you are proposing to do, my friend, is very dangerous. If I am going, we are going armed!"

Paul nodded his acquiescence but said, "The Lord will be our shield."

Titius ignored Paul's comment as he gave Alexander instructions. Alexander returned quickly with three other servants. They all were armed with short swords and carried unlit torches. He had torches and swords for Titius and for Paul. Titius took the scabbard and belted it to his waist.

"The Lord will protect us," Paul said as he refused the sword. He took one of the torches.

"You are a most unusual man, my Pharisee friend." Titius shook his head slightly. "Is everyone ready? We must stay together especially when it gets dark." Titius looked them over. "Let's go."

CHAPTER 6

STEPHANAS

"You know, brothers, that the house of Stephanas was the first fruit in Achaia, and that they devoted themselves to the ministry of the saints."

-Paul to the Corinthians

There was not one sin for which Paul could atone. But there were some things which could be repaired. Some of the sins he committed against others could be atoned on a human level though apology and restitution. Murder was not one of them. There was no restitution that would compensate for the unjust taking of an innocent life. Paul, Saul of Tarsus, was a murderer. There is no other adjective that can describe a person who did what Paul did to Stephanas of Jerusalem, more commonly known as Stephen, and to others who followed the way of Christ. Because Paul was acting with the authority of the Chief Priests and others, he was protected from the retribution of the law. But he stood condemned by the Law of God. The grace of God in Christ Jesus had procured forgiveness from the Law of God for Paul, a full and free pardon from Almighty God. But the temporal consequences of his sin remained. There was no undoing what he had done. There was no restitution possible. The face of Stephan being crushed under the rain of stones continually moved about in Paul's memory and testified that he was a murderer. But what Paul had done against Stephanas of *Corinth* could be undone *if* he could get there in time. It put the speed of Heaven into his feet.

When Paul and Titius and Alexander came to the rendezvous at the Olympia Taverna, Aquila and his people were nowhere in sight.

"We must go on," Paul said anxiously. "We cannot wait for them. Time is life!"

"We *will* wait here," replied Titius. "They will be here momentarily."

Paul was about to protest when the huge hulk of Aquila, sword strapped in a scabbard about his waist, moved out of the gathering shadows with five men. Everyone was armed. Aquila looked as dangerous as any gladiator.

Titius looked at Paul and nodded his head toward Aquila. "*That* is why we wait,"

"What is going on?" Aquila asked, breathing heavily from exertion.

Titius explained the situation briefly. Aquila looked at Paul as if in disbelief that they were on such a mission.

"We must go," Paul said urgently. "The Lord Jesus commands me to go to him. Stephanas can be saved! He must be saved!"

Aquila took a deep breath, expelled the air, and said, "Very well, let's go!"

Someone had produced a tinder box and lighted one of the torches from which the others were lighted. They moved more slowly as night descended and the streets became narrower. The sounds of living passed by Paul's ears as the group came to a slower pace and then stopped at the door of the brothel. Titius pulled on the rope that rang a bonze bell within the courtyard. The sound raised a chorus of catcalls, laughter, and whistles from the open windows of the neighbors.

"Luv, you must be desper't!" an old crone voice called from the window across the way, accompanied by more laughter and whistles.

A small speak-through door opened in the sturdy wooden door. "We are closed," a female voice said through the opening. The little door closed abruptly.

"They are closed, luv," the old crone's voice came from an upper window opposite the brothel door. "But it is alright though, luv, 'cause I ain't got no teeth! Come on up!" More laughter and whistles.

"That's disgusting!" exclaimed Aquila. Titius was suppressing his laughter and a couple of the men in the group laughed out loud. "Let's go back."

Aquila and Titius looked at Paul in the torchlight, looking for a decision. In answer, Paul stepped forward, grasped the rope, and pulled vigorously several times. The sound was answered by more hectoring from the neighbors.

The small door opened. "*What?*" It was the same female voice as before.

"I am not a customer. Your master is dying, and I am a healer. My name is Saul of Tarsus, also known as Paul. I have come to save him!"

"Paul? We already have a physician, the best in Corinth. I have never heard of you."

"I am not of Asclepius. I am a servant of the Living God, and I am the only hope for life for Stephanas."

"You are a sorcerer?" A male voice spoke through the door.

"No!" answered Paul. "I am a *healer*. The only hope for Stephanas."

"The physician says that there is no hope. Stephanas looks like death."

"Let me in, and my God will raise him to his feet. What have you got to lose?" Paul's voice carried urgency.

"What do you want? How much?"

"I want nothing," Paul said, "but to save him!"

There was a momentary pause. "Very well," said the voice. The man's face appeared as he gazed out upon the group. "You can come in, but you alone. And no weapons."

"I will need my assistant," replied Paul. "We will not be armed."

The small door closed, and there was the sound of a bar lifted and a latch opening.

"I want you to go with me," said Paul to Titius. "You need to see what is going to happen."

"You remain out here, Aquila, and take care of the group," Paul said as Titius handed his sword and dagger to Aquila. Paul was conscious of Aquila's Jewish sensibilities. "The scripture says that Israel will be a light to the Gentiles. That light is Jesus Christ. We must carry the light into the darkest places of the world."

"But, Paul," answered Aquila, "I do not want to listen to this filth!" He waved with Titius' sword in the direction of the laughter.

"Aquila, we must learn," Paul said, looking steadily in the eyes of Aquila, "to endure such things for the sake of the gospel of the Lord Jesus Christ." Paul felt a twinge of hypocrisy as he remembered how poorly he had responded to Stephanas in the Agora.

"Let's go," Paul said as he moved through the open door with Titius. As they came into the courtyard, they heard behind them the latch of the door closing and the sound of the bar dropping into place.

When Aquila heard the latch thrown and the door barred, he took a deep breath and prayed, "Lord Jesus, keep them safe." He looked around at the men in the street that had come with him and the curious ones who had come out into the street, "Lord Jesus, keep all of us safe."

"What's going on?" One of the curious came up to Aquila.

"Stephanas is near death. We have escorted a healer to see him."

"He already has a famous physician with him."

Aquila gulped. *Go ahead and say it!* At the prompting of the Spirit, Aquila raised his voice, "We have brought a healer to raise Stephanas up from his sickness. This healer is the servant of Jesus of Nazareth, who is the Christ, the Anointed One, the Word of God, the one and only Son of the one true God. In Jesus there is life, and to all those who will believe in Him, He will grant to them eternal life beyond death."

"Aye, man. Stephanas must be desperate to call in a spiritist! Everyone must die and then ... nothing, poof!" There was a general mummer of agreement from the growing crowd. "If I am to believe in this Jesus he must DO something!"

"Yes, Lord," Aquila said softly, "Please do something. For we all are in a desperate place."

Paul and Titius followed the man who spoke to them at the door through the inner gate into the atrium of the brothel. It was a large home with a spacious atrium. The man spoke over his shoulder, "My name is Belos, the steward. I am a servant of Stephanas. You are Paul, and who are you?"

"My name is Titius."

At this Belos turned around and looked at Titius as if seeing him for the first time. "Titius *Justus?*" Belos bowed his head in respect. "I'm sorry I did not recognize you at first! I am often in your shop purchasing supplies for the artists and sculptors that Stephanos employs here."

In the Agora, Paul had experienced the effect of one of the pornographic "books" that had bothered him so drastically as Stephanas had shoved it in front of his face.

Indeed, they were moving through the midst of a display of sculptures, paintings, and tapestries that were arrayed in a tribute to sensuality of every kind imaginable. Each of the second-floor support columns at the finial had sculptures of men and women in every position along with some that Paul did not think possible. The atrium was surrounded by rooms partitioned off with curtains for privacy, or not. There were some women in the atrium who looked at the men as though they were customers. In the closeness of the heat, they wore almost nothing. Their closely cropped hair, their nakedness, and lack of modesty offended Paul. He hated the reaction it brought to his mind and body. There were two men there as well, with long flowing hair, embracing each other as their tears ran down their cheeks for Stephanas. They were recognizable as men because of the state of their undress. The Greeks worshiped the body. Each of these prostitutes were a tribute to that ideal. Paul tried to look away from everything lewd or pornographic, but there was nowhere safe to look.

"This place was a favorite of the Emperor Tiberius when he visited Corinth," said Belos as he led them through the atrium to the stairs that led to the second floor where the living quarters were located. "Many children were brought in for him."

Paul shuddered at the thought of that extreme wickedness. The ceiling of the atrium extended through the second floor so that the rooms of the house surrounded the atrium. There was a banister along the walkway on the second floor that led to the room where Stephanas lay. Paul could hear the mournful tones of a flute coming from the entrance to the room.

As they entered the room they could see, by the light of numerous oil lamps, Stephanas lying on a couch. Lilia, the woman who had exposed herself to Paul in the market was kneeling beside the couch wiping the brow of Stephanas with a damp cloth. At the foot of that couch was another couch where the physician sat looking at Stephanas. There were others in the room watching as the flute music continued in its dirge.

"This man," Belos said as he motioned to Paul, "claims to be a healer and says that he can raise Stephanas from this bed and make him well."

The physician rolled his eyes. "What is *this*? How much did you give him?"

"Nothing! He claims he only wants to help and asked for nothing," said Belos. "Besides, he is a friend of Titius Justus, and that is recommendation enough for me. I am the steward of this house. I say, let him try. What have we got to lose?"

The physician shrugged his shoulders and motioned with his hand toward Stephanas. "Why do I have to suffer fools?"

I will gladly look like a fool in your eyes for the sake of Christ and for the sake of this man. Paul looked at Stephanas' pallid face in the light of the oil lamp, and it was obvious that he was at the point of death. His breathing was shallow and rattled in his throat.

"Don't touch him!" Lilia screamed at Paul, "Leave him alone!"

"Lilia." Belos took her arm and lifted her to her feet. "Let him try. I will not let Stephanas be harmed. Stand over here and watch. There's a good girl." Belos led her a few steps away.

"NO sorcery! Belos, don't let him give him any potions!"

"No sorcery, no potions," said Paul, "but I would like a little oil which is the symbol of the spirit of my God. Would you get some for me, Lilia? Quickly, now!"

Lilia rushed out of the room.

Paul stood by the couch of Stephanas praying quietly. The quietness of the room was only broken by the rattling breath of Stephanas and the doleful tune of the flute. Paul turned to the flute player. "Please! Stop that dirge! Stephanas will live and walk out of this room a healthy man. Think of something you can play at that time." The flute player laughed with some of the other people in the room, including the physician. Paul resisted the impulse to throw them all out as the Lord had done to those who mocked His healing touch. Paul wanted witnesses.

Momentarily, Lilia returned with a small flask of olive oil. "Place a little in the palm of my hand." Paul extended his left hand toward Lilia. "Thank you, Lilia." Paul lightly rubbed the oil in his palm.

"I am going to place my hand on the head of Stephanas." Paul put his right hand on the feverish head. "I want everyone to know that it is the power that is the name of Jesus of

Nazareth, the Christ of God, that will raise Stephanas up from this bed of sickness. It is not any power of my own."

"Ha!" The physician snorted.

Titius had been silently watching as all of this unfolded. He was becoming more nervous by the moment. As a Roman, his instinct was not toward compassion. He did not understand Paul's efforts toward Stephanas. Any Jew that he had ever met would consider Stephanas a loathsome, untouchable person. Titius' opinion of the man was not much better. Nor did he understand how Paul did not even think about what would happen if he failed to heal Stephanas. Paul seemed to be unfazed by the possibility of failure and the resulting ridicule, even danger. But mostly, Titius feared that he might appear, with Paul, to be a fool. He desperately wanted to stop Paul and leave the premises. But suddenly, he remembered the stories he had read in his treasured Septuagint Bible of the deeds of the prophets Elijah and Elisha who had even raised the dead. He began praying to God silently and fervently. Somehow, words he had read in Deuteronomy came in answer to his prayer, *It is I who put to death and give life. I have wounded, and it is I who heal!*

"It is in the name of Jesus Christ," Paul raised his voice, "That I command illness to leave this man! Raise him up to health! In the name of Jesus Christ!"

There was a momentary silence which was broken by the physician, "See, this charlatan has nothing to offer!"

"Silence! Have faith! God is working!" Paul felt the fever leave the brow of Stephanas. "God is working, He is working, bless the name of Jesus!"

Suddenly, Stephanas opened his eyes and sat bolt upright on the couch. He began gagging, convulsing as if he wanted to expel something evil from his body. The physician moved quickly to the couch.

"He's choking. Get him on his side. Bring that basin here!" The physician took control and moved Stephanas onto his side with his head draping over the edge of the couch. With every convulsion, Stephanas expelled quantities of stinking mucinous fluid into the basin until he had utterly expended his strength and there was nothing was left to expel. He lay back on the couch and took a deep breath, and then another, and another.

"I have never..." The physician looked at Paul and then at Titius and then at Stephanas. Titius was spellbound and felt paralyzed as if by fear.

"You live!" Lilia moved to the side of Stephanas as he sat up on the side of the couch with his feet on the floor. "You are alive!" Lilia was embracing Stephanas and sobbing uncontrollably. Then she fell at the feet of Paul and began kissing his feet and wetting them with her tears.

"Get up," Paul said. "I am just a servant of the One who has healed him." Belos lifted her to her feet and embraced her as his tears mingled with hers.

Stephanas was staring up at Paul. "I saw ..."

"What did you see?" Paul looked directly into his eyes.

"Someone," Stephanas' voice was gaining strength, "and another…"

"Yes?"

"He was awesome in his appearance. He stood right beside my bed. His eyes! They were like the flames of a fire. And His face shone like the noonday sun in the Agora. His voice sounded like the crashing of the waves of the sea, very loud, but I could not understand what he was saying. The other one I did not see but I could feel his presence behind me. Finally, the second one spoke to me from behind my bed …"

"What did he say?"

"He said," Stephanas stood and leaned close to Paul, "that my life was nearly spent on the banks of the Styx. Then all my bad deeds appeared before my eyes, every evil thing I have done to many people, and I could not deny a single one. I saw their faces, all of them. Then I heard a voice, a voice like a magistrate speaking, '*Ibis ad crucem!* You are going to the cross!' I felt life leaving me, and despair overwhelmed me."

Stephanas grasped the front of Paul's chiton. "And then I saw … *YOU!* The person standing behind my bed told me that *you* would come to me and save me and tell me how I could receive a pardon for every one of my many sins. I did not understand how that could be because of how I treated you in the Agora. The last I saw of you and heard from you was a curse to Hades. I do not even know your name." Stephanas buried his forehead in Paul's chest, "Thank you for saving me. Please forgive me."

"All is forgiven for my part, friend." Paul placed his hands on Stephanas' shoulders, "Will you forgive me of the unjust curse that I spoke to you?"

Stephanas nodded without lifting his head.

Paul pushed Stephanas back and held his face in his hands, "My name is Paul. I forgive you for what you did to me. But it remains for you to seek forgiveness of God. Just as the Angel of the Lord told you in a vision, I will instruct you. And I will tell you what you must do from this day forward. Today, salvation has come to your entire household. But at the moment, you need some nourishment. What do you think, Physician?"

The physician was standing by with open-mouthed astonishment. "Yes, yes, nourishment ... yes, get him some food. Nothing heavy, some broth and bread, water and a little wine, no barley." He nodded toward Lilia, and she started out of the room.

"And, Lilia!" Paul spoke. "Could you humor an old Jewish man by doing him a favor? Could you wrap your himation about you a little more modestly and ask all of the others to do the same? It would help me greatly."

"Yes ... I will." She hesitated then said, "I cannot remember any man, at any time, who has ever asked me to put clothes *on*. But I will," she said again as she pulled her garment about her and continued out of the room.

"Belos," Paul said, turning toward the steward, "would you be so kind as to bring Aquila and the others with him into the house? Assemble everyone in the house into this room. I want all to hear what I have to say."

Aquila's anxiety increased with every passing moment. After a while, a sizable crowd gathered in the street and noisily conversed about what was happening. Many pelted him with questions about Stephanas and about why they were there. There was a lot of derision and much name calling. The crone kept up a constant banter of embarrassing ridicule from her nearby window. It seemed like every word was an insult to the sensibilities of Aquila.

"They ain't lettin' you in, luv," the crone's screeching voice cut through the noise, "s'really 'spensive in there, luv, and you ain't got the coin for it! Take up a collection, luv, maybe you can get 'nuf to watch!" A huge outburst of laughter followed each of her taunts.

All the scoffs and mocking suddenly fell into silence as Belos opened the door and stepped out into the street. Belos needlessly held up his hands for silence.

"Stephanas lives and is taking food!" A gasp went up from the crowd as Belos made this declaration. "The healer, called Paul, prayed to his God, and an evil spirit came out of Stephanas. I saw it! He wants the rest of the group to come into the house."

The people immediately burst into a clamor and pressed toward the door. Their voices were both demanding and pleading. Belos raised his hands and tried to quell them to no effect.

Aquila moved toward Belos. Together with the men with him, they forced their way to the door. As he moved, the Spirit spoke to his spirit, *"Tell them Paul will come out after a while and speak with them."* Aquila immediately began to argue in his mind against it. *"Tell them, tell them!"* The impression of the Spirit won as he reached Belos and turned to face the crowd. Aquila's penetrating voice rose above the clamor. The words somehow came to his mind and out of his mouth.

"People of Corinth, listen to me! Silence!" The noise subsided as all eyes fixed on Aquila. "The healer is a man named Paul who is the servant of the living God. Paul will come out to speak to you as soon as he is finished in the house. Some of you know me. I am Aquila the Tentmaker, and I promise that Paul will be out here to talk to you."

"Swear it! Swear it!" shouted many voices.

"I promise on my honor as a Roman citizen!" That quelled the shouting. "Now, as it is presently, we could be accused of being a disorderly assembly. Please disperse except for a few who can call all of you back when we come out. I promise that Paul will hear you all."

Following Belos, Aquila and his company went in through the door, the courtyard, and the inner gate into the atrium. He kept his eyes on the back of Belos and did not look left or right as they moved through the brothel. They moved quickly up the stairs into the room of Stephanas.

While Stephanas was eating and the household was being assembled, the physician began questioning Paul. "How did you do that?"

"I prayed to my God in the name of—"

"I saw that. What did you *do* to heal him? Truly now."

"Truly! Your eyes and ears did not deceive you, nor have I," answered Paul. "You must believe what your eyes have seen and your ears have heard and your hands have touched."

"There is no physician from Parthia to Britannia who can do what you did. If you will teach me how that is done, I will quit my practice in Corinth and become an apprentice to you without pay."

Paul paused and looked at the physician's eyes. "Agreed. I could use another assistant ... what did you say your name was?"

"I didn't say," he said, extending his hand toward Paul. "My name is Luke."

Paul took his hand, "Well, Luke, there is one condition to seal our agreement. You must listen to everything that I am going to tell Stephanas and to everyone who will be assembled here in a few moments. You must believe with your whole heart in the name of Jesus Christ, the name that I called on to heal Stephanas. If you believe it sufficiently to leave all that you know to follow Jesus and will be baptized this night, you will be saved, *and*, you will become my student."

"Agreed ... If I believe."

While they were talking, Aquila and his group had entered the room. Titius was explaining to Aquila what had transpired.

Aquila looked extremely uncomfortable being in the company of the persons of this house.

Paul began speaking. "Stephanas, come stand here beside me."

Stephanas stood up, body erect, looking strong and healthy, moving to Paul's side as if he had never been ill. Everyone in the room looked in total amazement at what they were witnessing.

Paul continued, "I want everyone to know that it is by the name of Jesus Christ that this man stands before you whole and healthy. But I have a message for Stephanas and each of you that says that Jesus Christ came to heal more than the body. For we are all mortal beings, and all are made of corruptible flesh. All of us, with time and circumstance, will see the end of life. But Jesus Christ came to heal our souls and to give us life that extends beyond our natural life, eternal life with God!

"Each one of us have sinned. In the pride of our self-will, we have sinned against God. We have also harmed others and so have multiplied our transgressions against the Almighty. Without being reconciled to God, we all stand condemned and face eternal punishment. But Jesus came in the fullness of time, as a man born of a virgin, the one and only Son of God. He is not a son like the demigods of the Pantheon or like any of the gods of metal, stone, and wood. Jesus Christ is the Son of the One True God who created the earth and everything in it! Christ does not live in, or honor, any temple made with hands, but lives in those who believe in Him. He proved His divine nature with many miracles, even raising the dead to life. Because our offenses against God are so grievous, we cannot atone for even one of our sins. But Jesus was unjustly tried before Pontius Pilate in Jerusalem and was crucified, the Lamb of God hung on a cross. Jesus Christ became the sacrifice that atones for all of our sins, if we have faith in that atonement and the reconciliation to God that it brings.

"Jesus was buried and descended into the grave. But God did not let the body of His Holy Son see decay. God raised Him to life from the tomb. I am a witness to His resurrection. I have seen Him, and listened to Him, and have touched Him and witnessed His glorious divine nature. Over five hundred people saw Him ascend into Heaven to take His place beside the Father's throne. From there, Jesus will return to bring an end to this age and will judge the living and the dead."

Paul turned to Stephanas. "In your vision, you saw Jesus, glorious in His divinity. The Angel of God stood behind you and spoke to you about your condemnation. But the words he spoke, '*Ibis ad crucem*! You are going to the cross!', these words were the words that were spoken by Pontius Pilate to Jesus. Jesus took the punishment that you deserve for all of your sin, pride and evil deeds. I want everyone here to listen and respond to what I say to Stephanas."

Tears were flowing down the cheeks of Stephanas. Paul continued, "Stephanas, do you wish to be absolved of your sins and become a follower of Jesus Christ?"

"With all of my heart, yes!"

Everyone in the room, including Aquila, Titius, and Luke spoke their affirmation, "Yes! Truly! I do!"

"Do you turn away from sin and the world to be obedient to Jesus Christ and His commands?"

"Yes, I do."

"Do you confess that Jesus is the Son of God; that he lived a perfect life; that he was crucified for your sins; that he was buried and rose again and ascended into heaven; that the dead shall be raised to life everlasting or eternal punishment; that Jesus is returning to earth someday to judge the living and the dead?"

"Yes, yes, YES!" Everyone was joining in each confession with acclamation and tears.

"Now," Paul paused and looked around the room quickly at each face. "All of you who joined with Stephanas in repentance and confession, do you believe what I spoke with all of your mind, soul and spirit?"

"Yes, yes!"

To Paul, not a person in the room looked a doubter. "Please say this prayer after me."

Aquila joined in and repeated each phrase with fervor. He had learned that when someone receives Christ, it is helpful to them for some believer to join with them in confession of sins. Paul and Aquila opened their hands and lifted their eyes to heaven after the manner of Jews. Others assumed a posture and prayed as they were accustomed to pray. The Holy Spirit made all of the difference in the effect.

"Father in Heaven ... I come to you as a sinner in need of forgiveness ... I have sinned against you and I have harmed others ... I confess every sin to You ... please forgive me ... I believe in Jesus Christ ... I believe that all of my sins are forgiven ... not through my goodness ... but through your grace ... I receive Christ as the Lord of my life ... Amen!"

At the "Amen," Aquila began rejoicing and dancing the Priscilla hallelujah dance in an uninhibited display of joy. "Hallelujah! Praise Jesus forever!" He began pounding Titius and Luke and Stephanas on the back with hearty "amens" and praise. It seemed there was a holy presence in the room affirming their faith and doing "something," although they may not exactly know yet what was happening to them.

Stephanas' face was radiant as he spoke up, "I feel like a new person! It is as though a great burden has been lifted from me! My soul ... I feel ... clean! Everything has changed! And everything MUST change! Thank you, Jesus, for life! I know in my heart that this is all true! I can almost see Jesus in Heaven!" Paul was shocked as he saw the angelic face of Stephen the martyr in the face of Stephanas the convert. No longer would Paul be troubled by that face.

He placed his hand on the shoulder of Stephanas. "You have been born anew! You have new life and a new start! The new has come and the old has gone. Grace and peace be unto you and unto us all. Amen and Amen!"

CHAPTER 7

THE FRUIT
OF REPENTANCE

"Therefore, produce fruit worthy of repentance."

-John the Baptist

Paul had led many people in prayers of repentance and faith in Jesus Christ. Truly, he had found that a parable told by Jesus reflected the reality of evangelism. Jesus likened the evangelist to a farmer sowing wheat, scattering seed to the soil from the paths that run through the fields. The seed, He said, is like the Word of God. The soil represents the people who hear the gospel. Some of the seeds fall on the hard-trodden path where the birds quickly come and eat them up and the Word preached has no effect. Jesus said that the birds represent Satan who has so hardened the hearts of some people that they cannot be reached with the truth. Jesus said some of

the seeds fall on shallow soil that is mixed with rocks. The
seeds take root quickly and grow. But soon, because they had
no depth of root, they are scorched by the sun and quickly
wither and die. The rocky soil represents people who receive
the Word with rejoicing and begin well. But when the heat
of persecution comes, they fall away. There are other seeds
that fall among the weeds and thorns. The seeds take root
and grow but are eventually crowded out by the weeds and
thorns and produce no fruit. Jesus said that this represents
people who begin well. But the cares of life and the desires
of the flesh crowd out their faith and they produce nothing.
The seed that falls on "good soil," however, takes root and
grows and produces a crop many times what was sown, some
even a hundred-fold. The "good soil" are the people who are
fruitful. They are the ones who reproduce the Word, spread
the gospel, and bring forth the virtues that Paul called the
"fruit of the Spirit."

As Paul watched and rejoiced with the people, he saw the
joy of salvation on their faces. He wondered how it would
all work out. Who would be "good soil" and who would fall
away? Among the people in the room it would be exactly
as Paul understood the teaching of Jesus. It would become
evident to Paul who was "good soil." There was something
that Paul had learned about those who are truly born anew
and deeply rooted in the grace of God. In a newly reborn
convert, Paul looked for the first fruit of salvation, the fruit
of repentance. When someone has truly been born anew, they
begin, without prompting, to seek out those whom they have
wronged and try to make restitution of some kind. If they
have stolen, they will return the money or property. If they are

unable to pay immediately they will ask for time from those they have offended and begin repaying as they are able. The repentant person will try to restore torn relationships. The forgiven person forgives and asks for forgiveness. Jesus said that those who have been forgiven much, love much. Instantly, those who are saved and who had never before thought about Jesus begin to love Him supremely for His atoning death. In Paul's mind, the rush of first love and the unforced acts of restitution and forgiveness are the true signs of a redeemed sinner. When Paul saw the fruit of repentance in the life of the new believer, he knew that the seed had fallen on "good soil." Seldom would Paul see a convert that was more fruitful than Stephanas.

"Stephanas," Paul said as he placed a hand on the shoulder of a man who had, in an instant, left darkness to live in the light, "all that remains for the moment is for you to be baptized!" As Paul spoke, the tumult of celebration and rejoicing subsided.

"Yes, baptize ... what is baptize?"

"To baptize means to wash clean with water. Baptism is a ceremony for a new believer. It is more than a ceremony, it is a sacrament unto God. It is also a testimony to everyone that you are now a follower of Jesus Christ. It symbolizes the washing away of your sins, your death to sin, and your new life in Jesus."

"By all means, I want to baptize." Stephanas spoke with emphasis.

"You *will* baptize, brother!" Paul laughed out loud. "But first you need to *be* baptized. It is something that is done *to* you, not something you do to yourself. We need a quantity of fresh water like a bath, or a pool, or someplace near a drain."

"I have a bath in the house we can use."

Paul was skeptical about using the bath in a brothel, and it must have showed on his face.

"I have a personal bath," Stephanas said quickly, sensing Paul's discomfort.

"I am sure that will be adequate." Paul responded with a smile.

"Belos!"

"Yes, sir." Belos was instantly at the side of Stephanas.

"Belos, I want you to instruct the servants to have my bath prepared. Drain it out, clean it thoroughly and then fill it with fresh water. Do that quickly. Then, I want you back with me. I have some things that need to be done immediately."

"Yes, sir." Belos turned away and left the room with two of the women.

Paul could hardly believe that this was the same man who had accosted him in the Agora. Even though Paul had himself been changed in an instant, and he had seen it happen many times in others, he remained always amazed at the transformation that grace brought to the lives of people.

Stephanas raised his voice to the whole room, "How many of my household prayed with Paul to have your sins forgiven and to believe in Jesus?"

"All of us! All of us!"

"We are going to be baptized. It is a ritual of Jesus Christ. I am not sure of its significance, but I am sure of this: something happened to me that saved my life and has changed me forever, and I am not going back or changing my mind. I am following The Way of this Jesus who saved my life. Paul—"

"*Brother* Paul," Paul interrupted.

"Yes," Stephanas looked at Paul, "*Brother* Paul will instruct me in The Way of Jesus, and I will instruct you. But right now, there is something, or someone, that is telling me that everything about me and this house must change. We can no longer live the lives that we have been living. You must no longer engage in prostitution, and I must no longer profit from it. I do not know how that will work or how we will live differently. But If anyone wishes to follow me and be baptized, I will take care of you. I will not sell you in the market place or to some foreign slave trader."

"Yes, yes, we will stay with you and be baptized." Every one of his household spoke virtually the same thing.

"What about you, Luke?" Paul spoke to the physician. "Did you pray with me? Do you believe what you have witnessed? Do you believe that Jesus Christ has been raised from the dead and that He saves you right now? Can we perfect our agreement?"

Luke looked around at all and then back to Stephanas. "What I have witnessed here is much greater than a man brought back from the point of death. In my experience, the character of a person is infinitely more difficult to change than to bring healing to the body. I know you, Stephanas. I have often traded my service for the service of this house. I see the change in you, and I sense the same is happening to me. I too must change. I do believe. I will follow The Way of Jesus. And I will go with you, Paul, as your student." Luke offered his hand to Paul, and they shook heartily as men who make a lasting covenant.

"And how about you, Gaius Titius Justus?" Paul turned to Titius.

"Yes, I do believe. Jesus fulfills all the prophecy that I have read of in the Good Book that I have at my house. I have read it without real insight until now. I must confess something to you, Brother Paul. I thought in my heart to profit from what you have done and that your miracles would bring money into my business. I must change my way to The Way of Jesus. From this moment, I pledge not only my belief but all my business, wealth, and property to Jesus Christ. I will conduct my business as if it were owned by Jesus, and I am but a steward, so help me God!" Titius spoke with the intensity and directness that Paul would come to appreciate.

"Lilia?" Paul looked at her, and she looked directly back without lowering her eyes. "You are now a fellow follower of Jesus. Would you like to say something?"

Lilia was not only trained in the sensual "arts" but also in the social graces of entertaining. She was intelligent and well-spoken. "I was born to be a slave to prostitution, and I have lived that way to this moment. I do not have a thought about who my parents were. I was exposed as an infant and was "found" by a slave trader who raised me to be a sex slave. All my life I have done whatever men have told me to do. I now want to follow Jesus. I will not prostitute my body any longer, even if it means my death. It is the first free decision in my life that I can ever remember making. I feel *new*, free, and *unused.*" Lilia looked at Stephanas. "I love you, Stephanas, please do not send me away!"

"I will not send you away, I promise," replied Stephanas softly. "But things must change between us. We will speak later of it. Do not worry."

"Anyone else?" Paul looked at the other servants, male and female.

"I agree with Lilia," said one.

"Yes, yes," said the rest of the slaves.

The people in this room are My chosen instruments to bring the good news to Corinth and establish My Kingdom in this city.

"Well!" Paul expelled a breath of air. "This is the core of believers who will bring the Word of God to the people of Corinth! Stephanas, your household is the first fruit of my work for Jesus in Achaia. This means more to me than you can imagine. But you have much to learn of Jesus, of faith toward God, of grace, and of holiness. But now, you all must be baptized!"

Paul and Stephanas led everyone out of the room and down the stairway to the lower level. They met Belos coming up the stairs. "Everything is ready, sir," Belos turned on the step and walked down with the crowd.

"Belos," Stephanas waved his arm around the atrium, "all of the tapestries and the art work. Take them down immediately! Cover the frescoes and the column capitals with something or other. And, all of the idols and images of the gods. Take them away!"

"Sir, what shall I do with them?"

"Put them somewhere out of sight for now. Tomorrow, hire an oxcart, no, two. Load the tapestries and the art in one of them. We are going to burn them in the Agora. I have something to say to the people of Corinth. Put the idols into the other cart and conceal them well. Take them to that silversmith that I use. Tell him to destroy them all quietly. Let him keep the silver to remain silent about it."

"As you wish, sir." Belos' face showed his amazement.

At the insistence of Stephanas, everyone waited until the house had been transformed from looking like a den of iniquity into a somewhat pleasant Greek household. Paul's spirit soared as he witnessed a place that was formerly a place of drunkenness and debauchery being sanctified and changed into a building that would serve as a meeting place for the Church of Jesus Christ. He was amazed at how quickly the servants worked. When everything was done to Stephanas' satisfaction, he led them to the bath.

"Bless my soul," exclaimed Paul when he saw the bath, "A mikveh!" The small pool was like a ritual bath used by the Jews for purification. It was sunken into the floor with steps leading down into the water. The pool was constantly refreshed by a small stream of water coming from a bronze spout shaped like a lion's head that was attached to a hollow column next to the bath. Paul supposed that the column could be filled with warm water by the servants for a delightful bath.

As if knowing his thoughts, Belos said, "Sir, there was no time to heat water."

"It is perfect, Belos," answered Paul. "When a person is dipped into the water, it symbolizes the coldness of the grave.

When we come up out of the water it symbolizes being raised to eternal life. The water is perfect."

The luxurious bath reminded Paul that there would be a wide diversity of wealth in the church. The fellowship would be made up of the rich and the poor and everyone in between. Stephanas had a personal, private bath and surely, somewhere, a private latrine. The servants, and the ordinary citizens, and the poor of Corinth, who were gathering at the door in the street, used the public bath and the public latrine. In those places, there was no segregation of the sexes or privacy. No modesty was possible. If what one saw offended sensibilities, one was obliged to look elsewhere.

In such a diverse culture, how can the church be unified as one? Paul asked the Lord, as he prayed silently. *How will it be possible for Jew and Gentile, wealthy and poor, man and woman, slave and free, to have any unity at all? How will it happen? What must I do?*

The answer came to Paul as he prayed. *By MY GRACE and by MY SPIRIT, they will love one another, and everyone will see it!* Paul realized that the others had fallen silent and were imitating him in silent prayer. Paul said, "Amen."

"Amen, Amen!"

Paul instructed them in the process of Baptism. Each of them retreated to a place where they could wrap their himation around themselves like a tent with a clasp at the shoulder to hold the garment in place. Thus, there would be no cloth between their skin and the water as they stepped down. Paul took off his chiton and clothed himself similarly.

He went carefully down the steps into the pool and looked up at the assembled group.

"Stephanas, you are the leader of this house. We will begin with you. I would like for all of you who watch to say something together as people are baptized. When the person's head goes under the water, say, 'Dead to sin!' When they come out of the water say, 'Alive in Christ!' And, say it with *enthusiasm!*"

Beginning with Stephanas, one by one, they all came to be baptized. Each proclaimed their repentance and faith in Jesus with a few words. Then, Paul grasped their right hand with his left, placed his right hand on their head and said, "Because of your testimony of repentance and faith in Jesus Christ, I baptize you in the name of the Father, the Son, and the Holy Spirit!" The person closed their eyes and pinched their nose as Paul pushed their heads into the water. "DEAD TO SIN! ALIVE IN CHRIST!" the crowd shouted as each one went under and came out rejoicing. Aquila received them as they stepped up and gave them a towel that Belos had provided. Stephanas, Titius, Luke, Lilia, Belos, eleven men servants and eleven women servants, twenty-seven in all, entered the Kingdom of Heaven that evening through the grace of God in Christ Jesus. But Paul had just begun with them.

When all had been baptized, Paul spoke to them, "Now, I want to tell you about a wonderful gift that God has for His children. It is the gift of the Holy Spirit that will descend on each one of you. You will receive power to become the witnesses of Jesus Christ." Just at that moment the bronze bell at the outer door rang. "Tell them to be patient. We will be there momentarily."

When Belos started for the door, Aquila caught his arm, "I'll go. You need to listen to what Paul has to say."

Aquila strode through the atrium through the outer courtyard to the door and opened the speak-through window.

"*CASTOR!*"

"Sir, please, m' lady told me—"

"*I* told you to stay at the house … is that Priscilla?" Aquila was looking past Castor to see Priscilla talking, rather preaching, to the people in the street.

"Sir, she insisted! She was going to come here no matter what. Please forgive me!"

Aquila sighed heavily and wiped a hand down over his face. "Castor, you have nothing to fear. You are just doing as you are told. Brother Paul is not finished but will come out to the people in a few minutes. Look after Priscilla the best you can."

"Indeed, I will, sir!"

Aquila turned back to rejoin the group. He was both aggravated and pleased with Priscilla. He was just going to have to accept the fact that Priscilla was the preacher in the family.

Aquila had barely left their home with his armed servants when Priscilla began to get restless with waiting. While she was a faithful and respectful wife to Aquila, she exerted her will in the household with the force of her personality. With Priscilla, right was right and wrong was wrong and never would the two be reconciled. She had earned a place of equality with Aquila while still respecting his role as leader of the household. He saw her deep love of Jesus and the strength of the Holy Spirit in her. He had appreciated her intelligence and judgment and learned to rely on her advice in business as well as spiritual matters. Priscilla was not a large or particularly strong person, but she had the fighting spirit of a Spartan wife. She had listened to the message from the servant boy of Titius. Aquila had shown her the note from Titius that explained briefly Paul's mission to the brothel to save Stephanas. Aquila insisted that she stay at the house, and she had reluctantly agreed. She believed that it was proper for her to be obedient to her husband. But since the hour Aquila rushed out of the house with the servants, her resolve began weakening with each passing moment.

Priscilla knew that it would be considered very improper to go out of the home at night, even on a mission of mercy. To go to a brothel, even in the accompaniment of her husband was scandalous. She was sure to face criticism from others in the church. However, she sensed in her spirit the rightness of Paul's mission to save Stephanas. She understood grace and the power of the Holy Spirit to heal both body and soul. She believed that Jesus came to forgive sins and to redeem sinners who are in bondage to sin. Priscilla and Aquila had purposely sought out women servants who had been owned by brothels or individuals who kept them as sex slaves. The women were considered "used up," getting too old, or just boring to their previous masters. They actually had more servants than they needed. There had been many people who laughed at them and gossiped in the grossest way about it. But rescuing these women was Priscilla's mission of redemption, and she began to perceive in her spirit the urgency of the moment.

Go! Be strong and courageous, for I am with you wherever you go!

"Castor! *Castor!*" Priscilla called out through the darkened house. "Hera!"

Hera appeared immediately with a lamp. "Yes, m' lady? What do you need?"

"The children have yet to be put down for the night. You will need to do that without me tonight. You know what to do. I will remind them that you are in charge. Get a himation for me to go over my chiton and my walking shoes. I am going out to help Aquila and Brother Paul."

"But, m' lady," Hera exclaimed, "They went to—"

"Yes, I know where I am going. God will be with me! Get Syntyche to help you."

"M' lady." Castor came into the room.

"Castor, we are going out to help Aquila and Brother Paul. Aquila had them take torches, swords, and daggers, so you should do the same. I can carry a torch."

"But, m' lady, Aquila told me to stay here with the others to protect the house—"

"I am your master as well as Aquila, and I am redirecting you. No punishment or harm will come to you! Get some torches and a gladius and pugio from the armory. Strap them on, and let's be going!"

After kissing the children and telling them that she was going to help their father, Priscilla went out with Castor into the dimly lit streets of Corinth. She whispered prayers as they walked quickly over the cobblestones, "Lord Jesus, be a lamp to my feet and light for my path. Keep us from injury or harm. Help us to help Brother Paul and Aquila. I pray that you would give me favor with my husband for coming to him."

Their torches briefly illuminated figures sitting and standing in the shadows at the edges of the street, the homeless of the city of Corinth. The occasional walkers they encountered paid no attention to them as if Priscilla and Castor were unseen. As they came to the street in front of the Olympia Taverna, doubts began to enter her mind. In the believer, fear and faith seem to gage one another. When fear is strong, faith is weak. When faith is strong, fear is weak. "My faith is in you, Jesus. Give me courage for this moment!"

Have courage, do not fear! I am here!

"Here we are!" Castor exclaimed, "The Politeia are here also!"

Two members of Corinth's law enforcement were attempting to break up the gathering in front of the door of the brothel. The men were standing in front of the door arguing loudly with several angry men and women. As Priscilla and Castor got closer, they could hear the conversation.

"We are not leaving until they come out and talk to us!" A man was shouting at one of the officers. A loud roar of approval came from the crowd. "Aquila promised that the healer would come out to us and speak! The healer saved Stephanas! The steward of the house saw it! We want to speak to the healer!"

"I'll hav'ya arrested if you don't clear the street!" The officer looked out over the crowd.

"Arrest me!" The man offered his fists to be bound, "Go ahead, but you hav'ta arrest all of *them*! And there are several of us who vote in the city *Ecclesia*."

"Yes, yes, arrest us!" The crowd was nearly in unison.

The officer looked over the crowd and then looked at the other officer. The second officer returned his look with a grimace that said, "We're outnumbered."

"Castor," Priscilla tugged on the sleeve of his tunic, "Get me up to the door."

"M' lady! Hold on to the back of my tunic." Castor began pushing people aside as gently as possible and shouting, "Make way! The House of Aquila! Move! Make way!"

"My name is Priscilla," she spoke to the officer who seemed to be in charge. "My husband is Aquila the Tentmaker. He is in this house."

"Have you come to peal'm off one of the girls?" The officer laughed.

"Keep your tongue, slave!" Castor was in the officer's face. "Is this how you speak to the wife of a citizen of Rome?" Even in the light of torches, Priscilla could see the man's face blanche. The Politeia in Achaia were made up of slaves and freedmen because the citizens of Greece hated to police their fellow citizens. Officer or not, a slave who insulted a Roman citizen could face a capital offense.

"Please! M' lady! I meant no offense, please..."

"Have no fear, officer. I am here to save people, not to condemn them."

"My name is Fortunatus." The man who was arguing with the officer broke into the conversation and spoke to Priscilla with hands folded in front of his face. "I am a sorcerer. I live in a house down the street and came out to see a disturbance. Stephanas, who is the proprietor of this brothel, fell into a deadly illness. Aquila came with someone he called a healer to try to help Stephanas. The man went in while Aquila stayed in the street with us. He told us some about someone named Jesus while he waited. Then Belos, the steward of the house, came out and said that the healer had brought an evil spirit out of Stephanas and that now he was well. Aquila promised that the healer would come out to talk to us. We have been waiting out here. We want to see the healer!"

"Let me speak to them." Priscilla turned to talk to the officer. "I will keep them quiet and waiting patiently. They do not seem to be inclined to go home."

"M' lady, there is an ordinance against assemblies in the street at night—"

"Nonsense," interrupted Priscilla, "I saw plenty of people in the street as I came over here. These people are just needy and hurting. Castor, ring the call bell and let them know that we need them out here."

"Yes, that's right! We want to see the healer," Fortunatus began leading the crowd in a chant, "THE HEALER OR NOTHING, THE HEALER OR NOTHING!"

As Castor turned to the door, Priscilla addressed the crowd in the flickering light of torches.

"People of Corinth, listen to me." Her voice was strong and penetrated well beyond the light of the torches into the dark street and the chanting crowd. They quieted down to listen to Priscilla. "The healer is a man, Saul of Tarsus, known to all as Paul. What he has done for Stephanas he has done by the power of the name of one Jesus of Nazareth in Galilee of the Jews. Jesus appeared to us and showed by many miracles and signs that He is the Son of God."

Fortunatus and the people in the street listened as Priscilla told of the deeds of Jesus. She preached about His mockery of a trial, His unjust crucifixion, His resurrection, and the power of the Holy Spirit. In a brief but powerful sermon, she gave them The Way of Jesus Christ, the way of salvation. They were transfixed by her message that seem to be delivered with a supernatural force.

Fortunatus wondered aloud, "Who is this Sibyl, prophesying like an Oracle of Delphi?"

Just as Priscilla was finishing, the door opened, and out came Stephanas, Paul, Aquila, Titius, Luke, and twenty-four others. They all moved out into the crowd speaking of the glorious works of God in the house of Stephanas.

"By all the gods, this is trouble!" The officer let out a string of obscenities. He swore again as the other officer out in the crowd listened to all that was being said.

CHAPTER 8

CORINTH
AND THE CROSS

"We preach Christ having been crucified, to the Jews an
obstacle to faith, and to the Greeks an absurdity."

-Paul

"Today, in the Agora, we must know nothing among the
people of Corinth but Christ and Him crucified," Paul spoke
to Castor the next morning. "And you don't have to be here to
serve my needs. I can dress myself and put on my own sandals."

"Orders, sir," Castor replied. "Sir, please, allow me to do
this. It is more than a duty for me. It is an honor to serve you
in this way. In some way that I don't understand, I think Jesus
wants me to be your servant."

"That's wisdom, Castor." Paul spoke as his head went
through the opening of the seamless chiton, and it sank onto

his shoulders. "Always do the will of God. If you think He wants you to serve me, I will accept it. I like it, in truth, Brother Castor. You do a wonderful job." The garment was gathered about his waist and belted with a fine leather belt. Sandals came onto his feet. Castor began brushing his hair and beard. Never could Paul remember being attended to in this way. The expensive clothes reminded him of the prosperous days he enjoyed as a young man. *I must enjoy this while I have it. The day will come ...*

"Castor, stop with your work for just a moment. Sit here beside me." Paul sat on the edge of the couch, and Castor sat next to him. "I want to tell you about something that Jesus did on the night that He was betrayed, and His crucifixion the next morning. His disciples had gathered for a meal. As they arrived, there was no servant available to wash the dust of the streets off their feet."

"That is bad." Castor grimaced. "The most basic duty of a slave is offering hospitality to the table guests of the master."

"Yes, that is bad. But what was worse was that there was no one among the twelve disciples who was willing to take on this menial task for their friends. To be truthful, there was a great deal of jealousy among them as each of them were seeking leadership among the group. They were not about to wash the feet of one another. Jesus was observing them closely. He always knew what was in the hearts of people. During the meal, without saying a word, Jesus got up from the table. He took off his clothing and wrapped a towel about his waist, filled a basin with water and began to wash their feet."

"Like a slave," Castor's voice broke, and his eyes were moist with tears.

"Yes, Castor, just like a slave," Paul paused to let that thought have an effect. He continued, "As you know, the custom among the Jews is to recline on the floor on rugs and cushions to dine. The feet of the diners radiate out from a low table. Jesus knelt at the feet of each of them and washed the dust and grime of the world off their feet. When the Master got to the last one, it was a man named Simon Peter. Simon looked down at his feet where Jesus knelt and made an objection. He said, 'You will never wash my feet!'"

"That is what I would have said!"

"That is where you would have been wrong, Castor, and where Peter was wrong. This is what Jesus told him, 'If you do not allow Me to do this, I will have nothing to do with you.'"

"Then give me a whole bath! I would have said that, too!"

"You have insight, Castor. That is exactly what Peter said! But Jesus laughed and said, 'You are clean, you do not need a bath.' Then Jesus told them all, 'You call me Lord and Master, and I am that! I want you to know that I did not come to be served, but to serve. As a result, My body will be lifted up and offered as a redemption for many, an atonement for sin. I have done this for you so that you will all do the same for everyone, each of you serving the other. If you serve one another, as I have served you, you will do well.'"

"Brother Paul, you told me of the meaning of the cross before, and I believe it, but it is hard for me to understand. A slave being redeemed to become a free person? By Jesus being crucified? I will confess that I do not understand that. Why would God do that to His Own Son? Let Him be scourged half to death and then let Him be crucified? I would rather be burned alive, than to suffer for days, food for crows until death would finally take me."

"Castor, why is any person crucified? Those people who are hanging outside of the city of Corinth right now, why are they food for the crows? Why are they there?"

"Well, they have been condemned for rebellion against their masters, or for sedition against the government, or for crimes against other people."

"Yes, Castor, and I will tell you that all people everywhere are born rebels against God, we have sinned against Him, we have harmed others, and the judgment of God is just! Castor, do you remember the words of Jesus that I told you? Jesus said, 'I must be lifted up, so that everyone who believes in Me will have eternal life. For God so loved the world, that He gave His one and only Son, that everyone who believes in Him should not perish but have eternal life.' Remember those words, Castor. And remember that as Jesus came to serve us on the cross, so should we take up our cross every day."

"Be *crucified?!* No! Never!" Castor's face showed true terror.

"No, no!" Paul put his arm around Castor's shoulder. "What I mean by that is that just as Jesus gave His body as a sacrifice to God for the benefit of the world, so should we give our bodies as a *living* sacrifice unto God for the benefit of the world. It is a reasonable act of devotion unto God and love toward others. I will not lie to you, Brother Castor. The Lord has revealed to me that the Church of Jesus will suffer grievously in the coming years, and even now from around the

Empire, the blood of martyrs calls out to Heaven. I cannot promise that you will not suffer on the "cruel wood." But I exhort you, in the name of Jesus Christ, to hold fast to the eternal life that Jesus has given you, no matter what the cost. It is your only hope beyond death. Because of the eternal life that they possess, the martyrs love their testimony about Jesus more than they love their lives. God will help you."

Castor let out a deep breath. "I once overheard Priscilla say to Aquila, 'We have to take up the cross in this matter.' I did not know what 'matter' they were talking about. But, is that what you are telling me?"

"Yes, truly. Look, Brother Castor, Jesus taught us that if we want to be His followers we must take up our own cross and imitate him, that is, to always do the will of God no matter what the difficulty or personal cost. That is the obedient faith toward God that I live and preach among Jews and Gentiles wherever I go. It is the message of Christ and Him crucified."

Castor reflected for a moment and then spoke softly, as if whispering, "It is like I am crucified with Christ ..."

Paul stood to his feet and pulled Castor up with him. "Your own thinking did not reveal this to you, Brother Castor, but your Father in Heaven has opened the eyes of your heart to see this truth. I am going to pray for you that He will give you more and more insight into godliness."

As they began walking toward the workshop, Paul stopped and said, "Brother Castor, I want you to pray for me and me for you. We will make a prayer covenant. I want you to pray this prayer for me, and I will pray it also for you. Pray it sometime during every day for forty days. God will remind us if we forget. Here is the prayer,

> "Father in Heaven, I pray for Brother Paul,
> In the name of Jesus, I beseech You,
> Fill him with the knowledge of Your will,
> Be a light to his path and a lamp for his feet,
> Teach him to walk in your grace,
> And not in his own goodness,
> Help him to walk worthy of You, Lord,
> That he may please you in good works,
> Empowered to bear much fruit,
> Growing in the knowledge of You,
> May he have endurance and patience,
> With joy and thanksgiving,
> For you have rescued him from the darkness,
> And brought him into the Kingdom of Light.
> Amen!

"It is a lot to memorize, I know, but we can practice it as we work and go through the day." Paul had made this covenant with other Christians and there was one thing about it that he knew. When one prays with faith for spiritual blessings for another person, one can be assured of receiving the same kind of blessing.

"Brother Castor, forming this kind of prayer partnership with some other believer is one of the first things that a new disciple should do."

Castor wiped the tears from his eyes. "I will add that prayer to the prayer that I have been praying for you, Brother Paul. I prayed that you will be comforted in the loss of your wife and that you will not be disturbed in your sleep."

"I am truly touched in my heart by that, Brother Castor." Now, Paul's eyes were moist with tears. Castor slept just outside Paul's bedroom. He must have heard Paul's restless turning and every word muttered or spoken. Castor had been attentive to his every need. His love for Jesus and for Paul was evident. Paul was amazed that he was displaying the fruit of the love of Christ so soon after his conversion. Castor was good soil indeed.

"We are going to be a team, Brother Castor. This afternoon we are going to meet Stephanas and his household in the market place. I can sense a new adventure!" Paul was smiling and anxious to get on with the day's business.

Castor smiled and shook his head, "They will think we are out of our minds!"

"*Yes, they will*, Brother Castor. But *some* will believe. Never underestimate the power of the cross. It is the power of God for salvation to those who will believe!" Paul took a step toward the workshop and then stopped. "I forgot. Castor, would you please go back to the room and look in my bottle-shaped basket that I travel with? There is a small leather case that contains my tools. Get it for me please and bring it to the shop. Thank you. What is a tentmaker without awl and knife?"

Paul resumed his short journey to the shop. He loved his profession of tentmaking, and he looked forward to each day that he worked. He had served his apprenticeship under his father just as his father had served under his father. It was more than tentmaking. He had used a variety of materials to make all kinds of useful things out of skins and cloth. Once Paul had worked with the rarest of all fabrics in his day, silk. In Antioch, he even learned to be an expert sail maker. The profession was perfect for an itinerant evangelist as it only required a set of knives and awls that easily fit into his bottle-shaped basket. Paul was determined to work as he ministered so that no one could say that he preached the gospel for money. He had no trouble finding work anywhere that he went in the Empire. But today, work was to be found in the shop of Aquila the Tentmaker.

"Brother Aquila! I am ready to work!" Paul said as he walked into the shop. "Castor, I mean, *brother* Castor, is bringing my tools."

Luke was in the shop, standing next to Aquila. "Brother Paul, there was no sleep for me last night after what happened. I want to talk with you." As he spoke, Castor came running with Paul's tool case.

"Brother Paul, you have ministry to do," Aquila said with a large grin.

"You do not understand. I insist that—"

"*You* do not understand," Aquila said, waving toward the open side of the shop. "There is a huge crowd in the street outside of the shop. They say they are not going to leave until they see 'the healer'."

Paul walked to the side of the shop and saw people, men, women, children, slave, and free, shoulder to shoulder in the street as far as he could see in both directions.

Wherever you place your foot I will give the victory to you, for I am the Lord who heals and saves sinners!

"Praise the Lord!" Paul looked out into the street with open-mouthed wonder.

Behold, the fields are white unto harvest!

"Brother Castor, I will not be needing my tools. Today, we work in the harvest."

"Hallelujah!" Priscilla had appeared from somewhere. "Let's go!"

There had been no sleep in the house of Stephanas, but there was much prayer. Changes come into a person's life over the course of years. But humans are imperceptive to the body wasting away with the slowness of time. People become experts in denying their mortality. Gravity and time conspire to transform mind and body from youth into maturity into old age. In one day, Stephanas caught a true reflection of the truth and was stunned by the thing that had come upon him like a thief to rob him of life. Stephanas was a man who had lived any way that he wished. His father had given him an inheritance and the large home in which he did business. With that money, Stephanas had purchased some female slaves for the business of prostitution. He added in some young male slaves as he found the market for their service. Stephanas was smart and articulate, constantly in the Agora seeking out the well-to-do, procuring in the places of power and wealth. Drinking and debauchery were his merchandise. He trained his slaves to be entertainers rather than just bodies to be used. But Stephanas was merciless with his slaves. When they had finished their usefulness to him, but still valuable, he sold them. No number of tears or supplication could sway him from turning a profit. Soon, he had a clientele composed of the elite of Corinth. Even the High Priest of Aphrodite came to him, despising the temple prostitutes that served the masses. He had become exceedingly wealthy. Stephanas had never married. Why marry, he thought, when I can have a choice woman that can be discarded when I tire of her? His present favorite was Lilia. But things had changed for Stephanas, not over a length of years, but in the course of a day, in a moment of time. Stephanas had stared into eternity and realized that there was no rest in the grave for him, only judgment. He was going to go out of life the way that he came into it, naked and terrified. But, he had been given, by grace, the most precious of things: *hope*.

For the first time in his life, Stephanas had experienced love. He was one who was a merchant of what the world called "love." Stephanas had women who loved him with all their soul and body and proved it by word and deed. But, then came a Jew named Paul walking about in the Agora. Stephanas hated Jews because of the strictness of their morals and their judgment toward "people like him." He always thought that they had a prudish kind of moral superiority, and he despised them for it. When Stephanas saw Paul, he had launched a verbal assault of insults. If someone had insulted him in the same way, Stephanas would have left that person's life blood on the paving stones of the marketplace. Paul had cursed him to Hades, and Stephanas had quickly fallen into deathly illness. But when Stephanas was on the cusp of death, staring into eternity with a terrifying and awesome vision, he was brought back to the living. When he opened his eyes, who was the angel that he saw? Who was it that came through the dark streets of Corinth? Who came to his rescue when all hope was gone? Like a shepherd that braved any danger to find a lost sheep, Paul had come to save him. Paul had forgiven Stephanas for his offense before being asked. And then, to further astound him, Paul had sincerely apologized to Stephanas for cursing him. This was love like no other human being had shown him. Paul would teach him a new word for that kind of love. Stephanas had never heard or read of that word: *agape.* Paul told him that this was divine love, the kind of love that Jesus showed to us by taking our place on the cross. When Stephanas heard in his vision, "you are going to the cross," that condemnation was for Jesus, not Stephanas. Jesus took his place upon the cross. Stephanas knew it and experienced the pure and perfect love of God. And he loved Jesus for it.

"Belos," Stephanas called out through the atrium, "are we ready to go?"

"Sir, yes, sir," Belos said, coming from the street into the house. "I have the cart outside loaded to the maximum. I kept it covered as much as possible, but some of the neighbors who believed in Jesus last night added some items to be burnt."

"I wanted to keep it quiet until we arrived in the Agora!"

"Sir, the people were curious. It was hard to hide what I was doing."

"What about the idols?"

"Instead of two carts, I engaged one. I took the idols before dawn to the silversmith. I am using the same cart now for the Agora. The silversmith was greatly thankful for the silver. There was a *lot* of silver. It was hard for me to let it go! But I think we could get our money's worth out of the deal. He said that if you were going out of business, he would like to buy one of the women."

Stephanas shook his head, "No. We are not selling any slaves, including you, Belos. In fact, I need to find a way to free everyone without making anyone homeless or destitute."

There was silence for a moment as an incredulous Belos struggled to reply to his statement. "Our neighbor, Fortunatus the Sorcerer, believed in Jesus and he had nearly as much to put on the cart as you. He even told his customers about Jesus and many of them gave him their scrolls, drugs, and love potions. Fortunatus loaded them all on the cart, along with his scrolls and his *Annals and Interpretation of Dreams* and all the drugs. He threw in all the artifacts that he sells. It will make quite a fire. We will need to stay on the windward side of it or we will be staggering around the Agora like drunks. We may intoxicate the whole city!" Belos laughed.

"How will Fortunatus earn a living? Belos, he is not that wealthy. In truth, I think that he is in debt!"

"Sir, he told me he did not care, and that, if you can believe it, Jesus would take care of him," answered Belos. "Please, sir, may I ask, how are *we* going to earn a living?"

"Belos, I will tell you that, right now, I do not know. As my steward, you know that I am not in debt like Fortunatus, and I do have a substantial reserve of silver and considerable gold," Stephanas looked around about at the home, "and this house. We will need to help believers like Fortunatus. So, Belos, I will say, if you can believe it, Jesus will take care of us."

Belos snorted, "Sir, I wish I had your faith. I confess I do not."

Lilia and the other servants began gathering around. Stephanas had agreed to meet with Paul, Aquila, and Luke in the afternoon at the forum. Stephanas' people were going to go in procession following the ox cart into the forum area of the Agora. There they would find one of the fire pits used in the cool damp of the Mediterranean winter. It was well into spring weather so that an unused fire pit should be available. The things that they were devoting to destruction would be burned piece by piece. A crowd should gather at this unusual sight, and they would tell all of Corinth about Jesus. That was the plan. When Stephanas got out to the street, there was a large gathering of people.

Fortunatus greeted them, "We all want to go with you, Stephanas. I loaded your cart very heavily. Most of these people have been my customers. When I was praying to Jesus, He showed me how much harm had been done to them. I never partook of the drugs or potions because of what I saw that they did to people. The opium and the hashish even took my wife from me! Jesus has told me I must help them be free. And they want to be free! There are so many people who wanted to add to the cart that we had to stop them. So, they are carrying the things that they want to destroy. Stephanas, I feel His presence with me! What has happened to us?"

Stephanas pounded his fist into his palm. "We have been changed completely by Jesus *overnight*! I don't understand it fully, but, Fortunatus, like you, I feel His presence. I have been praying all night. Jesus does not need an image or a temple for prayer. It is like He was right with me, listening and answering my spirit. I know that what we are doing today is His will! Let us be on our way!"

They began their procession to the forum of the Agora. Stephanas, Lilia, and Fortunatus led the cart in procession like priests walking before a sacrificial ox or bull. Behind them came those carrying their books of sorcery, their drugs, and pornography. Some of them had received healing in their body. But all of them carried a new hope of eternal life. They were going to honor the One who had made it real to them. As they moved through the city, more people joined them as they clapped, praised Jesus Christ, and chanted His name.

At this same time, another procession was passing through the streets of Corinth. It was a sacrificial procession led by the High Priest of Aphrodite. Brass trumpets sounded to announce their passage. The priests proceeded before a young bull who was led docilely by the ring in his nose. The bull's horns were beautifully gilded, and garlands of flowers covered his neck and shoulders. Temple prostitutes and flute players followed in procession with dancing, songs, and laughter. They were headed for the forum to the place of sacrifice. The bull would be ceremonially killed, and the blood collected for sale to the mystery cults. The carcass would then be butchered for sale in the Macella, the meat market of Corinth. And so, Aphrodite, the goddess of love, would be sustained and enriched.

Paul, Aquila, Priscilla, Titius, Luke, Castor, and a large group of people met the procession shorty after they left the street in front of Stephanas' house. At Paul's insistence, Titius and Luke went to the front of the ox cart immediately behind Stephanas and Fortunatus while Paul, Aquila, Priscilla, and Castor joined the procession behind the cart. Paul wanted all of Corinth to know that what Stephanas and Fortunatus were doing was their idea and would not be able to accuse him, Aquila, or any other Jew of instigating trouble. He would stand beside Stephanas and Fortunatus before it was over. But the timing would have to be just right. He was very concerned about the reaction of the crowd, especially of the Priests of Aphrodite.

Have no fear! I am building My church. The gates of Hades will not be victorious against it. My servants will be victorious!

Some would say that it was fate, but Paul believed that it was the hand of God that determined that the two processions would enter the Agora at precisely the same moment and travel side by side for a time. The noise of the two processions melded together in a perfect jumble. The sight and sounds were beginning to attract a large crowd from the Agora. Stephanas and Lilia were well known to the priests. The Supreme High Priest moved closer to the believers' procession and threw a dark look and a gesture at Stephanas that said, "What are you doing?"

Stephanas laughed and went over to the priest, cupped his hands together, and shouted near his ear, "I am retiring from business. You should be happy. You can have my customers!" The look on the face of the priest was indescribable as he returned to the head of the pagan parade. At some point, the two processions parted. One proceeded to a place of sacrifice and the other proceeded to a place of sanctification. The curious crowd from the Agora turned away from the temple procession and followed Stephanas and Fortunatus and the lengthy line of believers.

When they arrived at the fire pit, Stephanas and the others began to unload the cart onto the pavement. The people who were carrying items walked by and threw them on the pile. The crowd came to silence as Stephanas climbed up into the cart and addressed them. "People of Corinth, listen to me! You all know who I am!"

"We know Lilia better!" wagged someone. There was a round of laughter from the men.

"No, you do not! You would not have survived, twig!" Stephanas laughed with all of them.

Paul covered his eyes with his hands and prayed, "Lord, I understand that he knows how to talk to them, but help him say the right words without being vulgar."

Do not be concerned. Stephanas has prayed through the night. I answered him. He is My instrument.

"Brother Paul! Brother Paul!" Voices broke into Paul's prayer. Paul had been distracted by his thoughts. "He wants you up there with him. Stephanas is calling for you."

Paul went to the back of the cart and several of the young men helped him up. From the higher vantage point, he was able to see across the Agora. He was astounded by the crowd that had gathered for what had become a spectacle. In the meantime, a fire had been started in the pit. Belos and several others were feeding the fire with parchments, papyri, and tapestries that had been cut into pieces for easier burning. They had thought better of burning the opium, hashish, and other drugs. Many the people put them under their clothing and disposed of them in a nearby public latrine.

"Two days ago, I assaulted Brother Paul in the marketplace." There was a murmur of agreement from the crowd. "I want to give him a public apology before all of you." The crowd fell into shocked silence.

"But Brother Paul is a man who forgave me before I ever asked. During that evening and the next day, I fell into a dreadful illness. As death overcame me, I found myself on the bank of the Styx. I realized that there was no rest for my soul but only a terrible and never-ending judgment. Then I saw a being who was awesome in appearance, whose face shown like the sun. I heard a terrible voice, 'You are going to the cross.' When I came out of my sickness, I saw the face of Brother Paul, who had come to me and prayed in the name of Jesus for my healing. From him, I learned that the judgement of the cross fell, not on me, but on Jesus. And that Jesus was offered as a sacrifice on the cross so that my sins against God could be wiped out! Not only my sins, but the sins of anyone in the entire world who would believe in Him. All who believe in Jesus will be raised from their graves to live eternally with Him!"

"You are out of your mind," one voice yelled out. Many in the crowd agreed in a clamor of voices.

"No, no, my friends," Stephanas was shouting. "As the believers who are with me here will testify, never before have we been in a right mind!"

"Truly! Truly! Truly," shouted the believers in the procession.

"Jesus has told me that we must turn away from the idols of wood, stone, and metal to only serve the Spirit of Jesus. We must not listen to the sorcerers with their trickery and drugs. He has told me that we must turn away from dishonoring our bodies one with another in fornication. That is why we are burning all of these things!"

"Madness! Stop burning them! We want them!" The noise of the crowd drowned the voice of Stephanas.

Paul saw that things were turning ugly and dangerous. He shouted by Stephanas' ear, "We must leave!" They jumped down off the cart and moved to the body of believers who surrounded them as a human barrier.

Some in the crowd had run across the forum to inform the High Priest of what was transpiring. He and the other priests came running to the smoke of the fire and the shouting crowd. Two of the priests lifted the High Priest on their shoulders so that he could be seen. He waved his arms for silence.

"Stephanas and those with him are nothing but ATHEISTS!" The Supreme Priest was in a rage and was hurling spittle as he screamed. "Stephanas has blasphemed the gods! Someone has bewitched him! AWAY WITH THE ATHEISTS!" Some among the priests who were afraid of causing a civil disturbance pulled at him to get him off the shoulders of the two priests. They began dragging him back toward the place of sacrifice.

"AWAY WITH THE ATHEISTS! AWAY WITH THE ATHEISTS!" Many in the crowd had been roiled and were chanting. But a considerable number of people were distancing themselves from both the priests and the believers. None of them wanted to face the magistrate about a riot.

"We have to get everyone out of here!" Titius shouted to the group that had gathered in the middle of the believers. "Paul, Stephanas, Fortunatus, Luke, come with me to my house. They will not be looking for you there. Aquila, Priscilla, Castor, look to your own house. Belos, dismiss the cart, then lead the believers back to guard the houses of Stephanas and Fortunatus." Taking charge in an emergency came naturally to Titius, and no one challenged his authority to give orders to them or their servants.

"Lilia stays with me," Stephanas said. "I have some questions to ask Brother Paul."

"Priscilla and I are going with Paul!" Aquila's huge presence would not be denied. "Castor, tell Achaicus what has happened and secure the house. Tell Syntyche to care for the children."

"Then come on back to Titius' house, Castor, I will need you." Paul had plans for Castor.

The group with Titius began melting away in the crowd and passed through without being spotted by those who had evil intentions. They left behind a smoldering fire pit where some men were fruitlessly poking through the ashes to salvage something. Paul was breathing easier as he was walking away with the others. "Thank you, Lord Jesus, for keeping us safe!"

No one will be able to harm you in this city. I have many people here.

CHAPTER 9

THE NEW CHURCH

"If to others I am not an Apostle, yet to you, in truth, I am an Apostle. You are the seal of my apostleship in the Lord."

-Paul to the Corinthians

When Paul returned from the Agora with the others, they walked through the establishment of Titius Justus without stopping until they had ascended the stairs to the second floor living quarters. In the outer courtyard, Alexander had simply looked up from his work and nodded a greeting as they passed through. The scribes were busy scratching at their parchments. Not one of the customers browsing the merchandise paid any notice to Paul or the group. To most of the group, the events of the day and the confrontation in the Agora was a great and unusual adventure. To Paul, it was just another day at work for the Lord. Civil disturbance, trouble with magistrates, persecution, dangers, and trouble of every kind followed him wherever he went. The Lord had told him, "Paul, you will find much tribulation in this world. But cheer up! I have been victorious over the world!" This had been a great comfort to Paul. He knew that no matter how much he suffered, Jesus suffered more. And Jesus had overcome it all. The Lord was always with him. But, the day was still young. The Sabbath would begin in a few hours, and Paul would be next door in the synagogue proclaiming Jesus as the Christ. There would be incredulity and faith, consideration and argument, love and anger, all together in response to what Paul would preach. Hopefully, there would be no violence as a result.

The group began talking about what had transpired over the last few days while Olivia and the servants of the house prepared a meal for them in the banquet room. Aquila and Priscilla seemed uncomfortable as they entered the room. A thousand years of tradition had forbidden them to enter the home of a Gentile. To recline at table with them was unthinkable. But they had already learned from Paul the Pharisee that, with Jesus Christ, things had changed. They followed the example of Paul and overcame their discomfort.

They took their place on the cushioned benches around the long table in the upper room that served as a place where Titius could entertain his friends. Everything was ornate and beautiful. A fresco surrounded the whole room with scenes of domestic life and nature. It was beautifully lit by soft sunlight reflecting off the architecture in pleasant ambient rays.

"We have had a very successful day!" Paul smiled as he spoke.

"*What*? Truly?" Titius and Aquila exclaimed at the same time.

"We are fortunate that we were not charged!" Titius had a look of consternation. "Where were the Politeia anyway?"

"I have no faith in fortune," Paul answered calmly. "The Lord Jesus Christ protected us from evil." Paul looked around at the group. "No one was hurt. The Politeia did not arrive. No one was arrested. The Supreme Priest will not lodge a complaint with the magistrates. There are many witnesses to testify that *he* was the one who stirred up the crowd. But look at what we have gained! By tomorrow, everyone in Corinth will be talking about what has transpired in the last three days! I will be going into the Agora every day with the message of the gospel to anyone who will listen. Most will, at the least, listen to me. Truly, the Lord has gone before me!"

The group received this in silence. Paul knew that they were absorbing a new way of thinking about everything. The Greeks believed that they were the elite of the world. The Jews believed that they alone were favored of God. Slaves lived as best they could in whatever circumstance they found themselves. Women lived at the pleasure of men. Rome ruled and oppressed them all, lording over one-fifth of the population of the Earth. The core of the new church of Jesus Christ in Corinth was in the banquet room of Gaius Titius Justus. They represented different ethnic and social groups. In ordinary circumstances, they would not even think of being in the same room to share bread and salt. But grace and the Holy Spirit were working a miracle. They were beginning to love one another.

Paul continued, "Each of us has been touched by an infinite Spirit. We will never be the same. The Lord is faithful. What He has begun in us, He will be faithful to complete, keeping us blameless until the day of our death or His return. He will raise us from the grave as His resurrection testifies. So, death has lost its terror for me! It has no sting left. I still am afraid of suffering, but God will take me forward into all things. I know that I will live with Jesus forever. But while I am living on earth, I am compelled to work as hard as I am able. I am driven to build His Kingdom and care for His church. Woe is me if I do not preach the gospel! But my words are only words spoken by human lips. It is the power of God that takes the Word to the minds and hearts of people to convince them of the truth. Consider the hand of God. When I came into Corinth, I was alone and did not know where to go in this city or what to do. As I wandered aimlessly through the Agora, Stephanas and Lilia found me."

"I am sorry," Stephanas' face was in his hands. Lilia was weeping quietly.

"No, do not weep. You meant it to harm me, but God used it for the good of both of us. I rushed off from you in a daze or a trance, I know not. Somehow, I came to the door of this house and then one thing led to another. You, Stephanas, and your house were saved and now all of Corinth will be curious about what we are doing. Praise God for His mighty hand!"

"What do we do now?" Titius asked. Paul could see he was a man who was always thinking about the next step and how to get ahead of the next problem. But he was completely at a loss in the present situation.

"I think that Brother Paul is going next door to the Synagogue as soon as the sun goes down." Aquila looked at Stephanas. "The Sabbath begins at sundown. Torah studies and lectures begin the Sabbath observance this evening. Tomorrow morning, we will have liturgy and a homily. We all bring food for a midday family meal. Tomorrow afternoon, there will be family worship with praise, singing, and dancing. Brother Paul belongs to a sect of the Jews called 'Pharisees.' The Pharisees are greatly respected among the Jewish people. He will have an opportunity to speak tonight and possibly give the homily in the morning. They may or may not accept what he has to say."

"Why would they not accept Brother Paul's words?" Stephanas said, mystified. "It is obvious that he is a man from the Most High God! No one could possibly do the things that Brother Paul does unless the Most High God is with him."

Paul spoke up, "From ancient times the Jews have been expecting a promised Messiah, one anointed by God to rule the nations. All of the prophesy pointed to Jesus of Nazareth, but He was not what they expected."

"Stephanas, I calculated the years from the ancient Book of the Prophesy of Daniel," Titius said, slapping the back of his hand in the palm of the other one. "I calculated right to the sixteenth year of the reign of Tiberius. I can show you the book in my scriptorium! When Brother Paul told me about Jesus, I knew that it had to be Jesus! He is the Messiah of the Jews, the Christ of God."

Paul shook his head, "They wanted a military leader to free them from the Romans and establish a new dynasty from the line of David, the greatest king of old. Jesus was of the royal line, but His family was of ordinary means from a no-account town called Nazareth. He was a *tekton* by trade, a worker in wood. He came to rule the hearts of men and that is how He will conquer the world. He is the Son of God, but He lived among ordinary people! He made Himself a sacrifice to God on a cruel cross for the benefit of the world. Isaiah the Prophet wrote that the Messiah would be a suffering servant and suffer death as an atonement for sin. But God raised Him from the dead so that we will have hope of eternal life! Many of the common people accepted him as the Son of God. But the greatest opposition came from those who were not going to accept any Messiah. The ones that ruled could not tolerate anyone who upset their religious tradition and their system of power and wealth. They are still suppressing the truth in unrighteousness!"

Paul looked around at the group. "I want everyone to hear what I am going to say now. We will have a great deal of opposition from the leaders and many others in the community of the Jews. You must understand their anger. The gospel of Jesus overturns centuries of tradition. Many of them even think that we are trying to destroy their faith. We must protect ourselves, but," Paul began clapping his hands with every word, "we must not return evil for evil, or blow for blow."

Paul let this sink in and then he said, "The Lord has revealed to me that in future years, there will be much suffering endured by the Jewish people. And, there will be much violence and persecution by some in the church against the Jews. This is very displeasing to the Lord, for the Jews are His chosen people. Remember always, that Jesus is a Jew! Remember that all of His apostles are Jews, and all of those who received Christ in the beginning were Jews. Without Judaism, there is no Christianity. Always remember to pray for the peace of Jerusalem. This is what Scripture teaches us to do."

There was a time of silence as each of them absorbed Paul's words. Paul supposed that most of them harbored the popular prejudice against Jews, but he was determined to get that out of their hearts and minds.

"How did Jesus become the Son of God?" Lilia interrupted the silence with her soft voice. In Greek society, women did not often enter men's conversations. Her question kept the group in the awkward silence that Paul had brought about with his words.

"I think her question should be answered." Priscilla, also, was not one who conformed to the conventional silence of women. "In our meetings of believers, we women are free to enter into any discussion among the group. Men do the teaching, but women can speak as long as we respect our husbands. Lilia has asked a good question that deserves an answer. Please, Brother Paul, answer her question."

Paul took a breath, let it out slowly and said, "Jesus was born of a virgin." He braced himself for the inevitable response. He was not comfortable talking to a former prostitute about virginity and childbirth. Paul could not keep the image out of his mind when Lilia had pulled aside her garment in the Agora to embarrass him and mock his red face. The thought was truly a messenger of Satan sent to torment him.

"How can that be, if she knew no man?" Lilia's face and tone told of the sincerity of her question.

In the momentary silence that followed, Priscilla spoke. "Brother Paul? Please." Aquila was sharing in the embarrassment of Paul. The others were anxious the hear the answer to a question that *they* wanted to ask. Titius' wife, Olivia, had joined them and was listening with an upraised brow.

"Lilia," Paul said, looking at her directly, "I will give you the same answer that was given to Mary, a very young girl in Nazareth of Galilee, when the angel Gabriel announced that she was going to be with child. Her question to Gabriel was the same as your question, 'How can this be, since I have known no man?' This is how Heaven answered her question and how I will answer yours, 'The Holy Spirit will come and fall upon you and the power of the Most High will overshadow you. Therefore, the One born will be called the Holy Son of God.'"

"Do you believe that?" Luke broke into the discussion. "I never believed in the gods of the pantheon, much less in the demigod offspring of gods and humans. I don't even have an ounce of confidence in Asclepius, the god in whose name I practice medicine. I believe in Jesus because of the astounding works I have seen you do in the name of Jesus. I feel the change that has come into my life. I know that some presence is with me, but I am a man who needs to know ... and I have doubts."

"I believe that God spoke, and the earth and all life came into existence," Paul answered. "I believe that God formed the first man out of the dust of the earth. It is not difficult to believe that this same God could create a pure human being, without sin, in the womb of a young virgin girl. It is not hard for me to believe that she would be His servant to carry His Christ and nurture the Holy One until the time was just right for Jesus to be revealed to the world. Brother Luke, you should consider these things yourself. I can introduce you to many witnesses. In fact, you could write an account of the life and teaching of Jesus. You could also chronicle the events and history of the Church. As my disciple, I might give you that task and you could serve as my amanuensis as well. I want to write many letters to the churches."

"So, Mary remained pure and undefiled by any man during her pregnancy," Lilia said, bringing the conversation back to the subject. "I suppose that God did this so that He could become human flesh without being defiled by the evilness of humanity. Therefore, I would think, Jesus was born pure and sinless ... holy!"

"*Exactly!*" Paul was amazed by the words coming from a woman that most people would consider nothing but gutter trash.

"And it was prophesied long ago in the book of Isaiah the Prophet!" Titius quoted the scripture from the Septuagint, "'Therefore, the Lord Himself shall give you a sign; behold a virgin shall conceive in the womb, and shall bring forth a son, and you shall call his name Emmanuel.' That name means 'God-with-us.'"

"Jesus, pure and sinless, the Son of God." Lilia's eyes welled with tears. "I am filthy and defiled! How can Jesus ever have anything to do with me?"

Paul spoke softly, "Never underestimate the grace of God..."

"You do not *UNDERSTAND!*" Lilia paused and gained control of her voice. "I was exposed as an infant. My first master was looking for females and found me. He did not raise me for his own use, but for money. He kept me untouched until I was a young girl. Then, he auctioned off my virginity at a banquet in the gymnasium. Some old goat was the 'winner.' He was disgusting! He really hurt me! I was crying and screaming. The other men watched ... laughing. They imitated his sounds and mocked my cries. They got down into my face and said things like, 'You will learn, you little wench,' and, 'you know you like this ...'" Lilia stopped, and Paul saw that Aquila had his face in his hands. Titius, Stephanas, and Fortunatus were shamefaced and looking at the floor. Olivia was staring at Lilia with her hand over her mouth.

Priscilla alone was looking at her with compassion. She said, "Sister Lilia, I am sorry that you have been so harmed and hurt. You have suffered much. You have also caused suffering to others. All people have sinned against God and harmed others." Priscilla moved to the side of Lilia. "Jesus came into this world because there was so much sinfulness and violence. He has forgiven your sins. Now He will heal your heart and soul. Jesus will change the men who follow Him so that they will not violate people as you have been violated. To those who refuse His grace and will not change, there will be *judgment!*" Priscilla looked around the room at each of the men.

Castor had returned and joined them at the table. The servants of the house were coming into the room bringing food. Paul noted they were stealing glances at Lilia, pretending not to listen to this fantastic conversation. He hoped they were catching every word as she was speaking. Paul could see the questions on their faces. What slave could speak up so forcefully? Who is the one they call Priscilla? What women could speak to men in this way? Slaves sitting at the table of the free?

"I will offer a prayer of thanksgiving to God before we begin our meal." Paul stood and looked at the ceiling with palms outstretched, in the manner of the Jews, but before eating, in the manner of Jesus. Titius had picked up a fig but put it down, being used to praying after eating. Paul prayed,

"Our Father in heaven,

Holy be Your name,

We thank You for the bounty of the earth,

That yields food to sustain our bodies,

I thank You for the grace extended to Sister Lilia,

That has made her my true daughter in the Lord,

As she has been given grace for forgiveness of her sins,

So may she forgive those who have sinned against her,

Heal her body and soul altogether,

Bring forgetfulness of hurt and remembrance of grace.

In the name of Jesus Christ, I pray,

Amen!"

Everyone paused to consider the prayer.

IN THE GRIP OF GOD

"Brother Paul, Jesus must have been a remarkable person," Luke said, "that His servants could speak as you speak and do what you have done."

"All of the glory goes to Him! I am but a vessel." Paul looked around the table. No one was touching the food. "Everyone, eat! The last time I was in this house I did not get to finish the meal! I am hungry. Thank you for your hospitality, Titius. Come now, eat, and be thankful, everyone. Aquila, Priscilla, you know the Lord has declared that all food is clean. What the Lord has declared clean, of both food and people, we dare not treat as unclean."

"Yes, that is what is right," Aquila answered, "but I would that you help us with the other Jews in our fellowship. We will face much criticism for this day, Brother Paul."

"I will help you. I will tell them of the vision of Apostle Peter and how he was condemned by many in the church for obeying the Lord. And I will tell them how I got in Peter's face when he backed off eating with the Gentile brothers in Antioch. That will be an appropriate time to share the letter that I am carrying from the Church in Jerusalem and James, the leader of the Church. The letter is instructive to the Gentiles, but it also speaks directly to Jewish believers. All of that will be a relevant story for the history that you will be writing, Luke."

"I have been thinking of that, Brother Paul. I will accept that task with gladness! I am naturally a curious person, and my mind is fairly aching to find out more about Jesus and about you, Brother Paul, and the other Apostles."

"I will tell you about what I know about the other Apostles and what happened to me and about my journeys up to this point. The Holy Spirit will be with you to inspire your writing and make sure that you get it right." Paul spoke between mouthfuls of the excellent dish that was set before them. "When Silas comes to us with Timothy, you must talk to him. Silas knew Jesus and His family and was there with the one hundred and twenty at Pentecost. He will tell you what happened. Then, you will accompany me after I have finished my work in Corinth. We will go to Jerusalem, and I will introduce you to many who were eyewitness to the things that Jesus did and the marvelous things that happened. Some of them were even healed by His hand. But right now, I want to tell you a story that was told to me several years after Jesus' resurrection by a fellow Pharisee, who is now a believer, named Simon. Be sure to include it in your account, Luke. The incident happened in Simon's home. Lilia, this story is for you to cherish in your heart.

"Simon told me that he was very curious about Jesus. So, he invited Him to his home for a meal. Simon did not give Him any honor at all, so he could see how Jesus would react. He let Jesus recline at table with his dusty feet. He did not offer Jesus or His disciples any water to cleanse their hands after the manner of all Jews. Nor did he anoint Jesus' head as one would do an honored guest. Jesus said nothing in reply but reclined as though He was not offended at all. There was a woman in the community who was known to be a very immoral woman, probably a prostitute, who heard that Jesus was reclining at Simon's table. She entered the house and began washing Jesus' dusty feet with her tears and wiping

IN THE GRIP OF GOD

them with her hair. She anointed His feet with perfume and kissed His feet. Simon could hardly believe what he saw. He thought, 'If this man were really a prophet, He would know that this woman is a filthy, immoral woman, and he would not let her touch him.' But Jesus could always discern the thoughts of people. So, He said, 'I would like to say something to you, Simon.' Simon said, 'Say it, Rabbi.' Simon was sure that he now had something against Jesus. But Jesus said, 'A certain banker had two debtors. One owed him five hundred denarii, and another owed him five. Neither one could repay what was owed. The banker graciously forgave them both. Which one to you think loved him most?' Jesus had a way of telling stories and asking questions to teach the truth and expose hypocrisy."

"Like Socrates," Titius interrupted, "and his method of teaching by asking questions."

"Yes, similar," Paul answered, "but with virtue and the wisdom that no man, including Socrates, ever possessed."

"Go ahead with the story! We want to hear the rest!" Stephanas, Lilia and Fortunatus spoke up at the same time. "How did Simon answer?"

"He answered in the only way that made sense. He said, 'I suppose it was the one who owed him the most.' Jesus said, 'That is the correct answer, Simon.' Then Jesus asked him another question that Simon could not answer. Jesus turned from speaking to Simon and looked to the woman at his feet and asked, 'Do you see this woman?' Simon told me that he was trying not to look at her at all! Jesus said, 'When I came into the house, you did not wash my feet, nor anoint my head with oil. But from the time this woman came into your home, she has not ceased from washing my feet with her tears and anointing them with perfume. Those who have been forgiven much, love much. Her sins, which are many, are forgiven!' Of course, Simon was horrified by this statement. But Jesus ignored his protestations and said to the woman, 'Your sins are forgiven. Go in peace.'"

"What a beautiful story!" Lilia's face was wet with her tears. "She was like *me*!"

"She was like all of us, Lilia!" Priscilla spoke forcefully. "God's commands are for us to love and respect Him alone as God; to forsake idols; to take one day a week for rest and worship; to respect our parents; to do no murder, to not commit adultery; to not steal; to not testify falsely about our neighbor; to not even covet what belongs to our neighbor. God gave these commands to Moses and has taught the Jews that to violate one is to violate them all. Lilia, all of us are sinners and deserve eternal punishment. Jesus came so that we could be forgiven. In Jesus, we have been saved and have a new life. We have lived very different lives, Lilia, but now we are your brothers and sisters in the Lord!"

"I love Jesus with all of my heart!" Lilia exclaimed. "And I love all of you!"

Paul resumed his story. "Jesus faced a lot of criticism because He associated with all types of people. He loved to sit at a meal and talk with His friends and disciples, just as we are doing right now. People called Him a glutton and a drunkard, a man who was the friend of sinners. He was no drunkard, and He never overindulged, but He *is* the friend of sinners. He told Simon, 'Those who are healthy have no need of a physician. I have not come to call the righteous, but sinners to repentance.'"

Luke spoke, "Jesus seems to have been a true physician, a healer of the whole person. I am naturally a skeptical person. People only change to become more like they always have been, and that not for the good. I have always seen in the human spirit the same thing that I see in the human body—deterioration over time. Will the people of Corinth *really* change? Will *we* truly change?"

"I must change," Fortunatus entered the conversation. "*We* must change, Luke. I have done nothing except lie to people and give them drugs. I pretended to have some occult power and tell them what they want to hear and then bend their minds with opium and hashish. Luke, they came to me because they could never afford a physician. There is no help or hope for them! When there is a plague, many people die because there is no one to provide them simple things, like nourishment and warmth! My heart is now crying out to the lepers outside of the gate. I want to show that I have changed by the actions that I take."

"I can't be the physician for the whole city!" Luke grabbed another citron and started to peel.

"But you can teach me!" Fortunatus thumped his chest. "And I can teach others. And we can teach the ones we help about Jesus. You know the truth, Luke! The people don't have physicians, only the wealthy. And, oh yes, Brother Paul can teach us how to lay hands on the sick and heal them in Jesus' name."

Before Luke could answer, Stephanas spoke, "I have in mind to free the men and women that I have forced into prostitution. But I don't want to throw them to the wolves. They would just return to selling their bodies as freed slaves. I want to set them up in some small industry that will support them. I could even hope that they could find husbands and wives."

"I could help with that!" Titius was catching the enthusiasm. "I have numerous properties around that could serve as small points of craft."

"I have something that Jesus is telling my heart about," Lilia said. "I want to go and find infants who have been exposed to die outside of the city. I want to save them from death and from being found by ogres like the one who found me. Stephanas, we could find parents for them from the people who are going to follow Jesus. Maybe we could care for some of them in your house."

Everyone began speaking and talking over each other. Paul's loud voice raised over the clatter, "People, people! These are all noble sentiments, and I think that we should plan to do each one of them. They are splendid ideas! But the change that you seek will not come through these good works. Being in Christ is what will change each one of you! If any person is in Christ, they are a new creature! It is a supernatural thing! There is a spiritual song that says,

> When Jesus comes to save,
> Our old person goes away!
> His life for new life He gave,
> A new person comes to stay!

"Not only do we have that new life when we receive Jesus, there is more. We are all being changed by the Holy Spirit, day by day increasing in the knowledge of grace and holiness. We are daily being transformed into the image of Christ!"

"So, what do we do *next*?" Titius said.

"We organize the church in Corinth." Paul was ready with an answer. "We have the first Council of the New Church in Corinth right in this room! Every group of people in Corinth, or most of them, are represented in this group. You will be the leaders."

"Leave me out of it!" Olivia stood up from the dining bench. "I think that you are all out of your minds!" She looked at Titius who had a look of consternation. "I am sorry, my husband, but I do not believe any of this. I do not like these people." She walked out of the door of the room.

"That ... that ... that is ..." Titius sputtered, "... outrageous! I ought to—"

"Be patient with her." Paul interrupted. "Do not put her away. Do not leave her if she consents to stay with you. Love her and pray for her. Do not harass her in any way. Be an example for her. Have faith that God will save her."

"What do I do now?" Titius face was red.

"We make a plan, Titius." Paul was smiling. "The followers of Jesus meet on the first day of the week for worship. We will need a place to worship. It can even be outside, but preferably under shelter. How many people do we have so far? Hundreds, I think, and many more in the future."

"I own a warehouse that I have just finished refurbishing," Titius said, gaining control of his emotions. "I will gladly give the use of it to the church."

"Andronicus and I can help establish worship," Aquila spoke. "We have been celebrating the Sacrament of Jesus in our worship. We can teach the significance of Jesus as the Passover Lamb. Brother Paul can preach."

"We can have a meal for all, everyone can bring food." Priscilla was beaming a smile that was a response to everything that had happened in the day.

"With your help," Paul said, "I will appoint overseers of the church. The gathered worship on the first day is essential and important. But the meetings that will take place on the third and fourth days of the week in the homes of believers are just as important. We will have small groups, men with men, and women with women. We will talk and pray together as we have been talking over this meal. We will confess our sins one to another and encourage each other to excel in faith and good works."

"We will need good leaders for those groups." Aquila was getting enthusiastic. "We can get busy this evening and tell everyone that we know from our neighborhood and the neighborhood of Stephanas that we will be meeting the day after tomorrow."

"I will need you, Aquila and Priscilla, and Titius, with me," said Paul. "I will be meeting the people at the synagogue this evening, and I want you to be there. Stephanas, Fortunatus, and Lilia can take care of spreading the word and getting everything prepared at Titius' warehouse."

The slaves of the house had moved from hiding behind the door to the entry of the banquet room, listening for quite some time. Neither Titius or Olivia reprimanded them or told any of them to go back to work in the house. When Paul dismissed the group with prayer, all of them prayed with him.

CHAPTER 10

THE SYNAGOGUE

"And Paul was dialoging in the synagogue every Sabbath, convincing Jews and Greeks."

-Acts 18:4

The shadows were lengthening as Paul, Aquila, Priscilla, and Titius stepped out of the door of the establishment. The door of the synagogue was just a few dozen steps to the left. Titius owned the entire block, and all the people and shops in the block were his tenants. The portion of the building that was occupied by the synagogue was next door to him, and they shared a common wall with his establishment. When he had let out the space to the Jewish people, he had no idea what Judaism was about or what Jews were really like. His prejudice was inherited and instinctual. But prejudice falls before friendship. He liked Crispus, the ruler of the synagogue, from the moment that he met him. Their negotiation for the lease wandered into discussion of religion and especially of the God of Abraham, Isaac, and Jacob. Titius was fascinated by history and prophesy. He thought about the validation, or invalidation, of one by the other. After the synagogue moved in, he accepted the invitation of Crispus to visit their worship service on the Sabbath. From the Godfearers' gallery, he looked through the lattice and listened to the Scripture reading. Titius watched as the Torah Scroll was presented, and a Rabbi carried the scroll around the assembly. He saw the Jews' respect for the Word as they touched it with reverence and some kissed it. After a time, he began donating the rent back to the synagogue and giving regularly to the poor.

When Titius learned that the synagogue possessed a copy of the famed Greek language Septuagint Scriptures, he asked Crispus if he could come and read on his own. He was a little disconcerted that he was not able to touch the Scriptures. The scrolls had been consecrated and sanctified. Being now holy, they could not be defiled by the touch of the Gentile. However, Crispus accommodated him by having Titius come during the week and listen from the gallery while he read from the floor of the synagogue. Titius asked questions through the lattice, and Crispus patiently answered from the floor. From what he learned in this fashion, Titius was determined to have a copy of the Septuagint. He also saw profit from being able to provide sanctified copies of the Septuagint to synagogues around the Empire. They would be beautiful works of art as well as true and accurate copies. Ordinarily, only scribes could reproduce manuscripts of Scripture. But, Titius' generosity to the synagogue and the poor facilitated a certain accommodation. He would have the blessing and oversight of Crispus, as well as the Rabbis, and have their contacts with other synagogues as well. The Scripture project had come together nicely, and with it, a friendship with Crispus.

Titius was surprised when Crispus asked him if he wanted to become a Jew. He had no idea that something like that was possible. He learned from Crispus that it was not his pedigree that separated him from God, but rather, his rebellion and idolatry. Titius came to believe that the Ten Commandments given to Moses were the best foundation of law for a truly just government. But when he found that to be a proselyte he would have to follow all the traditions of the Jews and be circumcised, he decided to remain a God-fearing Gentile. As he studied his own copy of the Scriptures, his mind was captured by the prophesies of the *Messiah*, as the Jews called Him, or the *Christ*, as the Greeks called Him. He continued to come to the synagogue and discuss what he was learning with Crispus. But Crispus could not answer many of his questions about the Messiah and the prophesies of His advent into the world. Aquila, a respected Jew in the synagogue and the community, knew about Jesus Christ and yet told Titius nothing about it. He was itching to ask Aquila, "Why did you not tell me about Jesus? We are friends, are we not?" He knew now that some Jews learned the truth about Jesus. But Paul was different than all the other Jews. Paul was not only a Jew, but the first scholar who was fully answering his questions. Paul came without hesitation into his house and shared a meal with him. He also brought Aquila and Priscilla to his table. And, Paul was the only Jew that he knew who was outspoken about Jesus. He loved Paul as a cherished brother and prayed silently for him as they all walked to the door of the Synagogue.

"Greetings, Aquila!" Crispus was standing before the door. He shook hands with Aquila. "Titius, it is good to see you, as usual." Looking at Paul, he said, "And who is this? A visitor?"

Aquila answered, "This is Saul of Tarsus, better known to us as Paul. He is a friend of mine and known to me. Paul is a Pharisee, as was his father and grandfather."

"Pharisee!" Crispus shook Paul's hand vigorously. "This is quite an honor. It has been an age since we had a Pharisee with us! Would you do us a great honor and lead the Scripture lesson? We have been studying Deuteronomy, but you can choose any text that you want."

"I would be honored by the opportunity," Paul replied, smiling warmly. "Aquila can read for me. My eyes are getting weak in the lamplight."

"Titius, I did not see you today when I came around for the collection." Crispus, the Ruler of the synagogue went around every sixth day of the week to collect for the widows and orphans of the synagogue. The synagogue then provided enough food for two meals a day during the coming week. It was his duty to see that all the poor were fed, sheltered and clothed. Titius' home was his best stop.

"I'm sorry," Titius responded, "I was occupied elsewhere and did not leave instructions for my steward. I will bring it in the morning and give it to you."

"That is not necessary. I will come around on the first day of the week. The commandment says, 'Remember the Sabbath day to keep it holy!'" Crispus changed the conversation. "Say,

Titius, as I was out collecting, I saw a disturbance in the Agora this afternoon. There was quite a bit of smoke going up. Do you know what that was about?"

"Yes, indeed, I do!" Titius looked at Paul, whose expression said, "Not now." "But it is too long of a story to tell at the moment. We can talk about it at our regular meeting."

Crispus did not have a chance to reply to Titius as there were many people now coming to the synagogue. When Paul and Aquila went into the main floor of the synagogue, Titius turned to the right and went up a couple of steps to the God-fearers' gallery. Priscilla turned to the left and went to the women and children's gallery. There were tiered stone benches in each of the galleries on which to sit with cushions provided for comfort. If they could walk, boys accompanied their fathers by the hand into the floor of the synagogue. The main room was laid out from east to west so that as the worshipers entered, they would be facing toward Jerusalem. The length of the floor was enhanced by a double row of columns from back to front. A magnificent fresco covered the front and the sides of the room with depictions of Bible stories and the characters that carried the Word of God to the people of Israel. The fresco on the back wall of the main hall was dedicated to paintings of the three temples of Solomon, Ezra, and Herod. The room was beautifully appointed with furnishings. There were ornate chairs for the Ruler, elders, and rabbis. There were stone benches scattered around the room with cushions similar to the ones in the galleries. The men sat on the benches, sat on the floor, or stood. The men kept their heads covered at all times. At the front of the room was a platform ringed by three steps. In the middle and on the back edge of the platform was a cabinet, called the "ark." The ark contained the scrolls of the Scripture. Above the ark was suspended a lamp that was kept burning continuously. In front of the ark was a pulpit on which the selected scroll was rolled out to be read. To the right of the pulpit on the platform was a chair from which the preacher could preach or the teacher could teach. To the left of the platform on the floor stood a large silver menorah with its nine lights. The chairs for the Ruler, elders, and rabbis were arranged in front of the platform facing the congregation. The platform was well-lit with many lamps.

Priscilla worked to keep her composure. She was expected, with the other women, to listen silently on the other side of the lattice. The children were not with her this evening. She missed having her daughters sitting next to her. She wanted to see her son sitting on the floor in the front row before the chair of Aquila. She greeted the other women as they began settling in to their seats. As she waited, Priscilla's thoughts took her away from the scene on the synagogue floor. In her imagination, *she* was sitting in the chair of the preacher. Her husband was standing at the pulpit ready to read from the prophet Joel. She nodded to him and he was reading,

"And it shall come to pass afterward,

That I will pour out My Spirit on all flesh,

And your sons and your daughters will prophesy,

And your old men shall dream dreams,

And your young men shall see visions,

And on my servants and on my handmaids,

In those days will I pour out of My Spirit."

Priscilla was preaching and in her mind's eye, she saw every kind of face imaginable looking back at her. Men and women, children, of every age, race and tribe known on the earth. They were all listening and believing ... *you are my chosen instrument, preach the gospel, proclaim the Holy Spirit, let no one despise you!*

"Priscilla! *Priscilla!*" Junia's voice brought Priscilla out of her fantasy. "Are you well?"

"Junia! I was just wrapped up in my thoughts."

"There is much to think about this evening. We must pray!"

Among the women of the Jewish believers, Priscilla was very outspoken. She was able to speak frankly and openly with her husband. In the congregation, however, it was another story. The Holy Spirit seemed to be pushing Priscilla to speak out boldly as she had spoken in the street outside of the house of Stephanas. She was wavering between determination and fear. She sat beside Junia and took her hand as they prayed together for Paul and their husbands. The other women in the gallery looked at them curiously. *Paul is my apostle! As I have sent him, so am I sending you!* Wondering if she was hearing the Lord or her own flesh, Priscilla squeezed the hand of Junia and prayed fervently. The muted sounds of their prayers began filtering through the lattice down to the floor of the synagogue.

Paul was ushered up to the front and given a seat of honor before the platform. Aquila sat to his right and Crispus to his left. He looked out over the men and boys who were gathering. How he loved his fellow Jews! He recognized the believers that he had met at the love feast in the home of Aquila. These men would give him a great advantage in his efforts. He looked at both galleries and nodded his recognition to those who were praying. Paul looked around the beautiful synagogue. He loved this place and its traditions! How saddened he was that the Law, the Temple, the synagogue, and complex traditions had become substitutes for the faith of their father, Abraham. Abraham had no law, no temple, no synagogue, no tradition, and not even a permanent home in the land that had been given him by God. But Abraham was justified before God because of his simple faith in the promises of God. And, a promise came from the Lord that one of Abraham's descendants would be a blessing to the whole earth. "Now people are justified by faith in that promise fulfilled in Jesus Christ," Paul spoke softly. "How difficult it is to turn from tradition to a new and living way in Christ!"

"SH'MA!" All stood at the call to worship. Everyone recited together the proscribed prayer that every Jew repeated twice a day, morning and evening. Each phrase was given in Hebrew and then in the common Greek. Paul recited it with conviction,

> "SH'MA, YISRA'EIL! ADONAI
> ELOHEINU ADONAI, ECHAD!"
> "Hear, Israel! The Lord is our God, the Lord is One.
> Blessed be the Name of His glorious
> kingdom for ever and ever.
> And you shall love the Lord your God,
> With all your heart,
> And with all your soul,
> And with all your might,
> And these words that I command you
> today shall be in your heart,
> And you shall teach them diligently to your children,
> And you shall speak of them when you sit at home,
> And when you walk along the way,
> And when you lie down,
> And when you rise up.
> I am the Lord, your God. AMEN!

Crispus remained standing and addressed the assembly, "We have the distinct honor at the beginning of this Sabbath, to be visited by Saul of Tarsus, a Pharisee. He is known by his cognomen, Paul, 'the small.' There seems to be nothing small about him, though. Aquila has been telling me that Paul is a third-generation Pharisee who received his rabbinical instruction at the feet of the great Gamaliel in Jerusalem. Paul has also held, for a time, a seat in the Sanhedrin. Paul will conduct the scripture lesson for us. Aquila will be reading for him. Rabbi Benjamin will assist them at the ark. Rabbi Philip will now lead us in the Blessings.

While the congregation recited the Blessings, Paul and Aquila stepped up to the platform. The Rabbi helped them find the Scroll of Isaiah. The Rabbi raised his brow when Paul told him the two passages of Scripture that he wanted Aquila to read. Paul took the seat of the preacher while Rabbi Benjamin rolled the Septuagint scroll out in the prescribed way on the pulpit. Benjamin and Aquila found the first passage. They waited while the Blessings continued.

From the chair, Paul prepared his mind and spirit. He gave a hearty "Amen" with the congregation as Philip recited each blessing. Between the "Amens", he prayed, "Blessed are You, O God. I give thanksgiving for all of the blessings that we have received from You. You are the shepherd of Israel. You have loved us with a never-ending love. You have loved us by sending Messiah Jesus to us. You sent us Your very own Son. You offered him up as a sacrifice, an atonement for our sins. Just as You showed Abraham, who was willing to offer Isaac as a sacrifice, help me to show Your precious people that You have provided the blood to be offered on The Day of Atonement. Help me to proclaim salvation for Israel and for the people of the whole earth. Amen."

When the Blessings were finished, Aquila spoke from the pulpit, "Paul has chosen three passages from the Prophet Isaiah. The first is found in the seventh chapter,

"Therefore, the Lord Himself shall give you a sign: Behold, the virgin will be with child and bear a son, and you will call His name Immanuel."

"The second is found in the fifty-third chapter of Isaiah." Aquila and Benjamin took a moment to find the second scripture. Paul looked around for a reaction to the Scripture. It was a little hard for him to see in the lamplight, but he could imagine their response.

Aquila resumed reading,

"'O, Lord, who has believed our report?
And to whom has the arm of the Lord been revealed?
We brought a report as of a child before Him,
He is a root in a thirsty land,
He has no form or comeliness,
And we saw Him, but He had no form or beauty,
But His form was ignoble,
And inferior to that of the children of men,
A man in suffering,
And acquainted with the bearing of sickness,
For His face is turned away,
He was dishonored and not esteemed,
He bears our sins and is pained for us,
Yet, we accounted Him to be in trouble,
And in suffering, and in affliction,
But He was wounded on account of our sins,
And was bruised because of our iniquities,

The chastisement of our peace was upon Him,

And by His wounds we are restored.

All we as sheep have gone astray,

everyone has gone astray in his way,

And He, because of His affliction,

Opens not His mouth,

He was led as a sheep to slaughter,

And as a lamb before the shearer is dumb,

So He opens not His mouth,

In humiliation His judgment was taken away,

Who shall declare His generation?

For His life is taken away from the earth,

Because of the iniquities of my people,

He was led to death.'

"May God bless the reading of His Word, Amen," Aquila spoke with conviction as the congregation gave a muted, "Amen." Aquila and the Rabbi remained at the pulpit.

Paul began, "In times past, God has spoken to us by means of Moses and the Prophets. In these last days, he has spoken to us through a Son." Paul paused to let the words have their effect. "This Son has not abolished any of the Word of God given to us, but has fulfilled the message of God for Israel and for all the people of the earth.

"We have heard the reading of the Scripture. These are passages that we have not often heard read in the synagogue. Some of you may never have heard this read. The reason is that these words of God that have come to us from the prophet Isaiah have been very difficult to understand. These prophesies pertain in some ways to a person in the time of the prophet. But it is obvious that they also apply to the Expected One; the Holy One of God; the Son of David; the Son of Man; the Messiah. But how could a virgin ever conceive? How would her child be called 'God-with-us'? How is it possible that Messiah would be rejected by His own people? How could the suffering of a man atone for sin? It is impossible, in our minds, for Messiah to be 'cut off' as it says in the scroll of the prophet Daniel. His kingdom is to be an 'everlasting kingdom.' Because Scripture cannot be broken, these have been unanswerable questions to us. So, we have had to lay these questions aside and wait patiently until the day that God Himself will reveal the interpretation to us. I am here to proclaim that an answer to these questions has been found. An answer that God has given, to which I am a witness. Brother Aquila, will you please read the third passage for consideration?"

"This is also from the fifty-third chapter of Isaiah." Aquila resumed reading,

"And I will give the wicked for His
burial, and the rich for His death;
for He practiced no iniquity, nor deceit with His mouth.
The Lord also is pleased to purge Him from His stroke.
If you can give an offering for sin, your
soul shall see a long-lived seed,
The Lord also is pleased to take away
from the travail of His soul,

To shew Him light, and to form Him with understanding,

To justify the just One who serves many well,

And He shall bear their sins.

Therefore, He shall inherit many,

And He shall divide the spoils of the mighty,

Because His soul was delivered to death,

And He was numbered among the transgressors,

And He bore the sins of many,

And was delivered up because of their iniquities.'"

Paul continued, "The Scriptures tell us that there is One to be born of a virgin and is to be named Immanuel, being interpreted, 'God-with-us.' It tells us that the Messiah is not coming to us as a conquering warrior and King, but rather, a suffering servant who will be an atonement for our sins. It proclaims that He will be the Prince of Peace who will become the King of Kings." Paul raised the tone of his voice. "In the days of the census commanded by Caesar Augustus, One *was* born of a virgin in Bethlehem of Judea, the town of David. This One, namely, Jesus of Nazareth, fulfilled all the prophesy that has been read in your hearing. It was fulfilled in how Jesus lived His life, the marvelous signs that He performed, and what Jesus did to become a sacrifice to God for the benefit of the world. Jesus has made clear that which was hidden from the foundation of the world. He proved by His life and His miracles that He was indeed, Immanuel, God-with-us.

"Many of you, I trust, have heard of John the Baptist. His disciples are preaching in Asia and probably in Achaia as well.

In the days of the governorship of Pontius Pilate in Judea, John came preaching a baptism of repentance for the remission of sins. Almost everyone came from Judea and Jerusalem to hear him. He baptized thousands in the Jordan River. The people believed that John was a prophet. But wicked King Herod, the Chief Priests, and the religious leadership hated him because he preached against their sin and hypocrisy. He was finally executed by Herod because John condemned Herod for taking the wife of the King's brother. John proclaimed that he was preparing the way for the Messiah. When he saw Jesus coming to him, he proclaimed, 'Behold the Lamb of God, who takes away the sin of the world!' When Jesus was baptized, the heavens were ripped open and a great voice was heard, 'This is My Son, whom I love!' And, the Holy Spirit came from heaven in the form of a dove and rested on Jesus' head. When John heard the voice, and saw the Spirit come and remain on Jesus, he proclaimed, 'I have seen, and I declare, that this is the Son of God! I have baptized you with water, but He will baptize you with the Holy Spirit and with fire!' With these and many other words he proclaimed Jesus to be the Messiah, the Son of God."

Paul paused for a moment and then continued, "Jesus has become our Pascal Lamb! Just as the blood of the lamb sprinkled on the lintels and door posts protected our ancestors from the Destroyer in Egypt, so the blood of the Lamb, Jesus Christ, shed on the cross, protects us from eternal death and gives us a new life. His blood not only serves as an atonement for our sins, but also for the sins of the entire world.

"God did not consent for His Holy One to see decay, but raised Jesus from the grave. He appeared to many, including myself, afterwards. I proclaim to you, that Jesus Christ is the Son of God. If you will change your mind about these things and confess your sins; if you will confess Jesus as the Son of God; if you will believe in Him; if you will receive Jesus as your Savior; you will be saved and possess a new life. Then you can receive the purifying baptism of the Holy Spirit. Remember! Repent; confess; believe; receive Jesus and be baptized in His name!"

Paul looked around at the assembly, "I know there are many questions, and I am ready to answer."

Rabbi Philip moved quickly to the platform and skipped the bottom step in his rush. "Paul, this is a fantastic and unbelievable claim that you have made! There have been many in Judea and Galilee who have claimed to be Messiah. They all ended the same way! Scattered by the Romans. The ones that survived the fight were crucified along with whoever claimed to be the Messiah. These events that Paul has been speaking of happened over twenty years ago! By now we would have been informed by the Elders in Jerusalem and the Chief Priests if they were true. I say, put Paul out! He should not be speaking!"

"Excommunicate a Pharisee?" Crispus spoke up from his chair, "You go too far, Rabbi. We should consider these things that Paul has said. He has answered many questions that I have had in my mind about the scriptures that Aquila has read. Please, Rabbi, will you descend from the platform and make your comments from the floor?"

"Perhaps it is Crispus that needs to be put out!" The lamplight did not illumine Philip's red face, but it did display his anger.

"Please, Rabbi, follow decorum!" Crispus looked straight ahead, not turning his head back to look at Philip. "I serve at the pleasure of the Elders, not the Rabbis."

"I can make a petition!" Philip started to descend the steps but stopped and reversed his direction. Those who ascended the platform had to descend from the opposite side. There were a few involuntary sounds of laughter that came from the congregation as Philip walked across to the other side.

"There's a good fellow," Crispus said, as Philip reached the floor.

"This has not ended," Philip said softly as he passed by Crispus' chair.

"What Rabbi Philip has said is true." Paul leaned forward in his chair as he spoke. "The Council in Jerusalem and the Chief Priests have not accepted the testimony of John the Baptist. They have rejected Jesus, just as Isaiah prophesied. They have actively opposed the Church of Jesus Christ in Jerusalem. In truth, I, Saul of Tarsus, violently opposed the followers of The Way in the year following the resurrection of Jesus. I instigated a mob against a righteous man, Stephen. I held their coats while they stoned him to death. I obtained warrants from the Chief Priests and pursued the followers of the Way in Jerusalem, Judea, and even to Damascus. But Jesus appeared to me on the road to Damascus and struck me to the ground. He blinded me with a flash of light and asked me, 'Why are you persecuting me, Saul?' I said, 'Who are you,

Lord?' And He said, 'I am Jesus, the One you are persecuting.' Jesus instructed me to go to a believer in Damascus. I had to be led by the hand by my servants. I could see nothing. The believer was very kind to me even though I had a warrant in my basket for his arrest. He laid his hands on me in the Name of Jesus, and I received my sight. I received Jesus in faith and was blessed with a baptism in the Holy Spirit. Since then, I have preached Jesus Christ, the Lamb of God crucified and resurrected from the dead."

"Another fantastic and unbelievable story!" Philip was standing in front. "Besides yourself, are there any others you can name among the leaders in Jerusalem who have followed this Jesus?"

"Yes, as a matter of fact, I *can* name them. Nicodemus, Simon of Bethany, and Joseph of Arimathea are fellow Pharisees among many others who have followed Christ. Nicodemus was among the rulers. Even Gamaliel, my teacher, and a Pharisee, warned the Council about opposing the followers of Jesus. My hope is that even he, the great teacher, will receive Jesus as Messiah. There have also been many priests who have been obedient to the faith. But it is the common people among the Jews who have received Jesus as Messiah and Savior. They number among the tens of thousands in Jerusalem alone."

"I have something to say," Aquila said as he stepped down from the platform and stood in front of his chair. "I am a believer in Jesus Christ, and I follow Him. You know that we came from Rome when the Emperor expelled the Jews from the City. But you do not know why, other than the ongoing and unjust prejudice against the Jewish people. There have been many believers in Jesus among the Jews in the City of Rome. There was much anger between those who believed and those who did not. There were hot heads on both sides. Actual fights and even riots broke out. It was unseemly, brothers. Caesar had no concept of what it was about and simply expelled us all. I want to testify that in Jesus Christ, I have found peace with God and in the Holy Spirit, I have found joy in the Lord."

Aquila looked around at the congregation and to the gallery of the women and the gallery of the God-fearers. "I want to apologize to all of you! I have been keeping my faith a secret for fear that conflict may arise among us. But now, I am testifying to the power of the cross of Jesus Christ! I urge each of you to listen to Brother Paul. Repent, confess Jesus as the Son of God, receive Him in obedient faith, and be baptized in His name!" Aquila sat down.

"Hallelujah, husband!" Priscilla's voice came through the lattice.

"Amen! Amen," came from several voices from the floor and the galleries.

"*You?*" Philip was looking incredulously at Aquila.

"I have something to say!" All fell silent as an elderly voice pierced the room. Pamphilos began shuffling toward the front of the synagogue, with the aid of a staff. Everyone was surprised as the old man who never said anything in the synagogue came to the front to speak. Pamphilos was a man of few words. He had everyone's attention as he moved slowly to the front. The only sound heard was the "tap, tap, tap" of his staff on the floor. At the front of the synagogue, he turned to face the congregation, leaned on his staff, and spoke.

"Twenty-two years ago, I made my lifetime pilgrimage to Jerusalem for Passover Observance at the Temple. The Passover that I attended was the one where Jesus of Nazareth was crucified. I saw him enter the city on the foal of a donkey. The people loved him! They laid their coats in the road and cast palm branches before him. They praised God and welcomed him as they would a King! I followed the crowd as they went immediately to the Temple. You cannot believe what I saw! Jesus went into the market place in the Court of the Gentiles. He had a scourge with him, and he beat down those rascals that sold overpriced sacrificial animals and the crooked money changers. He turned over the tables of the money changers and the coins went rolling across the Temple floor." Pamphilos laughed. "You should have seen those swindlers on their hands and knees going after the money while Jesus striped their backs! He was yelling, 'You have made my Father's house a den of thieves!' I think, *that* is what did Him in. Jesus threatened their source of riches. They had him on the cross before Passover. When He was crucified, I thought no more about it until Pentecost.

"I stayed in Jerusalem until Pentecost. I was at the Temple, and I heard a commotion. The disciples of Jesus were preaching that Jesus had been raised from the dead. They were speaking in many languages all at once. Each person was hearing in their own native language. Simon, called Peter, was the main preacher. It was like the Holy Spirit possessed him. Thousands were baptized that day, but I was not among them. But when

I saw with my own eyes a man who was crippled from birth brought to his feet by Peter in the name of Jesus, I became a believer in Jesus Christ! I was baptized that day.

"Tonight is not the first time that I have seen Saul of Tarsus. I felt the heat of his persecution. Stephen was the godliest man I have ever known, a righteous Jew in the best sense of the word. Saul, Paul, had Stephen stoned for his faith in Jesus! Then he started going after us all! When Paul entered our synagogue this evening, I thought that he was here hunting the followers of Jesus. I left Jerusalem in the midst of that persecution and returned to Corinth. I want to join Brother Aquila in apologizing to you for my lack of courage. I am sorry that I hid this from you for all these years. I also want to advise each of you to listen closely to Brother Paul and do exactly as he says. Believe in Jesus and be baptized in His name! That is all I have to say."

"Amen! Rubbish! Hallelujah! Blasphemy!" A cacophony of voices erupted from the floor and from the galleries, some saying one thing and some saying another.

"Silence! Silence!" Crispus brought the synagogue to order.

"That is *all* you have to say?" Phillip was speaking loudly at the back of Pamphilos as he shuffled slowly back to his seat.

"Crispus, you have to say something!" Philip turned to speak to Crispus, "You have to stop this *nonsense*! Crispus! *Say something!*"

Crispus took a deep breath, stood to his feet, turned to face Paul, and said, "I want to be baptized!"

CHAPTER 11

THE FIRST DAY

"Crispus, the Ruler of the Synagogue, believed in the Lord along with his whole household. And many of the Corinthians, who were hearing, were believing and being baptized."

-Luke

The baptism of Crispus and his entire household shook the Jewish community in Corinth. But it also had its effect on the Greeks. Paul's gospel message was trembling the culture, rolling across the country like an earthquake from Thessalonica to Corinth. Crispus was well-known in the city as the leader of the Jews. Although he kept an appropriate "distance" from the defilement of the culture of Corinth, he nevertheless was friendly and courteous to all people. The occasional anti-Jewish slurs and insults that were thrown at him in the Agora he deflected with good humor. He took for his attitude the Proverb, "A gentle answer turns away wrath, but a harsh word stirs up anger." Many of his brothers in the synagogue thought it a better policy to return insult with insult. But the way of the soft answer to angry, hurtful words had yielded large results for Crispus personally, and for the Synagogue as well. Crispus had a good relationship with the administrators of Corinth and with the City Assembly. He had cultivated relations with Gallio, the Proconsul and Chief Magistrate of Achaia. All these associations enlarged Crispus and the synagogue. His friendship with Titius was an example. However, Crispus' attention to Titius was not solely done in selfishness. From the first time that he spoke with him, Crispus recognized that in Titius was a desire to know the God of Abraham, Isaac, and Jacob. He found Titius' fascination with the Scriptures to be amazing. He felt as though he was learning as much as Titius was learning from him in their one-on-one study sessions. As Titius asked penetrating questions from the gallery about the Scriptures that Crispus read from the floor of the synagogue, Crispus' mind and spirit were stirred. He began opening his mind to think about passages that he had closed off simply because he had no answer to the questions they brought forth. It had prepared his mind to receive the words of the Apostle Paul about Jesus Christ. Crispus not only received Jesus as Messiah, he grasped Him with all his heart, soul, and mind.

There was much consternation among those Jews who were doubtful about Jesus. But there were enough people who believed that Jesus was indeed the Messiah, that the Messianic Jews endured in the synagogue for the time being. The fact that Aquila and Priscilla had come out for Christ, and that Crispus became such a strong advocate for Jesus, made a fortress for them in the congregation. It worried Crispus that Paul asked him to serve on the council of The New Church in Corinth. Paul seemed to think that Crispus would have no problem being a part of an organization that had such radical ideas about Gentiles, women, and slaves. Crispus remained skeptical about his ability to have *close* personal and spiritual relationships with Gentiles.

"Thank you, Lord," he prayed, "for your hand in my life. You have opened my eyes to the Messiah. Jesus, your love for all people is amazing. I do not know that I can change. Help me! Give me a portion of Your love that I may love and accept Gentiles as you have loved and accepted me. I have always prayed for protection from them. Now, I pray, help them to love and accept me, also. Amen."

In the evening after the Sabbath meeting, Paul held a meeting with the Council of the New Church in Corinth. He brought them next door, to the establishment of Titius. Business was done for the day, so they had the lower floor area to themselves. Crispus had often been in Titius' establishment for the purpose of business, so he did not have any problem with the location of the meeting. However, he refused the offer of water or wine and kept his distance from the Gentiles, especially Stephanas and Lilia.

"I loved your homily today, Brother Paul." Crispus glowed with enthusiasm. "I had never really understood the story of Abraham and Isaac at Mount Moriah until today. Why would God ask Abraham to take such a drastic and sinful step as to sacrifice his own son? Didn't God already know that Abraham loved Him? I did not understand that story because I did not know Jesus! Isaac trudging up the mountain with the wood for the fire on his back. This is a type of Jesus carrying the cross up to the place of execution! The purpose of the story is not to let us know that Abraham loved God, but, when we see what Jesus did, *that God loves us!*"

"Hallelujah!" Priscilla was about to break out in a hallelujah dance. "You are a preacher, Brother Crispus!"

"And the part about God's provision! The ram caught in the thicket for sacrifice. God has indeed provided the once for all atonement for sin!" Crispus was showing the passion that would make him a powerful preacher.

"There are many things about faith in Jesus that go beyond what I said, Brother Crispus," Paul spoke and raised the cup that was in his hand. He had received the water and wine mixture from the hand of Titius' servant, Alexander. "What occurred between God and Abraham happened before there were any Jews. It would be centuries before there was a code of Law, or a temple, or the priesthood, or synagogues, or the body of traditions, or a nation called Israel. There was just Abraham and his tribe of Hebrews. Abraham was not even circumcised until he was one hundred years old. Yet, Abraham had a relationship with God. Without the Law of Moses, Abraham understood sin and obedience. God was teaching

Abraham how to be justified—by faith in the promises of God. He was showing him how his sins could be atoned—by a perfect sacrifice that God Himself would provide. Abraham was a Chaldean of Ur. He was living as a nomad in the land that God promised him and his descendants. He died, never seeing the promises fulfilled. But Abraham died in faith, believing that when the time was just right, God would give his descendants the land and provide a perfect sacrifice for sin. This is how Jesus could say, 'Abraham saw the day of My birth and rejoiced in it!'"

Crispus' eyes were moist with tears. "I know in my heart this is true! When you laid your hands on me, Brother Paul, and I received the Holy Spirit, it was like heaven came down to me. Jesus with me! I feel His near presence, like when Abraham and Moses talked with God."

"Yes, that is what we have experienced as well," Paul answered. "It is the experience and testimony of Jews and Greeks, Romans and Barbarians, men and women, slave and free. And, we have become one community in Christ Jesus, brothers and sisters in the Lord. The church meets on the first day of the week because Jesus was raised on the morning of the first day. Brother Crispus, I am not asking you to stop being a Jew or leave the synagogue. God forbid! But I am asking you to join with the church tomorrow in sharing with all of the believers at the Lord's table. It is a ritual that is similar to our Passover meal. I will explain it to everyone tomorrow. I want you to be willing to eat at the love feasts of the church at the same table with Gentiles. I want you to be able to enter their houses to minister to them. As a first step, I am asking you to take a cup of water from the hand of Alexander, a fellow believer, and to drink of it."

Crispus looked at Aquila and Priscilla, both of whom had received cups. Both looked back at Crispus and took a sip of water. Crispus said, "This is very difficult. I have always believed that such things defile me. How can I change that in a moment?"

Paul answered, "Jesus said, 'It is not what goes into your mouth that defiles you, but what comes out of it. That is what defiles a man.'"

"Brother Paul!" Titius spoke up, "It seems to me that we Gentiles have more to apologize for than the Jews. The Jews have been oppressed by every nation on earth! Brother Crispus, I hope that you will forgive us for all of the offenses. But since we have become friends, I have longed for you and your wife to join me and Olivia at my table. I would never serve anything that is detestable to you."

"Besides," said Lilia, who, after all, had no difficulty interrupting the conversation of men, "some of the men of the synagogue were my 'customers.' They put on Greek clothes and tried to hide the facts. But when they fornicate, they cannot hide that they are Jews. It is the mutilation, you know, the circumcision that gives them away. Jesus forgave prostitutes of their sins. So, if there are prostitutes in Israel, there must be customers for them. Who is better? The one who sells or the one who buys? You are no different than us, sinners who need Jesus."

Luke and Fortunatus laughed out loud at this statement. Titius rolled his eyes in exasperation. Aquila's face was red with embarrassment. Priscilla looked at Lilia with her closely cropped hair, styled after the fashion of prostitutes, but Lilia had adopted a new modesty in her clothing.

Paul winced at the boldness and crudeness of Lilia, and prayed with his thoughts, "Lord help me deal with this woman!"

Let her speak! She has spoken truly!

Stephanas spoke up, "My apologies to you, Brother Crispus. Lilia has been trained to speak in this direct way to men. We are all learning a new way of speaking. She meant no disrespect for you! Please forgive us, Brother."

"Apologies are not necessary," Crispus answered. "Sister Lilia has simply spoken the truth. I know that. The Law of God is good. His commands and precepts are right. But we have heaped laws upon the Law, and regulation upon the laws, and tradition upon the regulations. I have not lived an immoral life, nor have I been a thief, or a murderer, nor an idolater. But, Sister Lilia, I *am* a sinner. To keep the Law is to keep *all* the Law, *and* the laws, *and* the traditions. To violate in one is to violate them all. It is a burden of transgressions that I cannot bear nor could my ancestors. Because I thought to justify myself by keeping the Law, I have lived as a hypocrite, as an actor in a Greek tragedy. But in Messiah Jesus, I believe, now, I have found a new way to be justified and reconciled to God. Through faith in Jesus Christ, I am able to seek holiness in truth! I want to thank you for your words, Lilia. They came from God."

"The grace of God in Christ Jesus has come to Jew and to Gentile alike!" Paul looked at Crispus directly. "Brother

Crispus, we Jews are the natural branches in the tree of the Lord. These believers have been grafted in by the grace of God through their faith in Messiah Jesus. We must receive them as brothers and sisters in the Lord." Paul spoke to the others, "And the Gentiles must give respect due to the Jews as those who have carried the light of God to the entire world."

Paul looked at Alexander, who was standing nearby with a chalice of water, and said, "Alexander?"

Alexander stepped over to Crispus. He held the chalice up to Crispus, bowed his head with respect, and said, "In the name of Jesus."

Crispus took the cup and answered, "In the name of Jesus!" He tipped the chalice high and drank the entire contents in a single draught. Some of it splashed out and trickled down his beard.

"Amen! Hallelujah! We love you! Praise the Lord! Well done!" Everyone was giving their acclamation. Everyone drank in a salute to a new unity that only the grace of God could bring.

They all moved into the garden area to take their seats on the cushioned benches that the servants had brought. The servants pretended to leave the group to their privacy but stayed close enough to overhear. Paul knew that he could not keep the slaves of the house from eavesdropping and would not prevent them anyway.

The group chatted noisily in the way that friends do, paying no attention to what might be overheard. Paul brought them to order and said, "What just happened among us tells us of the difficulties and the wonderful possibilities that we face as we establish the church in Corinth. The believers, *Christians* they call us in Antioch, meet for worship and communion on the first day of the week."

Priscilla spoke to Lilia, "That is because Jesus was raised from the tomb on the morning of the first day of the week." Priscilla held Lilia's hand as she sat next to her on the bench.

"Yes, that is true," Paul continued, "Tomorrow morning is the morning of the first day of the week, and we must be ready to receive all of those who have proclaimed their faith in Christ. We must teach them about the Lord's Table and be ready to serve them all."

"What is the Lord's Table?" Stephanas and Lilia said at the same time.

"The Lord's Table is a ritual, a sacrament that Jesus established for His church." Aquila spoke up. "It is based on the Passover observance that we Jews celebrate in the spring of the year. It is sort of a long story ..."

"Perhaps I can help explain!" Crispus had a look on his face as one who has had an enlightening thought. "If I may, please, Aquila? Brother Paul?"

"Yes, indeed, Brother Crispus," Aquila answered. Paul nodded his approval.

"In the time of antiquity, the descendants of Abraham became slaves to Pharaoh in the land of Egypt."

Lilia interrupted, "The Jews were slaves?"

"Yes, indeed, Sister Lilia, the whole nation of us. The Jews are one tribe of twelve original tribes. Only Judah and Benjamin survived as tribes, and we are one, now known as

Jews. The other ten are lost because of the oppression and cruelty of the nations around us. Israel has been persecuted and killed for centuries by people who have hated us without a cause."

"We will never do that to you, Brother Crispus. We love you!" Lilia was close to tears. Priscilla put her hand on Lilia's arm to urge her to let Crispus speak.

"Thank you for that, Sister. But I fear that there is going to be a great conflict between the Jews and the followers of Jesus. It will not turn out well for my countrymen. But, where was I?" Crispus continued, "Yes, the Jews were slaves in Egypt. God had mercy on us and sent us a man named Moses to lead us out of Egypt and claim the homeland that He had promised to Abraham. When stubborn Pharaoh refused to let the people go, God sent plagues upon the Egyptians. Finally, on the night that they were freed, the Israelites were instructed to paint the lintels and doorposts of their homes with the blood of a lamb. When a Destroying Angel came through the land, the first-born of every home died except where the blood was on the door. Pharaoh *sent* them out of the land! They ate the lamb for their last meal in Egypt along with flat bread made without yeast because they had no time for the bread to rise. So, to this day we celebrate their escape in a ceremony called Passover. I am sure that the communion of the church recreates that ceremony in some way to celebrate the atoning death of Jesus.

"Yes, Brother Crispus, that is it!" Aquila continued, "We Jews, who follow Jesus, came to Corinth as refugees from Rome. We follow the sacrament that Jesus gave to His church.

Jesus, on the night that he was betrayed, took some of the unleavened Passover bread and broke it. He distributed it among his disciples and commanded them to eat of it saying, 'This is my body which is broken for you. Eat of it and remember me.' Then, He took the cup, called the 'Cup of Redemption.' He held the cup up and said, 'This is my blood which is given for the redemption of many. Drink of it and remember Me.' So, like Crispus said, we recreate that moment at our First Day Services to remember what Jesus has done for us on the cross.

"Some have called this sacrament, "Thanksgiving." I *am* thankful that the blood of Jesus has redeemed me from the bondage to sin. But the sacrament tells me of God's love for me, just as the words of Jesus have come down to us. The words are in one of the songs we sing while taking the unleavened bread and cup. Priscilla, sing it with me, you know it, 'Thus, He Gave.'"

> God loved the world,
>
> Thus He gave,
>
> Thus He gave,
>
> His One and Only Son,
>
> That everyone,
>
> That everyone,
>
> Who believes in Him,
>
> May not perish,
>
> May not perish,
>
> But have eternal life.

"That's beautiful!" Lilia was clapping her hands. "Everyone, sing it again! Priscilla! Aquila! Crispus! Titius! Fortunatus! Luke! Stephanas, I *know* that you can sing, I have heard you!"

"Do I *have* to sing?" Luke was shaking his head. "You will be sorry if I do!" Everyone laughed.

"Come now," Paul began badgering Luke, "You Greeks love to sing! Make a joyful noise!"

"Oh, I can make noise singing!" Luke was laughing with them all. "But, if there is a seven-string lyre in the house, I can play well!" There was a seven-string lyre in every well-educated Greek's home. The eavesdropping servants produced one in short order without being asked. Priscilla said something to one of them, and they brought her a tympanum, a small drum that she played with her fingers.

Aquila and Priscilla began singing and drumming the rhythm, stopping frequently to teach the lyrics. Luke strummed and picked out the music. By the time that they had gone through it a second time, everyone was singing and playing like they had been doing it together for years. Paul motioned for the servants to come in and join them. Aquila and Priscilla taught them some hymns and psalms. Paul taught them some spiritual songs. They sang, played, and made melody unto the Lord into the night by lamplight.

The fountain garden of Titius had a privacy wall. But what could not be seen by the neighbors could be heard as it wafted over the walls and through the cool spring evening and into the windows of the block. Soon, Paul heard some voices from somewhere over the wall, and beyond sight, joining them in singing. After a few minutes, there arose a chorus singing to the God that was unknown to Corinth. But He would not be a mystery for long.

Paul thought about the Stoics and Epicureans he had confronted in Athens before he had sojourned into Corinth. They sought to persuade men by logic and philosophy. But people held their view of truth somewhere hidden in their hearts, not their minds. The "great minds" of the Areopagus were simply justifying what their hearts wanted to believe. Their own preconceptions and fleshly desires were their foundation of truth. Their minds worked to justify their heart. Even the Stoics could not avoid their own prejudices as they sought to bring the desires of their body under subjection with harsh discipline. Pilate spoke from his heart when he asked Jesus, "What is truth?" Paul used reason and the Scriptures to move people so that they could receive Christ. But he knew that it was the story of the cross and music that were the keys that God used to unlock the will from the imprisonment of sin. Then, people could abandon long-held preconceptions and beliefs to receive the truth of Jesus. Of all the plans and preparations that had been made for the service in the morning, the most important was what they were doing now.

After a time, Paul saw Olivia come into the garden. She was carrying a double flute of a type that many Greek and Roman women played. She walked over to Titius and sat down next to him. She laid her head on his shoulder and looked up at him with respect as a wife to a husband. Titius' face looked as though he was the happiest man on earth. Olivia straightened up and began playing with great skill.

"Lord, help us!" Paul was praying, "Help us never to lose our music! May we always sing unto you!"

Then, never forget the One of whom you sing!

If the music and singing was a joy and blessing to many on the block of Titius, it was a curse and blasphemy to others. The lyrics filtered over Titius' garden wall into the courtyard of the synagogue, through doors and down the corridor to a room where Rabbis Philip and Benjamin were praying. They were bringing the Sabbath to a close as shadows began to grow to bring in the first day of the week. Several lamps were lit and began pushing back the night.

"We have to do *something*!" Philip was becoming more agitated by the minute. "That music is blasphemous!"

"What can we do? Crispus has taken up with Paul and embraced Jesus as Messiah." Benjamin seemed calmer than Philip.

"Jesus of Nazareth, the *Messiah*?" Philip began pacing back and forth and wringing his hands. "Paul has given him the Greek name, *Christ*! They are making this Jesus equal with God! By Paul's own words, this Jesus has been dead for over twenty years! And Paul, what kind of a Pharisee is he? He has defiled himself with heathen food and has entered the house of Gentiles to eat with them. I am sure that he eats without washing his hands! Our traditions are *everything*! The Son of God indeed!"

"The arguments that Paul makes from the Scriptures are powerful," Benjamin said carefully.

Philip looked incredulous, "You are not one of them also, *are you?*"

"No, I am not." Benjamin kept his voice calm. "But the prophet Isaiah does say that Messiah will be God-with-us. And, He will be in the form of a suffering servant. The Prophet Daniel also says that Messiah will be "cut off." And clearly the grave cannot hold Messiah, for He is destined to bring the Nations under His foot *forever*. The question becomes, 'Is Jesus the One?' The best argument that you gave was the first one that came out of your mouth when you said, 'By now we would have been informed by the Elders in Jerusalem and the Chief Priests if it is true.' I recommend that we write a letter—"

"*Yes*, by the Temple, we will!" Philip smacked his palm with his fist. "I will tell them what a vile character this Paul is and how he is destroying our synagogue! I will tell them how he associates with Gentile sinners and even eats with them and encourages others to do the same. He must be stopped!"

"I think, rather, we should write a simple letter of inquiry without hostility. I am sure that we will receive an answer that will inform us of what to do. We can write a letter to the Synagogue of the Freedmen in Jerusalem and to the Elders and Chief Priest. I will deliver the letters. It is time for my lifetime pilgrimage to Jerusalem. I am going to stay for a full year. I plan to study with the scribes and attend all the festivals and then return after Pentecost of next year. Someone said that Paul came here from Macedonia. I can travel by way of

Macedonia. We have synagogues at Beria and Thessalonica. I will write to you from there. I am sure that Paul, Saul of Tarsus, has left wreckage all along his path—"

Benjamin was interrupted by the sound of the bell at the door of the street.

"Who could *that* be?" Philip waved with his hand in the general direction of the door, "Rabbi, go see who it is, please!"

Benjamin took a lamp and walked to the door, leaving Philip to begin assembling parchments and writing materials. After a few minutes, Benjamin retuned. He hesitated to speak.

"What is it?" Philip held his lamp up to the face of Benjamin.

"There are many people out in the street. Corinthians! They are asking for the healer—"

"There is no physician here!"

Benjamin sighed. "They are asking for *Paul*!"

At that moment, a servant in the house came to Titius as he was singing and praising the Lord. He said something to Alexander and the three of them left the celebration and went to the door of the street. After a few moments, Titius returned with Belos, the steward of the house of Stephanas, and spoke to Paul. Paul shook his head in understanding and continued singing until the song was finished. Belos went over to Stephanas and spoke quietly with him. Paul stood to his feet and looked around the group.

"We have had a wonderful time here together, singing and praising Jesus! We must replicate what we have done here tonight in the morning at our first service. It is how Christians worship! We will celebrate God's love for us at the Lord's table and remember what Jesus did for us. In the bread and wine, we will spiritually partake of the Lord's body and blood. We will offer prayers and teach statements of faith that we will recite together. We will hear the brothers and sisters testify about the grace of God in their lives. The Word of God will be proclaimed by a preacher. But the work we do for the gospel will not only occur in our meetings, where we try to convince inquirers who come out of curiosity. The work of Jesus happens outside of our assemblies, in the Agora, in homes, and in the streets. Evidently, the street outside is full of people seeking a healing touch from Jesus."

"I am sorry," Belos blurted out, "I did not know what to do! People showed up at the door of Stephanas, ringing the bell, and shouting for the healer. I went out and tried to do what I could. I prayed in the name of Jesus for a small girl who was crippled in her feet. When I laid hands on her and prayed, her feet were straightened out! She began to walk about! In front of my eyes!"

"Hallelujah! Praise the Lord!" Priscilla danced the hallelujah dance.

"That's when they swarmed me like a bunch of angry hornets. And then, I saw the covered litter that some servants were carrying. It was Chloe, daughter of Gallio. She has had The Fever for several years, and she is very sick. They said she is dying. I do not know how she heard about you, Brother

Paul. Truly, I could not touch her! She is the daughter of the Proconsul." Belos sighed. "So, I brought them all here."

"You have done well, Brother Belos," Paul said, smiling warmly.

When Belos said that Chloe was out in the street, Olivia immediately got up and headed for the door. She and Titius were friends of the Gallio family and knew the serious condition of Chloe.

Belos kneeled on the floor in front of Paul, "My faith has been weak! Please forgive me!"

Paul brought Belos to his feet. "Your faith is stronger than you think, Brother Belos."

Then, Paul said to them all, "Only God can forgive sins. And He does that according to our faith in the blood of Jesus Christ! This is what we are going to *do*. We are going out into the street to minister to the people of Corinth, just as we did when the Lord healed Brother Stephanas. Some will be healed, some will begin healing, and some will show no effect. It will be according to the will of the Lord and their faith. But the goal of our ministry is the healing of peoples' souls. The gospel brings new life and reconciliation with God. To be saved, the people of Corinth must forsake idolatry and the evil deeds of the flesh and turn to Jesus in obedient faith. Jesus is faithful to bring them a new life now and eternal life to come. And, it is through Jesus *only*! Understood?"

"Understood! Yes! Amen!" everyone answered.

Paul led them out into the street where they began ministering, bringing hope to people who thought they had no hope. The power of God broke the fever of Chloe and won her heart as Olivia prayed for her. The first day of the New Church in Corinth would dawn on the evening of the seventh with miracles and signs in the power of the Holy Spirit. Salvation had come to the City.

CHAPTER 12

INTO THE FIRE

"But, there comes an hour when everyone who kills you supposes that he is doing a service of worship to God."

-Jesus

There is no fury like the fury born of jealousy and righteous anger. There was a great crowd of new believers in attendance on the first day in the warehouse that Titius had provided. But there was an unexpected visitor who had come to church. He was one who had not come to worship, but to intimidate the worshipers. He was the High Priest of the Temple of Aphrodite. What he was seeing was not right in his mind, and the flames of envy were burning him alive. He was astonished at the crowd that had assembled only days since Paul's encounter with Stephanas and Lilia in the Agora. He had sent his priests and acolytes out into the city to find out what was going on with this cult and why it was spreading like a plague. He did not like what he heard back from them. These people believed in an invisible spirit god that was not even represented by any image or idol. They were speaking some nonsense of a god that died and lives again. And they were trashing their idols! The Priest's people had already found some of the household gods of these new believers in the city dump. He had heard that the new believers were being taught to abstain from eating the meat from the Macella that had been sacrificed to the gods. That was just like those despicable Jews! And worse, they were being taught that they should abstain from joining with the prostitutes of the Acrocorinth. In just a few days, they had convinced hundreds of people to join them. If this cult grew, there would be a great loss of revenue for the goddess Aphrodite. And, they had some sort of occult power to heal people that he wanted to know about. It was probably a trick of some kind or a drug that the stupid sorcerers had not yet discovered. He was at the assembly with some of his priests and acolytes to see what everything was about. He had to stop this 'religion' before it got out of control. He was furious, and it showed in his face.

Paul had prayed far into the night and had only a few hours' sleep. But in those hours of sleep, Paul had received a vision from the Lord who appeared to him and said, *"Paul! Fear not and keep speaking! Do not be silent! I am with you! No one will attack you to harm you, for many people are Mine in this city."*

Paul awoke refreshed by the repetition of this promise and grateful that he did not dream of Lydia or Sarah. But he was concerned as he watched the Priest of Aphrodite scowling at the people who were assembling on this first day of the New Church in Corinth.

"We are going to say something to him before this gets started," Titius said as he walked up to Paul with Aquila, Crispus, Stephanas, and Fortunatus.

"I know the High Priest personally." Stephanas looked back at the Priest who looked back at him with complete malice. "The people fear Him. He is very powerful and up to no good!"

Paul nodded his agreement, "Just remember, do not repay evil with evil."

The people were beginning to gather in the large room that was lined with columns on each side. There were no benches, so they had been told to bring cushions or mats to sit upon. As they assembled, the men and boys took their place on the right side and the women and the children on the left side with a separating "aisle" down the middle. Except for the aisle, the room was solid people. Some stood along the walls or leaned on the columns.

The Priest of Aphrodite and his male and female acolytes remained standing conspicuously near the front. Defying custom, the Priest stood with his painted face on the women's side of the aisle. Titius and the others walked over to greet the Priest.

"Greetings," Titius did not offer his hand. "I am Gaius Titius Justus. I hope there will be no trouble."

"Trouble? These … *people* are trouble. They have all become *atheists!*" The Priest waved his hand at the crowd as though dismissing them all.

"We are not atheists!" Stephanas moved in front of Titius. "Our God is Jesus Christ who has commanded us to forsake idols and worship spiritually and truthfully."

"*You!*" The High Priest's face was inches from Stephanas'. "You are the one who has led them astray! If you are not an atheist, then prove it! Offer some incense to the spirit of the Divine Caesar."

Titius put his hand over Stephanas' shoulder, pulled him back, and stepped back in front to face the Priest. "These people are a sect of the Jews! They are exempt under the Edict of Caesar."

"These people are *not* Jews! I want to see if they are circumcised! I wager every one of them has a proper foreskin!"

"It is true! They *are* exempt," Crispus spoke up. "I am the Ruler of the Synagogue in Corinth. These people follow Jesus, a Jew of the province of Galilee. They are all proselytes to Jesus Christ. This sect does not require their followers to be circumcised."

The High Priest looked around at the crowd and then at the men who were confronting him. "You have some fine friends, Gaius Titius Justus. Some dirty Jews, a pimp, and an accursed sorcerer!"

Aquila moved to the side of Titius. His imposing bulk towered over the High Priest. The acolytes moved a little closer together, as if hoping they would not be required to fight.

Titius spoke, "We welcome the High Priest to observe what we do here, we have no secrets. But, listen to me now! If you disturb this service in any way, you will be tossed out of here on your priestly kolos. It is unlawful to disrupt proceedings at any temple or place of worship. If you cause trouble in this place, I will press charges, you can be assured!"

The High Priest looked up at Aquila. "We haven't any cushions on which to sit."

"I'll get you some." Aquila turned to go get some cushions.

The entire auditorium had fallen deathly silent while the confrontation was taking place. As the priestly group was getting settled, the musicians began playing to change the mood. But the presence of the High Priest of the Temple of Aphrodite could not be ignored.

It had been decided that Stephanas should open the service with a greeting. "*Hail*, people of Corinth!"

"*Hail*, Stephanas!"

"We welcome you all in the name—"

Stephanas was interrupted by a murmuring of the crowd. By this time, the crowd was spilling out into the street. In the auditorium, sound was amplified by some large vessels partially filled with water. Beyond that, "repeaters" carried the message outside. The people outside were parting before a procession that was coming into the building.

"Chloe! It is Chloe! *Chloe!*" The mummering of the crowd grew louder as Chloe walked down the aisle followed by her servants. She had not been able to walk anywhere in Corinth for months. She had walked the entire distance from her home, with her servant holding a sunshade over her head, as the noble ladies of Corinth were accustomed. She was very thin, but looked healthy, and her steps were steady and firm. The people began standing and clapping as she walked, bejeweled and radiant in her finery.

When Olivia saw that it was Chloe, she left her flute and walked up the aisle to meet her. Olivia had gone out to see Chloe the night before, and she was shocked at the condition of the young woman. Where it came from Olivia did not understand, but she put her hand on the feverous, sweaty brow of Chloe and prayed in the name of Jesus, "I am not one who is worthy, Lord. But, just as You healed Stephanas, Jesus, heal Chloe! *Please, Jesus!*" She felt the fever leave immediately. Chloe sat up and looked at Olivia as if seeing her for the first time. Olivia wiped the sweat off her brow and embraced her. Olivia told Chloe what she knew about Jesus and how she felt changed and forgiven for her sins and had a promise of eternal life. Before her servants took her home, Chloe had received Jesus with joy.

Now, Olivia embraced Chloe in the aisle. "Come, sit with me and my children. I am playing my flute for the worship. I will join you after the music is finished." She escorted Chloe and her servants to the front, near where the High Priest and his acolytes were sitting among the women. When they were seated, Olivia cast a look at the Priest and gave him a triumphant smile. His face flushed with a redness that even the paint on his face could not hide.

"We welcome all of you this morning," Stephanas continued, "to the first meeting in Corinth of the Church of Jesus Christ. Most of us are very new to this faith. I, myself, only days ago, knew nothing of Jesus. But I have been healed in my body. And, my soul has been touched by God. I know that I now belong to Jesus. Brother Paul came to Corinth as an Apostle of Jesus. He has been sent to bring us the Word about Jesus, about forgiveness of sins, a new life today, and eternal life to come. Brother Paul, with Brother Aquila and Sister Priscilla, have planned this service. They are going to teach us what to do and how to worship. We will be taught some new songs. We Greeks love to sing, yes?"

"Yes, yes! Truly." The people were clapping, and some stood as though they would begin dancing.

"There will be prayers offered. We invite you to pray along with those who lead in prayer. We will be taught a simple creed to recite. We have some people who will testify to the grace of God in Jesus Christ. Brother Paul will address us and tell us about the Lord's Table. Then, after the service, we will go to the Public bath for baptisms. How many of you have been healed by the name of Jesus?"

Many hands went up and a chorus also, "*Thank you Jesus! Praise be to Jesus!*"

"How many of you did not receive healing of the body but received healing of your soul, and so, believe in Jesus anyway?"

Many more hands were displayed along with thanksgiving and praise.

"Now, we have two simple rules that govern our fellowship. The *first* rule is to love Jesus with all of our heart. The *second* rule is to love the brothers and sisters as we love ourselves. Not with the *eros* love of Aphrodite, nor even with the *philadelphia* of brotherly love. We must love one another with the *agape* love that God has shown us in Jesus Christ. So, let us worship in song, and let us love Jesus supremely and love one another sincerely as God has loved us!"

Paul looked at Stephanas and listened to him in wonderment. The man was speaking like an apostle! These were the words of a mature preacher of the gospel. One week had not passed since Paul had walked down the Lechaion Road into Corinth, trembling with weakness and fear. He had known no one in Corinth and despaired of his ability to bring the gospel to this pagan city. Much could be accomplished by just beginning to spread the Word and then letting God take control. In Corinth, Paul had not known where to start. But the Lord had sent Stephanas and Lilia to him, and then sent Paul to Titius, and then he was sent on to Aquila and Priscilla. Paul felt as though he was in the grip of God, being carried along in a runaway chariot.

That first service in Corinth was blessed with a demonstration of the Holy Spirit. Paul kept everything at a simple level, knowing that these were infants in Christ and needed milk and not solid food. But, Paul was sure that while he was offering prayer, he heard among the clamor of prayers of the people his own native dialect of Tarsus. Many of the inquirers testified later that they heard the prayers and Paul's sermon in their own native language. Many were convinced by this to come to repentance and receive Jesus. Paul knew that it was not him, but God that spoke to Corinth. It was the Lord that was bringing the word of faith to the city. Paul and the others were merely the instruments that testified to the grace of God.

Paul's message about Jesus and the grace of God for the forgiveness of sins and the gift of eternal life was well received. But, the crowd got smaller as Paul began to proclaim that people must repent and turn from their idols to serve the Living God. There was quite an exodus when he said that people must no longer join with the prostitutes of Aphrodite. More left when he spoke of sexual purity. There were some men who got up and went to the women's side and took their wives and children and walked them out of the assembly. As people were leaving, the High Priest of Aphrodite was laughing and turning around to the congregation to show his mocking face. Paul knew this process was necessary to separate the wheat from the chaff. There still remained a multitude of people.

Behold the threshing floor! The wheat will be gathered up unto eternal life! The chaff is carried away by the wind! Look upon the harvest and rejoice!
At the end of Paul's sermon, an invitation was given to any who wanted to repent, confess their sins, and receive Christ in faith. Paul asked those who wanted to receive Jesus to stand.

They soon were surrounded by believers who were praying with them for their salvation. Paul then explained the Lord's Table which was loaded with flat bread and diluted wine. He thanked those who had listened but had not received Jesus. He dismissed them with an invitation to come again to the next first day service.

As the High Priest walked out, he paused before the Table to look at it. He turned to the assembly and shouted, "It is a poor banquet this Jesus serves! Jew-bread and watered-down wine!"

"Leave! Shame! Shut up!" Many voices came back at him.

The Priest turn back to face Paul. "You have not offered any incense to the Spirit of the Divine Caesar."

Crispus cried out, "We are *exempt!*"

"That's questionable," answered the High Priest as he walked out of the building with his acolytes. He did not notice, until later, that two of his company remained behind to receive the grace of God in Jesus Christ.

Paul moved immediately to the Table. He addressed the people, "Jesus said, 'My body is real food and my blood is real drink.' Jesus spoke these words in a spiritual sense. This is spiritual food and spiritual drink to nourish our souls and strengthen our faith. I am going to pray and bless this table. After the prayer, each of you should come by the table, and we will give you of the bread and wine. The bread represents the broken body of Christ and the diluted wine represents the water mingled with blood that flowed down from the cross. After you have partaken, walk down to the public bath where those who have not yet been baptized will be baptized."

Paul began his prayer and soon was praying fervently for the believers. He asked God to remember the threats they had received and to give them boldness to speak out in the name of Jesus Christ. Suddenly, he thought that there was a small earthquake occurring, but he realized that it was the Lord who was shaking the place. The church was experiencing an outpouring of the Holy Spirit. He heard the wonderful works of God being praised in the language of his birth. Many others testified to the same thing, but no one could identify who spoke what. Some of those who had left without taking communion had lingered outside, listening to the prayers. When they heard the gospel in their native dialect, they were amazed and returned into the church to proclaim their faith and take communion. The church was transformed in an instant. The gospel had come in power with full conviction to the people of Corinth.

The people moved joyously through the streets to the public bath for the baptisms. It was a large pool that was constantly refreshed by the aqueduct. At the bath, Paul arranged for the ministers he had appointed to do the baptisms while he oversaw everything. It was not yet noon, but it seemed that too much was happening in each day for Paul to handle. He was anxious to return to the house of Titius for some rest and prayer.

"There he is! *Seize him!*" The Politeia had arrived in force, accompanied by the High Priest of Aphrodite and reinforcements of priests and acolytes. Paul's stomach drew up into a knot as the officers of the Politeia moved toward him. But they passed him by and laid their hands on Belos. "You are arrested by order of the Magistrates of Corinth!"

Stephanas came quickly up out of the pool, dripping with water. "This man is my servant, my steward! What charges do you have against him?"

The High Priest stepped forward, "The charge is criminal atheism! And malicious destruction of images of the gods. It should be enough to get your servant crucified, if justice is done."

One of the officers brought a man by the arm to stand in front of Belos. "Is this the one?"

The man looked down at the feet of Belos, "Yes, he is the one."

"The silversmith," Stephanas blurted out.

"The silversmith, yes!" The High Priest glared at Stephanas, "He is in trouble also. But he has agreed to join in the accusation against your servant so that he may escape punishment. But it will be "ad crucem" to the cross, for Belos. You should dry off and make haste. The Magistrate is taking the case immediately. You must see your servant condemned."

Then, the Priest turned and gave all the people a hateful look, "And I will see that all you atheists suffer likewise!" He left with the officers of the court who had arrested Belos.

Paul, Stephanas, Lilia, Luke, Titius and Olivia followed the Politeia who were leading Belos with his hands bound and tethered to one of the officers. Chloe walked with them, along with her servant. Fortunatus and Crispus continued with the baptisms and formed a prayer meeting for Belos. Many of the people began weeping and crying out to God for him. The fellowship had passed from triumph to tragedy in moments.

Paul blurted out, "Why are they in such a hurry to condemn Belos?"

"The Isthmian Games are beginning," Titius answered, "The first ceremony is this afternoon. They will be executing the condemned in the arena."

"That means that Belos will probably not be crucified," Paul said, "but will be offered to the wild beasts or burned. I hope Gallio is presiding as magistrate today."

"No," answered Chloe, "My father is presiding at the games as the Proconsul of Achaia. Belos will certainly be judged guilty and be in the procession of the condemned. We must go out to the Isthmus and appeal to my father. I have sent my servants to fetch my carriage to the forum court. We must be at the arena to talk to my father well before the procession arrives."

"Who will speak for Brother Belos at the court?" Paul was well-conditioned for the road and not winded at all by the brisk pace they were keeping. "We must be sure that Belos is not sent to the cross! Is he really guilty of 'malicious destruction of the gods?'"

"Yes, he is guilty," Stephanas answered. "When I was healed, I instructed Belos to take my household gods to the silversmith to be destroyed in the forge. I told him to give the silver to the silversmith to keep quiet about it. Evidently the investigators of the High Priest found out about it and coerced the silversmith to join them in accusing Belos. I feel as though I have brought the Acrocorinth down on my servant's head. Forgive me, Jesus!"

Lilia was weeping and clinging to Stephanas' arm as they walked along. He squeezed her arm and said, "I will speak for Belos. He is my servant."

"Sister Chloe," Paul moved to her side, "do you think your father will show mercy?"

"I do not know," She answered. "From the time I was a child, I have heard my father say, 'Chloe, The Senate and the People of Rome did not commission me to be merciful but commissioned me to be just.' He says it all the time. I do not know what he will do."

When Paul arrived at the court, the Magistrate was offering judgment to some offender, who was standing in front of the Bema, shoulders slumped and staring at the ground. He could see that Belos was next on the docket. They would waste no time in condemning him. Paul could see a group of condemned people, bound and being arranged in line for the procession. Placards were being hung around their necks proclaiming what kind of a criminal they happened to be. They would become a spectacle to the people of Corinth as they were marched to the arena. They would hear jeers and insults as they arrived. They would hear applause and cheers as they died. They would perish by the sword, by being pulled to pieces, or by fire, or being torn by wild beasts or dogs.

"Sometimes, Lord," Paul prayed quietly, "I think that, in this world, we Apostles are all like the condemned in procession, being nothing to the world but a spectacle. Please save Belos, your servant. Keep all of our believers in Corinth steady as they witness this sight."

Belos is my witness! I am with him! Fear not for him or the people! The people of the church are mine!

Belos was taken by the arm before the judgment seat. He appeared sober-minded and did not look as though he was terrified. His hands were still bound, and he remained tethered to the officer. The officer handed a slate to the lector of the court who read, "Belos, servant of Stephanas, you are charged with criminal atheism and malicious destruction of the gods. The penalty is death by whatever means is deemed appropriate by the court. What do you have to say to the court?"

"To the charge of atheism, I am innocent. As to the destruction of gods, I am guilty, Honored Sir." The admission drew a groan from the believers who were present.

The Magistrate spoke directly to Belos, "Do you realize that such an admission makes defense of any charge against you moot? You have said enough to be crucified! Do you wish to retract your plea and make a defense?"

"Honored Sir, I follow Jesus Christ, the Son of the Most High God. There is salvation and eternal life in no other god. He has commanded his followers to turn their backs to idols and serve the living and true God. So, Honored Sir, I am no atheist. But I *did* burn the wooden idols in the forge of the silversmith, melt down the metal ones, and broke the stone idols with a hammer on his anvil. As I was praying to Jesus this morning, He told me I must always tell the truth. And I must testify about Jesus, even though it may mean my death."

"It *will* mean your death, Belos, slave of Stephanas!" The Magistrate made his face hard and looked out to the people. "I am ready to pass judgment on this man. Are there any who wish to speak in his behalf?"

"Yes! Honored Sir." Stephanas moved quickly to the Bema.

"Stephanas, master of the house of pleasure," The Magistrate responded. "And Lilia, your associate." He gave her a very injudicious wink which drew some laughter from the crowd.

"Honored Sir, I ask that you would be merciful to my servant. I also am a follower of Jesus Christ, and I was attempting to obey the command of our God. I told Belos to take the idols to the silversmith for destruction. I told him to give the silver to the silversmith."

The Magistrate asked, "Did you go with your servant and destroy the idols?"

"No, Honored Sir, I did not actually do the destruction, but—"

"Then the crime is Belos' alone. Charges against you, Stephanas, will be taken under advisement by the court. I charge the Politeia of the Court to seize the silver in question until it can be determined who is the owner of said silver." The Magistrate then turned his sight to Belos and proclaimed, "Belos, servant of Stephanas, you are guilty of acts of sacrilege! You will be taken to the arena of the Isthmian Games and this day be offered to the wild beasts or other such means of execution as the Master of the Games will determine. Let the charge read, 'Atheist', and 'destroyer of the gods.' Done! Next case."

"Honored Sir! Honored Sir," The High Priest hurried up to the court. "If you please, Honored Sir, let the inscription read, 'He *tried* to destroy the gods.' No one can actually—"

"What I have written, I have written. I don't think you want me to ask you how you and your ... *people* ... got mixed up in this. Stephanas is a good citizen of Corinth, and Belos was his steward. Do not push this court! Next case!"

The High Priest of the Temple of Aphrodite melted away from the face of the Magistrate behind a cloud of perfume. When he had backed away from the court, he found Stephanas, "This will end up costing you much! Perhaps more than you can pay."

Stephanas made no reply but turned away so that his tears could not be seen. The laughter from the priest followed him. It would echo in his mind for years. Stephanas had no confidence in any appeal for Belos. He could not go out to the games to see his steward torn to pieces and dragged around the sand of the arena. He went back to the house with Lilia, depressed and feeling guilty. He had ordered Belos to his death as much as the Magistrate. Belos could have recanted and offered incense to the spirit of Caesar and possibly have gotten away with a scourging. "But he was trying to protect me," Stephanas spoke his thoughts aloud. And then the Spirit spoke to his spirit with a voice that would become familiar to him.

Take heart! Belos testified about ME, Jesus! And he has more to testify of before this day is out!

Stephanas was startled by this voice. It did not come through his ears or mind, but somehow through his soul. He knew instantly that it was the voice of the Holy Spirit. Stephanas felt as though Jesus was speaking to him. He could feel comfort and peace flooding his being. He, Lilia, and the men and women of the house did nothing but pray for the rest of the day.

CHAPTER 13

CARRYING THE CROSS

"Whoever does not take up his own cross and come behind me, cannot be my disciple."

-Jesus Christ

Paul, Crispus, and Chloe, along with Titius and Olivia, rode noisily along the bumpy cobblestone road in the carriage of Chloe. Talking was impossible and Paul soon gave up the attempt. The driver was keeping a brisk pace which challenged the leather strap suspension of the vehicle. The road from Corinth to the games was crowded. Even with the noise of the road, Paul could hear the cries of the servant who was riding a horse ahead of the carriage. He was shouting people out of the way in the name of the house of Gallio. The first day of the games was going strong when they arrived. Musical contests and the women's events attracted large crowds of men and women. When the men's events began, the women would not be allowed to attend. However, the procession of the condemned would soon arrive and the blood sports would begin for the enjoyment of all.

Paul and the others entered the arena from the back, through the gate of the dignitaries. Chloe was known to the soldiers who were at the entrance. As Paul entered the building, the noise and cheering of the crowd echoed throughout the structure. Gallio was in one of the rooms behind the grand reviewing stand of the arena. He was receiving some petitioners who had given a large amount of money to the games. A centurion was keeping the gate for the Proconsul along with a quaternion of soldiers.

"M'lady!" The centurion bowed his head with respect when he saw Chloe. "It is so good to see you well. We have been offering prayers to the gods for you."

"Thank you, Valerian, for your prayers. It was Jesus who raised me up. I think He heard your prayers for me. I will tell you about Jesus later, but, at the moment ..." Chloe looked past the centurion to the door, "Is my father in the way of receiving me?"

"Yes, he is always in the way of receiving you!"

The centurion turned and nodded at Titius and Olivia who were known to him. He looked at Paul and Crispus. "I do not know these men. Who are they? They are dressed like Jews."

"They are respected men of the Jews," Chloe said, motioning with her hand to Crispus and Paul. "Crispus is the Ruler of the Synagogue in Corinth and is known to my father. This is Saul of Tarsus, known as Paul. He is a Pharisee, a holy man of the Jews."

The centurion looked at the soldiers. By some silent order, they knew to begin searching the clothing of Paul and Crispus. Paul hated the indignity of a body search. He had been subjected to it many times and spread his arms out without changing the expression on his face.

"Some of your countrymen are causing much turmoil in Galilee and Judea," the centurion spoke to Paul as though he were examining him. "The zealots will be the death of your country. I have served in Palestine before and, from reports I am hearing, I will serve there again before I am retired. Do you have sympathy with those seditious maggots?"

Paul looked at him steadily. "I follow one Jesus of Nazareth, who taught us to pay our taxes and to pray for Caesar and for all those in authority. I teach people that you are the servant of God sent to punish those who do evil. You do not carry that sword for nothing ... sir."

The centurion stared at Paul, blinked, and then turned to speak to Chloe, "M' lady, your father will be delighted to see you ... and your guests. I will go in and run the cockroaches out. Wait here, please."

The centurion went into the room. Shortly, the door opened, and out of the door came the High Priest of the Temple of Aphrodite with two of his acolytes, escorted by the centurion.

"Ah, the atheists!" The High Priest smirked. "You are too late. We brought a very large gift to the Isthmian Games from the Great Aphrodite of Corinth. What have you atheists brought from Jesus?"

"Have some respect when you speak to your betters!" The centurion spoke sharply, "Get out!"

Paul had to close his mouth from the shock of seeing that the Priest had arrived well ahead of them. They must have come on horseback. The High Priest gave Paul a smile, threw back his head, and started to walk down the corridor to the reviewing stand.

"Not that way!" The centurion moved to block the Priest. "Go out the back, the way you came in. *Now!*"

"But …" It was the Priest's turn to look shocked.

"The reviewing stand is for the family members of Caesar, the Proconsul, and their guests."

"But I—"

"You," the Centurion said sternly, "smell like a whore. Go sit with the mob."

One of the soldiers took the High Priest by the arm and hustled him and his acolytes out of the back entrance of the arena. The soldier spoke to the quaternion leader who was guarding the entrance, "The centurion says, 'Do not let them back in.'"

Paul and the group were ushered into the presence of Gallio. The Proconsul's face lit up at the sight of Chloe. He cared not for the appearance of dignity as she moved quickly into his open arms. "Daughter," he said softly, "I feared that you were dying!"

"But look, Father!" Chloe pulled back and stood arms stretched out to her side, "I am well. My appetite has returned, and soon, I will not be able to count my ribs!" Her laughter was like music in the room.

"How did it happen? I had been given no hope!" Gallio was looking her over.

"This man," Chloe pointed to Paul, "Saul of Tarsus, known as Paul, brought us good news about Jesus Christ, the Son of God. He has prayed for people in the name of Jesus and many have been healed. So many, that he has been called "the healer." My maid servant heard about him and took me to him. But it was Olivia who prayed for me in the name of Jesus, and I was healed! But more than that, Father, I am made new in my being! I have received the Spirit of Jesus, and He has given me new life!"

"I have heard of the followers of Jesus, a man referred to as 'Cristus.'" Gallio looked closely at Chloe. "Some sect of the Jews. I have just received Imperial dispatches requesting information concerning his followers. Nothing bad in them, just information gathering. Are you a follower of *that* Jesus, Daughter?"

"Yes, Father," Chloe answered, "and although it has just been a short while that I have been with Jesus I have known nothing but virtue in that way. But, Father, I have an urgent matter to bring to you. There is, among the procession of the condemned, one Belos, the Servant of Stephanas, who is a believer in Jesus. The crime that Belos committed, destruction of the gods, he did at the command of Stephanas. Belos refused to turn and condemn his master because of his love for him. We are asking for clemency for this good man."

"This is quite an extraordinary situation!" Gallio had a bemused look on his face. "The High Priest of the Temple of Aphrodite was just in here to ask me to ensure that Belos die in the most painful and humiliating way possible. The foolish man came to bribe me. I took his gift for the games. It is much needed. But he insulted me. He did not need to pay me a denarius for justice to be done."

"Then, you will free Belos?" Chloe embraced her father, but he did not return the affection.

"I cannot, daughter," Gallio replied evenly. "From what I have learned of this case so far, I have no reason, or legal precedent, for clemency."

"Please, Father," Chloe was crying, "have compassion."

"I have been sent to Corinth by the Emperor, the Senate and the People of Rome as an administer of justice, not a minister of compassion. Belos has been judged by a magistrate of Rome. I cannot overturn that judgment on a matter of personal privilege. It sounds as though compassion is a virtue to the followers of Jesus. That is well. But, to the Magistrate of Rome, compassion is weakness. The slave must die."

Paul expected no less. But he always expected victory in Jesus Christ. Paul had kept silent and listened to the scene play out. This was just the type of situation that he had experienced before. When it seemed the world and the devil were triumphant, and the church of Jesus would be stopped in its path, the Kingdom of God was advanced, and the world and the devil were pushed back. He anticipated victory for the Kingdom of God. Paul was not hopeful for the life of Belos, but he was expecting a triumph of faith. Paul waited patiently for the Lord.

Gallio continued, "There is something that I *can* do for your Jesus. I can give you some relief from the High Priest of the Temple of Aphrodite. Titius, will you ask the centurion and the amanuenses to come in, please? I am going to issue an injunction against the High Priest with respect to the religion of Jesus. And, I will also declare that the followers of Jesus are a sect of the Jews and under the exemption until such time as the Emperor shall determine otherwise. You are safe with Claudius, but not so safe with his heir, Nero. Belos will be offered a chance to recant and give a pinch of incense to the spirit of Caesar. If he will do so, his death will be swift, by the sword. If he refuses, he will be torn by the beasts. Do you think he will give incense to Caesar, Daughter?"

Chloe hesitated, then said softly, "I do not know, Father."

"Caution, Daughter." Gallio spoke as a father and a magistrate, "Do not speak to me again of Jesus or your faith. If you do, I cannot protect you when things turn against you."

"Yes, Father." There was sadness and affection in her voice at the same time.

Paul resisted the temptation to speak. He did not think that he could add anything that had not yet been addressed. He knew that he could greatly complicate the situation. Gallio greeted Titius and Olivia who were friends. Gallio knew Crispus from the intentional relationship that Crispus had pursued seeking peace for the Jewish Community. When Gallio came around to Paul he drew him to the side for some private words. Gallio had a friendly, but serious expression.

"Are you the leader of the Jesus cult?"

"I am one of twelve, Honored Sir," Paul answered.

"You can call me 'Honored Sir' at the Bema, but in casual conversation, please call me Gallio. I am very grateful for what you have done for my daughter, and I count you my friend. But I want to caution you, friend, that I want my daughter protected. I am placing her in your hands, and I am holding you responsible for her safety. The High Priest of Aphrodite hates you and has made many detestable accusations against the people of your way."

"The High Priest knows that your daughter is among the believers, Gallio." Paul voice carried urgency, "He came to harass us this very morning at our worship service. Chloe had a place of honor among us and was very near to the Priest and his acolytes. I thank you for the injunction against him, but I fear that he will come against all individually, including your daughter."

"So, he *knew* that Chloe was among the believers!" Gallio spoke angrily, "I will have Valerian serve the High Priest the injunction, and more!"

"O, please, Gallio, I would not have him killed," Paul pleaded, "Jesus wishes us never to repay evil with evil!"

"No, he will not be killed … now. But the centurion will come to serve him the injunction and say, 'The next time you see me, my message will be, 'Caesar wishes you to die!'" Gallio paused and asked, "What did you call your cult?"

"They are beginning to call us Christians."

"The centurion will then tell him to leave the Christians in peace or else. The Priest will piss on his own sandals, and you will never be bothered again by him."

Paul could think of nothing to say as the Proconsul turned to talk to the others in the room. Paul could only revel in the providence of God. His Pharisaical training taught him that in most things, men had free will, but in others, God's providence was supreme. But now, more than ever, it seemed as if Paul was again in the very grip of God and being carried along by His will. Paul began praying in the spirit, "O Father in heaven, how inscrutable are your ways! How mysterious your thoughts! You are the only Wise One! Who has known Your thoughts? Who has been Your advisor? Just as Jesus offered his body up for you as a sacrifice for the benefit of the world, so I offer my body as a living sacrifice to you that I may take your glorious gospel to the world." Tears were coming to Paul's eyes as he prayed. He continued praying and pleading for the life of Belos as the group left the room and walked down the corridor to the reviewing stand.

I have gone before Belos in the way of suffering. Through many persecutions will my servants enter the Kingdom of God. Belos is sanctified unto Me!

As Paul stepped out with Gallio onto the reviewing stand with the group, the hair on the back of his neck stood up as he saw the vast crowd in the arena. The noise and the cheering of the crowd was like thunder coming from a dark cloud. He took his seat with the dignitaries and the other guests of Gallio. Paul had heard that some of the family of Caesar were attending the games, but he could not identify them.

Gallio went out onto the porch of the reviewing stand to greet the crowd. They responded with thunderous applause and cheering. The Proconsul waved his hand in response.

The last of the women's events was coming to conclusion as a woman ran into the arena. It was the end of the longest cross-country race and the finale of the women's events. Wishing to cast off every encumbrance, the male athletes wore no clothing. Women, however, competed with a minimum of clothing, a cloth binding their breasts and a loin cloth bound up around the waist for modesty. The men competed completely naked, and when those events began, women would be barred from the games. Nevertheless, Paul appreciated the events of the games, especially the running events. Paul watched as the woman, well ahead of her competitors, ran with a patient, beautiful stride around the track receiving the adulation of the crowd. She, however, did not look at the crowd or acknowledge their cheers. As she neared the end, she fixed her eyes on the finish line. The Master of the Games stood there with the victory crown. As she crossed the finish line, the crown was placed on her head, and she began to walk around to cool off. Flowers rained down around her, and she held her fists in the air to acknowledge the crowd. Gallio stepped forward and saluted her. Paul could not applaud enthusiastically because he knew that Belos was the on the way to the arena.

My servant, you are surrounded by a vast cloud of witnesses. Lay aside every weight and every entangling sin and run with patience the race that is marked out for you. Fix your eyes upon me, for I am the source and the perfecter of your faith. Run the course, finish the race. A crown of righteousness awaits you!

After a while, the wavering blast of trumpets brought Paul out of his communion to the scene in the arena. The procession of the condemned had arrived. Centurion Valerian led the procession into the arena. Eight quaternions of his legionnaires escorted the condemned as they were led slowly around before the stands. The presence of the centurion and the legionaries told of Rome's justice and that only Rome could dispense the ultimate penalty. The trumpets continued their wavering minor notes. Drums beat at every footstep of the soldiers. The condemned, mostly men, were bound with their hands in front and each was tethered single-file to the one in front and the one in back. Hung around their neck was a placard that proclaimed their crimes. Their only consolation was that, because of the games, they would not die on the cruel wood of a cross.

Paul strained to identify Belos as the procession entered the arena. Belos was the last in the line. He came in among the jeering crowd who were hurling insults of every kind at the pitiful line. But Belos appeared anything but pitiful. He held his head high, and his steps were steady and even. He did not look at the crowd but held his bound hands up to his chest as though praying. One of the soldiers made Belos put his hands down so that the placard could be plainly seen. As the procession came around, Paul was able to see the peaceful expression on the face of Belos.

"Away with the atheist! Away with the atheist! Death to the blasphemer!" The crowd began chanting such things as Belos

was led by. Belos seemed not to hear them at all but looked at the back of the head of the one in front.

When the centurion came to the front of the reviewing stand, he stopped and faced the Proconsul. He handed up a scroll containing the indictments to the Amanuenses. The centurion then brought each one of the condemned to stand before the Proconsul, pulling on the tether to drag each one in place. By means of a speaking trumpet, the Master of the Games announced the names and crimes of each one, reading them from the placards around their necks. The Amanuenses then spoke the condemnation and means of death through the trumpet. One by one, the condemned were brought before the Magistrate, a string of miserable creatures being drawn to a horrible death. At the last, Belos stood before the Proconsul.

"Belos, the servant of Stephanas," the Master of the Games announced. "Atheist, destroyer of the gods." The crowd responded with jeers and whistles.

"He is condemned," shouted the Amanuenses, "Belos will be torn by beasts!" This drew a tumult of cheers and applause.

Gallio said something to the Amanuenses and then raised his arms to quiet the crowd.

The Amanuenses shouted to the crowd, "The great Gallio, Proconsul of all Achaia, Chief Magistrate of Corinth, has offered a small measure of clemency to Belos." The crowd fell silent, not daring to express their disappointment. The Amanuenses continued, "If Belos will recant and give a pinch of incense to the spirit of the divine Caesar, he will receive a swift death by the sword. What say you, Belos?"

The Master of the Games asked Belos, "Well? What do you say?"

"I cannot recant. I cannot deny Jesus who has given me eternal life." Belos' voice was strong and steady.

"Eternal life?" The Master was incredulous. "Slave, your life is soon to end! Have some consideration for yourself. Those lions will begin devouring you before you are dead. I can tell the soldiers to give you a gladiator's death, a swift thrust down to the heart!"

"You threaten me with suffering because you do not know Jesus, who suffered to bring us eternal life. I will not recant."

The Master of the Games shook his head slowly, "Religion has made you mad!" He turned and announced through his trumpet, "Belos says, '*no.*'"

The crowd erupted with deafening jeers, whistles, and shouts. They began chanting, "*Away with the atheist! Away with the atheist! Away with the atheist!*"

Gallio let the crowd keep up the chant for several minutes. He looked around at the crowd and then at the dignitaries on the reviewing stand. His eyes finally rested on Paul and Chloe. He shook his head slightly and then turned to the crowd and quieted them with upraised arms. Gallio spoke to the Amanuenses and said, "Away with the atheist."

The Amanuenses repeated through the trumpet, "*Away with the atheist!*"

Paul could hardly hear Chloe shouting at him for the noise of the crowd. She was crying and holding onto Olivia's arm. Belos was led with the other condemned into an iron stockade on the side of the arena floor. What Paul, along with Chloe,

Crispus, Titius, and Olivia, witnessed next was a testimony to the depravity of man. Paul spotted several believers in the arena who had followed Belos and the procession to the arena. They were watching and praying. Paul also saw that the High Priest, along with his feathered entourage, was seated right behind the stockade. They were shouting obscenities and making lewd gestures at Belos.

One by one, Paul saw the objects of Roman justice brought forth to suffer tortures that only the most hateful of minds could think up to inflict on another human being. One was thrown into a cage of snarling feral dogs. Another was nailed to a stake, covered with pitch and set afire. He burned for the duration of the event, the stench pervading everywhere, incense offered to Satan. One was pulled to pieces by horses, another dragged to his death. But by far, the most popular entertainment were the offerings to wild beasts. The animals were trained to human flesh and properly starved before the event. Goaded and provoked, they were in a hungry rage when they were set loose.

Belos was the last. When he stepped out of the stockade, the floor of the arena was splashed with blood and littered with bloody garments. The burning man continued to pour forth black, acrid smoke. Belos was stripped down to his loincloth and led to the center of the arena accompanied by a crescendo of sound from the spectators.

"Stand here, cat crap," said one of the soldiers gruffly.

The other soldier laughed. "You think this'n' 'ill run? I hope so."

"Don't think it'll matter. You been listening to that cat? Don't think he'll be inclined to play with his food, ha-ha!"

Belos said, "I forgive you. If you will receive Jesus, you will receive eternal life."

"Jesus? Forgive me? If Jesus can keep me from going to Germany or Palestine, I'll think about it. And *you* can't forgive me for *nothin'*."

"I will pray for you," Belos replied, looking steadily and unafraid at the soldier.

The soldiers looked at each other and laughed maniacally. They ran off to the expectant cheers of the crowd, leaving Belos to face his fate. The crowd got louder as the door of the cage was opened and out came a magnificent male lion. The animal was experienced in the arena and after looking around and snarling at the crowd, the lion let out a roar that could have been heard for a mile. Belos was standing motionless in the center of the arena with his hands outstretched and eyes to heaven.

Paul could see that Belos was praying. When the lion spotted Belos standing alone, the big cat came to attention, then crouched down and fixed its eyes on the solitary figure. The cat paused at the unusual behavior of the man. His victims usually ran or sank to the ground in fear. But this one just stood there looking into the sky. The lion began to move toward Belos, tail twitching, stalking him until he was at his feet. The lion crouched down. Belos stood motionless, never looking at the lion. The lion's whiskers brushed him, as it sniffed at his legs and groin and then around his chest. Paul and all the believers were holding their breath.

"*Get him! Eat! Jump on him!*" The multitude of spectators were getting impatient.

"That lion is not going to eat Belos," Paul said, under his breath.

The lion backed off a few yards, looked around and roared. He went over to a tangled mess of bones and half eaten flesh, picked up a bone and carried it off trailing the whole body like a trophy. The lion trotted back to his cage, head high, dragging the body. The big cat entered and lay down for a meal as the cage door fell shut. Belos remained, unmoved and praying.

The Master of the Games came out from his shelter onto the floor of the Arena and looked up at Gallio. Gallio glanced over to his daughter with a raised eyebrow. He looked back at the Master and made a cutting motion across his throat.

The Master of the Games shouted through his trumpet, "Belos has a bewitching power over animals. He has enchanted the lion. Belos will be dispatched *pelekizo.*" There was a small smattering of applause that Belos' head would be separated from his shoulders with a sword. A superstitious cloud was settling over the crowd.

The High Priest was screaming from the seats, "Throw him in the cage! *Throw him in the cage!*" The crowd picked up on the chant and continued for several minutes.

The Master of the Games looked up again at Gallio as if to ask what to do. Gallio shook his head, "no," and made another cutting motion across his throat. When the High Priest looked over at Gallio and saw the dark, angry face of the Proconsul, he got the message, even from that distance. He stopped screaming, and so did the crowd.

The soldiers came back out to Belos, who was standing in the same position. Slowly, they approached motionless Belos with drawn swords. They were cautious of this strange man, a slave who forgave his torturers, and mesmerized lions. One of them had a long *rhomphaia* sword in his hand, leaving the shorter gladius in the sheath at his side.

"I told you we shoulda picked up that last body. The lion went for that!"

"No, that cat never goes for leftovers. He likes to kill!"

They stood in front of Belos, who had not moved an inch. "Belos, sir, we have to do this!"

"Yes," said Belos, lowering his arms, "you do have to do your duty. I want to say something before you do. It was Jesus Christ who closed the mouth of that lion. If you receive Him with faith, you can be assured of eternal life, just as I have been. You can ask Paul, an Apostle of Jesus. He is sitting up near the Proconsul. Now, do your duty, I am ready. You do not need to bind me. What do you want me to do?"

"Please, sir, kneel down. Put yer hands on yer knees. That's it, sir. Now look up at the sky like you was. I'm gonna grab yer hair and hold yah in place. We'll make this quick, sir, so don't throw no spell on us. We're jus' doin what we're told!"

"I SEE JESUS, STANDING BY A THRONE!" Belos' voice thundered throughout the Arena, "I SEE JESUS STANDING BY A THRONE! I SEE JE..."

Paul watched the long sword strike a mighty blow on Belos' neck. The blade landed perfectly and severed Belos' head with a single stroke. The soldier who was holding his hair snatched the head away and put his hand over the eyes of Belos. Paul did not know if the soldier thought to spare Belos the last few seconds of conscious sight or to keep him from looking at him to curse him. Belos' body remained kneeling with blood spurting six feet into the air. The soldier who had swung the sword pushed Belos over with his foot and rolled the body over on its back. The soldier then stepped on the chest and pumped away, expelling huge quantities of blood until none flowed. The head of Belos was then placed on the sword and the soldiers walked around the arena displaying the head of the servant of Jesus Christ. No one cheered. No one whistled or jeered. When they arrived at the reviewing stand, they lifted the head for Gallio to see.

"Away with that!" Gallio looked sick. "Get it out of my sight!"

Gallio got up immediately and left the stand and walked back down the corridor. Paul walked behind him followed by the Chloe and the others. About half way down the corridor Gallio turned and got close to Paul's face.

"Do you wish to make my daughter into a fanatic like *that*?"

"We will protect her. I will pray for her and Jesus will—"

"That is not the answer I wish to hear!" The Proconsul sounded exasperated. "*Your* head is not on *your* shoulders that securely, Saul of Tarsus! If Claudius does not snatch it off, Nero certainly will!"

"I would love to tell you that there will never be any danger to Chloe." Paul tried to keep his voice calm and even. "But in all truthfulness, there is something that you need to know about the followers of Jesus Christ. To us, our testimony about Him is more important to us than our life. That's just the way we are."

"Father," Chloe embraced her father's sagging shoulders, "I love you. Everything will be well. I can feel it!"

"Daughter, I will do what I am able to protect you. Just do something for your father. Keep your faith in this Jesus, whoever he is, *private*. Please? For your father?"

"Yes, Father." Chloe looked in his eyes. "But I am still going to meet with the assembly of Jesus, and I will never deny Him."

"Very well." Gallio sighed, "Wait for Valerian. I will order an escort for you for your journey back to Corinth."

"If you please, sir?" Paul asked, "May we have the body of Belos? We wish to bury him."

"I will order it. Now, leave me, please!"

The journey back to Corinth was more leisurely than their trip out. They were able to talk about Belos and the grace of God. Paul, however, became engrossed in conversation with the soldiers who walked beside the carriage. They were the very ones who executed Belos. They wanted to know all they could about the One who forgave the soldiers who were crucifying Him. Paul told them story after story about Jesus and His love and grace for sinners. By the time they got to Corinth, both wanted to be baptized.

Much had happened in a few short days. But now, Paul and the church had peace. It would extend beyond Paul's stay in Corinth. They were free to minister in the marketplace and hold public meetings. Small groups could be organized to meet in homes scattered throughout Corinth. Paul had a chance to assign and train leadership. Thanks to Crispus, Paul continued to minister the gospel in the Synagogue. But, Rabbi Philip would become increasingly hostile. He was organizing the opposition to Paul. Timothy and Silas would catch up with Paul before long. And, so would his enemies, who had lost track of him after Thessalonica. Until then, Paul thought, there is a lot of work to do, both in the city and the synagogue.

CHAPTER 14

WORKING

"The things that you have heard from me through many witnesses, entrust to trustworthy people who will be able to teach others."

- Paul to Timothy

Paul was not accustomed to having time to take deliberate steps in establishing the church. It seemed that he was always being thrown out of communities, jailed, beaten down, or asked to leave before he was able to teach sound doctrine or organize a fellowship of Jesus followers. His enemies dogged him from city to city. But in Corinth, after the first tumultuous week Paul was there, things settled down into a routine of work and ministry. The martyrdom of Belos did not scatter the church but had the opposite effect of binding the fellowship together. Paul instructed Luke, who was writing an account of Paul's journeys, not to write of the events surrounding Belos.

He did not want any kind of trouble to come to Chloe or Gallio for his service to the fellowship. Chloe had become a leader in the church and hosted a mid-week group. Gallio remained resistant to the grace of God despite the pleas of Chloe and the friendship that was formed with Paul. Ministry in the synagogue continued, Sabbath after Sabbath, with much debate and rancor.

When Paul first entered the city, the Lord immediately sent him to the people who could help in the seemingly impossible task that had been given him. Aquila and Priscilla, Titius Justus, and Stephanas became the pillars of the church. If the church were to prevail over the pagan culture, it must be filled with the Spirit and overflow with love for the fellowship and for the people of Corinth. Paul knew that they must establish a sound doctrine, a strict ethic, and build a tight, disciplined organization. In this regard, they would have to maintain a certain intolerance among themselves, not compromising their beliefs or ethics, but be tolerant toward the world. To achieve this end, Paul formed a court of arbitration so that believers could maintain discipline and settle disputes within the fellowship. Titius, Stephanas, and Crispus were formed into the first tribunal of the court. The courts of the church gained such a reputation for justice and fairness, that pagans began subjecting their lawsuits to its arbitration. These kinds of courts were instrumental in the church's ascendency over Rome as Rome's vaunted justice system became increasingly corrupt and waves of barbarians overwhelmed the Empire. The New Church in Corinth would have many problems in its formation years, but the Lord would use its courts to bring the fellowship though many tribulations.

Paul united Stephanas and Lilia in marriage. Even though Stephanas emancipated Lilia, their union was not recognized by law. But, since their covenant to each other was sincere and made before heaven and the church, Paul solemnized the marriage. Theirs was the first of many contracts held by the church. Lilia followed the vision that the Lord gave her. Because of the crude abortion procedures that she had been subjected to, Lilia never conceived after her marriage to Stephanas. She mourned for her unknown children. She began searching out the places around the city and outside the gates of the city where people exposed infants in the night. She did everything she could to rescue the children from death, or worse. Most of them were female. Without her intervention, the survivors, like Lilia, would become sex slaves. The brothel was transformed into an orphanage. As the church grew, Lilia was constantly finding Christian couples to adopt these infants who were rescued from hell on earth. After a time, people began laying infants at the door of the former brothel and ringing the bronze bell. Although she never had a child of her own, the people of Corinth named her, "Mother Lilia."

Paul insisted that he work for the money that Aquila was giving him. Paul felt he must be genuinely useful to Aquila. He worked at it daily, save the Sabbath. So, he arose early every morning to work with awl and knife. By being quite skillful and working enthusiastically, Paul's purse became healthy. It would not be long until he could return to Antioch with enough money to finance another journey. His skill and arduous work inoculated him from the charges that he was using the gospel to enrich himself. He refused to be distracted by the people who would come by the shop to have "the healer" pray for them. Some of the sick were not willing to wait a few hours, so Paul would give a believer the sweat band from his head, or the apron about his waist, to lay upon the sick as an aid to their faith. They soon learned that Paul was not some sort of magician but a man of faith. It was the prayer of faith that raised people up, bringing healing to some and salvation to all. The afternoons were spent in ministry in the Agora and the Forum, speaking to whomever would listen to him. Late afternoon and evenings were spent teaching and training the new leadership of the church at the home of Titius. Sabbath days were spent in the synagogue, contending with the Jews and the Godfearers, trying to convince them of the truth of the gospel of Messiah Jesus. Nights were spent in prayer and the pursuit of sleep. Paul immersed himself in work and tried not to worry about Timothy, Silas, and the rest of his companions.

Despite Paul's protests, Castor became his shadow. Paul began teaching him the tentmaking trade and urging Castor to seek his freedom. The wide world, however, can be a frightening thing to a caged bird. Castor saw more security in becoming a valuable slave than being an employable free man. So, Paul began training him to be a minister to the many slaves that would become believers in Jesus. By some peoples' count, there were more slaves in Corinth than free people. Almost all of them would never realize freedom and would die slaves. They could not run away. There was literally nowhere in the known world where they could run. Paul could see no way to change the system of slavery. But Castor could teach slaves to honor God, serve Jesus, and serve their masters as well. Paul believed that God had grace even for the sex slaves.

If the ministry to slaves was extremely difficult, the Lord made Castor just the man for the job.

Luke was becoming a valuable associate and was serving as Paul's amanuenses. He also began writing an account of Paul's journeys and adventures. He constantly questioned Paul about the life of Jesus, about Paul's conversion and the history of the church. He also sought out people among the Jewish believers who might have had personal knowledge of Jesus or the events related to His life and ministry. Luke closely questioned old Pamphilos who had witnessed Jesus' crucifixion and had become a believer after the day of Pentecost. He began praying to God for truth, and to send him many reliable witnesses to the grace of God in Christ Jesus.

Paul found a method of teaching that produced the closest thing to a systematic theology that the Apostles produced. Aquila and Priscilla, Andronicus and Junia, and others from among the exiled Jewish believers from Rome, urged Paul to write a letter to the Church of Rome. Paul formed an instruction group of Aquila, Priscilla, Luke, Titius, Stephanas, Lilia, Chloe, Andronicus, Junia, Fortunatus, Castor, and several others who would be able to evangelize Corinth and teach the whole church about faith, grace, and holiness. It was Paul's idea to send the letter to Rome by way of Aquila and Priscilla, who wanted eventually to return to their home city. Titius supplied an amanuensis named Tertius to record the letter. Luke wanted to be free to take his own notes and ask questions.

Paul began dictating his letter to the Romans and teaching the concepts of sound doctrine to the group, asking and receiving questions. The plan was for the scribes of Titius to make faithful copies of the letter and send a number of manuscripts to Rome. The church in Rome, according to Aquila, was fractured into splinters of Jews, Romans, Greeks, barbarians, and slaves. Paul wanted to circulate one letter to each of the numerous small groups of disciples. It was quite a challenge to keep a unified, consistent message that would speak to all groups. But, like Joseph and the prophets of old, the Lord was with Paul. The letter would become more than a message. It would be more than Paul's intellect and skillful teaching. Paul could feel himself led of the Spirit as he spoke. There was no rough draft or rewriting of the letter for clarity. The epistle stood as it came from the heart of God to the mouth of Paul. Paul also carried with him a copy of the letter that he had written to the believers in Galatia, contending with the enemies of the gospel of faith and grace. Together with the Septuagint Scriptures, Paul felt as though he had plenty of resources. He used these instruments to teach the group.

Spring melted into the oppressive heat of a Corinthian summer. Paul was writing and teaching the entire leadership group. The letter to the Romans was going much slower than he had expected. There were many questions and discussions of the letter so far, especially among the Jewish believers. The lessons of law, grace, and dead works did not go down easily with the believing Jews. Now, it was time to disturb the Gentiles with holiness and personal responsibility. After they had prayed, Paul had Tertius read the continuation of the letter that Paul had dictated in preparation for the lesson.

"What then will we say? Should we continue in sin so that grace will overflow? May that never come about! Do you not know that as many of you as were baptized unto Christ Jesus were baptized unto His death? Therefore, we were buried unto death with Him in baptism. So that, just as Christ was raised from the dead through the glory of the Father, so also we might walk about in newness of life."

Tertius, at the instruction of Paul, read the passage with the same syntax, rhythm, and emphasis as he heard from Paul. This was how Paul wanted the letter to be read, as if he were speaking. Tertius could imitate the voice of Paul so well that the group would begin to laugh.

"We have been speaking of the futility of trying to find justification and reconciliation with God by obedience to the law and the 'righteous' deeds of our own flesh." Paul paused as Alexander came into the banquet hall and whispered in Titius' ear. Titius said something back, and Alexander left the room. Despite the distraction, Paul continued, trying to keep the irritation out of his voice, "I spoke of this in the letter to the Galatians. However, we are obligated not to follow the flesh as we did before we knew Christ, but to follow the Spirit who will lead us in the way of love and—" Paul stopped speaking abruptly as Timothy and Silas walked into the room. Timothy, although he was well passed his twentieth year, looked as though he was a mere youth. Silas appeared to be about the same age as Paul.

"Timothy! My son!" Paul rushed over to Timothy and embraced him and kissed him on both cheeks. "And Silas, my friend, it is so good to see your face." Tears filled the eyes of Paul as he embraced the men.

"This is Timothy, my true son in the Lord," Paul beamed as he introduced him. "And this is Silas, my partner in ministry. God set us apart for ministry, that we should work together. We have been beaten side by side by the lectors in the Agora, been in jail together, set free together. Luke, Silas is an important witness to Jesus Christ. He knew Jesus personally. He witnessed Jesus' ascension into Heaven and was among the one-hundred-twenty who received the Baptism of the Spirit on the day of Pentecost."

Then Paul spoke to Silas, "Luke is a physician of Corinth who has received Jesus and has been filled with the Spirit. He is writing a history of my travels and of the church and wants to write a narrative of the life and teachings of Jesus." Paul introduced everyone around to each other.

"Father, you look well," Timothy said, "you look like you may have even gained a little weight. You were very thin the last I saw you."

"The Lord is good. These great people," Paul waved his hand around the room, "have taken wonderful care of me. But, tell me, how are the believers in Thessalonica doing?"

"First of all, I want all of you to know that Paul is my spiritual father, and more of a father to me than my own." Timothy looked fondly at Paul. "The believers are doing remarkably well, really. But they need further instruction. And they have some questions. A few of them have died and the church wants to know from *you* what that means, especially because of what you said to them about the return of the Lord. I have a letter from them."

"Come, come. Sit here and tell us all about what is going on in Thessalonica!" Paul urged Timothy to sit in the chair of the teacher. The next task that Paul would take on would be to write to his beloved brothers and sisters in Thessalonica. They had accepted the gospel so readily and from every report, they were faithful and fruitful. But he longed to instruct them in grace and holiness. Timothy would always tell Paul that the letter should be entitled, "What Every Believer Needs to Know."

"I will relate all. But, I have quite a bit more for you." Timothy motioned to a man who was carrying a large wicker basket. The man came forward and took two scrolls encased in leather and several flutes that contained letters rolled tightly inside. "While we were in Thessalonica, dispatches and manuscripts began catching up with us. Here is a letter for you, Paul, from Jason of Thessalonica and one from Lydia of Thyatira." Timothy handed the letters to Paul.

Paul's ears began burning as he received the letter from Lydia. He resisted the overwhelming urge to pull the letter from the flute and read it immediately. He could feel the eyes of Aquila and Priscilla looking upon his red face. Paul gulped, and said, "Thank you."

"We have also received some things that are very special from the Church of Jerusalem." Timothy did not seem to notice Paul's embarrassment. "We have a letter from James, the brother of Jesus. He is the Leader of the Church of Jerusalem.

He is asking that the letter be read in all the churches. Also, we have received from the hand of Mark an account of the life, crucifixion, and resurrection of our Lord Jesus Christ."

"Mark?" Mark was the nephew of Barnabas, Paul's former ministry partner. Mark had been with Paul and Barnabas to begin their first missionary journey. Mark had lost his courage and left them to go home when they were on the island of Cyprus. Paul thought that this was cowardice. He made no allowance for Mark's youth and inexperience. Paul spoke all his thoughts to Barnabas frankly and without much charity. When Barnabas wanted to take Mark along on their second journey, Paul exploded with objections. Barnabas objected back, defending his nephew and saying that he needed another chance. When Paul said that Mark would cry for his mother within two weeks of starting their journey, the argument deteriorated to a point of non-reconciliation. Silas was then teamed up with Paul and propelled out on their way through Asia. Barnabas and Mark were sent in a different direction.

"Yes, Mark," replied Timothy. "The manuscript is accompanied by a note from Apostle Peter. It is addressed to you and sealed with Peter's insignia. I recognize the emboss. May I break the seal and read it?"

"Yes, by all means." Paul fought feelings of guilt and regret for the harsh words he had uttered two years ago. Also, Paul had not been bashful about getting into Peter's face. He had confronted Peter with what Paul considered to be hypocrisy in Peter's dealings with the Gentile believers. Paul tried to combat the feelings of guilt by the fact that he felt that he was right at the time, both about Mark and Peter.

Yes, you were right! So right that you became wrong!
Timothy began reading,

> "Simon Peter, the bond-servant and Apostle of Jesus
> Christ to my brother servant and Apostle, Paul.
> Greetings! I hope in the Lord Jesus that this letter
> finds you well. We have received a copy of your letter
> to the believers of Galatia. We are reading it in all
> the churches. I am sending you two manuscripts.
> One recounts many of the things about Jesus that
> I witnessed, both of His ministry and the events
> surrounding His crucifixion and resurrection. Mark
> wrote it, faithfully writing the account as I have told
> him. I would ask you to accept this as the Word of the
> Lord. We also are sending you a letter from James,
> the Brother of Jesus. We ask that these manuscripts
> be read to the churches that you have founded. The
> last we heard, you were in Macedonia, possibly as far
> as Thessalonica. Greet Timothy. Greet Silas and your
> other companions. Grace and peace to you."

Timothy rolled the letter up tightly and inserted it in the
wooden flute. "Father, I have read the account of Mark several
times over. I think that it should be entitled 'Gospel,' that is,
'Good News.' It has really helped me construct the life and
teaching of Jesus in my mind. I think every believer should
hear this account read."

"That is where I can help," Titius spoke up. "Manuscripts
are my business. The Lord directed Brother Paul to my door
the first day he was in Corinth. The Lord has revealed my

path, day by day. I will publish all of these works, as many as you need, Brother Paul."

"Wonderful," said Paul, "But I want to hear about the church In Thessalonica. Come, Timothy, tell me all." What Paul really wanted to do was find a private place to read the letter from Lydia. He hoped it did not show in his face.

As if he could discern the thoughts of Paul, Timothy said, "I will tell everything, but first, we would like something to eat. We have had nothing to eat this day but a few pieces of barley bread."

"I will see to it," said Titius. The servants of the house, who were constantly eavesdropping at the meetings in the house, responded to a nod of Titius and hurried off to the kitchen. "You can use our triclinium, Brother Paul, I don't think anyone is in there."

"I think it is wonderful that Lydia has become a believer," Priscilla informed the group. "She is a dealer in purple cloth from Thyatira and a very good person. Her father did business with us before he died. Now *Sister* Lydia carries on." Priscilla looked at Paul as if she were some kind of matchmaker. "And she is *very* beautiful."

Paul knew that his face was ruddy with embarrassment. He looked around at the group and saw that everyone was genuinely pleased that he had received the letter. He thought, *does everyone know about my affection for her?* Words escaped him, and he just gazed at the group as they looked back.

Timothy broke the awkward silence, "Father, be sure to read this letter from Jason, also. It is sealed for you. Jason said that it was urgent." He handed the letter to Paul.

"Then," Paul sighed, "excuse me, please." Paul took the letters and left the room to walk to the family dining area.

When Paul had exited the room, Castor stood and spoke, "I am the servant of Brother Paul, but he treats me as a friend and associate. We should pray for him and not annoy him, even if we think we are encouraging him to find the comfort of a wife. I have taken my station outside of his door at night. I have heard him crying out to God in every watch of the night. I have heard my name, and each of your names, and the names of many of the saints lifted up to God. I have heard Brother Paul in a mighty struggle with his desire for a life mate. I am a slave. My desires must be subject to the desires of my master. Brother Paul is the slave of the Lord Jesus Christ. I know what he is going through. I am going to take my station outside of the door and pray for my brother."

Silas spoke up, "It is just like the Lord when he prayed to the Father in the garden, 'Not my will, but Yours be done.' His sweat fell mixed with blood in his agony. He asked his disciples to pray for Him, but they failed Him in their humanness. Go, Brother Castor, take your place for Brother Paul. We will pray here."

Aquila spoke as Castor left the room, "Brother Castor and Brother Silas are right, we must pray." He looked at Priscilla, "*And* we must strive to mind our own business."

Paul laid both letters on the table in the triclinium. He sat on the couch and looked across the table and out over the roofs of Corinth. He had been wildly successful in planting the Church of Jesus Christ in this pagan city. This had all been in the power of the Lord. "Why can I not conquer my own heart?" Paul prayed, "Help me, Lord, to be your servant. I know not what to do. Please, free me from this desire."

Paul reached forward and took the flute containing the letter from Lydia. His fingers trembled as he slid the letter out of the container. The letter was tightly rolled up with the message written inside. A thin thong of leather was threaded through a hole in the parchment and tied in a knot to keep the letter rolled up and secure. A wax seal covered the knot and bore the embossing of Lydia's signet ring. On the outside of the scroll just over the seal was written, *Lydia of Thyatira to Paul, Saul of Tarsus.* Paul took a breath, broke the seal, unrolled the parchment, and began to read.

> "Lydia of Thyatira to Paul, Saul of Tarsus. Grace and Peace to you in our Lord Jesus Christ. By the time that you receive this letter, I will have returned to my home in Thyatira. I thank God that I have met you and that our hearts were so tuned to each other. I have prayed to the Lord about this, and I have received a word from the Lord for myself and a word of prophesy for you, my dear Brother. For myself, I know that my desire for

you is not in the will of God. I am surrendering my will to the will of the Lord. I am going start a church in Thyatira. The Lord will help me in this work. As for you, The Lord has shown me how much you have been hurt and the difficult path that lies ahead of you. I will pray for you every day. The Lord wants you to forgive Sarah from your heart. He wants you to forgive the members of your family who have harmed you. I know that must be difficult for you, but you must do what the Lord wills, my Dear Brother. Surrender to Him, I beg of you. Please do not respond to this letter. Greetings to Silas and Timothy. Farewell."

Paul bowed his head over the letter that was spread out on the table. He had to move it away so that his tears would not stain the letter. Sister Lydia was truly a prophetess. The Lord had shown her the darkest corners of Paul's soul, and she had ministered to him. And she had, with mercy and kindness, cut off all possibility of a relationship between them. Surrender! How easy it is to preach cross-bearing Christianity, and how difficult to it is to walk the Way of Sorrows with the Lord. Somehow, though, Paul did not have to pray for hours. Like the Lord, events were catching up to Paul. Jesus, as He prayed in the garden, could see the torches of the Roman Cohort and the Priests winding out of the Eastern Gate, and hear the noise and tramping feet of six hundred soldiers. Time was short, and the hour had come. Likewise, Paul could sense that Sosthenes was on his trail again. The crisis was at hand. Paul sank into the will of God. He confronted his anger at Sarah and his family. He forgave them from his heart before the Lord. Paul poured himself out on the altar of God. A wave of the Spirit passed over Paul, and the love of God seemed to flow over, around, and through him.

An hour passed thus with Paul. Castor stood at the door praying and guarding Paul's privacy. When someone wanted to bring food in, Castor held his hand out and shook his head. He knew that Paul would come out when he was ready.

When Paul was able, he opened the letter from Jason.

> "Jason of Thessalonica to Paul. Greetings in the name of Christ. The Church of Jesus in Thessalonica has you in our prayers continually. I must inform you of certain threats that have been made against you. I am sure that Silas and Timothy will tell you of all the events that have transpired in Thessalonica. When Silas and Timothy returned to us without you, Sosthenes thought that you had returned to Asia or possibly to Antioch. He left, searching for you in those places. Some days ago, one Rabbi Benjamin of the Corinthian Synagogue came seeking information about you and

saying that you were in Corinth causing a disturbance in their synagogue. He went on his way to Jerusalem. Your whereabouts will become known to your enemies. Certain ones here have sworn to kill you on sight. I am looking to see Sosthenes return at any time. Be on your guard, Brother Paul. Greetings to Silas and Timothy."

Paul laid the letter out on the table just as he had with the letter of Lydia. There were no tears, however, shed upon this epistle. Instead, he raised his eyes to the ceiling, and prayed to God. "Lord, look at this letter! I pray in Jesus' name, give me boldness in the face of these threats! Give your servant courage. I am yours! Send me to the ends of the earth. In You, I have lost nothing, but gained *everything!*" With these and many other words, Paul reaffirmed his total commitment to the will of God, no matter the personal cost to himself. Just like Jesus.

Fear not! Keep speaking boldly! As you have testified of me in Macedonia and Achaia, so will you testify of me in Rome.

Paul walked out of the room and embraced Castor. "Thank you, Brother Castor, for standing prayerful watch for me. You are indeed a friend to me. You are truly a free man, no matter what man holds the deed to your life. You belong to the Lord, Castor, and that is the best freedom anyone can have."

Paul and Castor walked back to the group. Shadows of the late afternoon lengthened as strong beams of light came through the western windows. Silas and Timothy stood before the group. Timothy told them of all the fantastic adventures of Paul. Silas knew Jesus personally and witnessed His crucifixion. He saw the Lord ascend to Heaven, along with 500 other witnesses. His experience in the upper room at Pentecost made each of the group long to walk with the Spirit as Paul had urged them to do. When Paul walked back into the room, everyone stopped talking and looked at him expectantly.

"All," Paul looked at each of the people in the room, "I repeat, *all* of the true children of the Lord undergo discipline. If we are not disciplined, we are as bastards, and not true children. I have been disciplined by the Lord. I confess to you and will confess to all that I did not treat Barnabas and Mark with love. I have especially harmed Mark, and I will seek his forgiveness and try to repair the damage that I have done. I have never spoken of my family troubles, and I will not speak of them now, except to say that I have forgiven them from my heart and will seek their forgiveness whether they will forgive me or not. As to my personal affairs, it seems that everyone knows of the affection between Lydia and myself. Although it is lawful for each of us to seek marriage, it is not in the will of the Lord for us to do so. The Spirit has revealed this to both of us. Lydia has returned to Thyatira to establish the work of the Lord. I would just ask each of you not to speak of these things to anyone outside of this room. I will continue as I am, the bond-servant of the Lord Jesus Christ."

"Hallelujah! Praise the Lord! Amen," came softly from everyone in the room.

Paul's heart warmed as he sensed love emanating from the whole group. Taking a moment to control his emotions, he spoke, "I believe that we are about to face a crisis in the synagogue. There is a deep division among the Jews over Jesus. Rabbi Philip has led the opposition against us, but the council has held firm in its support of Crispus. We have been blessed by the Lord with many converts from among them. Crispus may correct me, but I think that we have done about as much as we can do. Silas and Timothy will help us out and perhaps we can convince a few more. But Jason has written to me," Paul held up the letter, "about death threats that have been made toward me. Those things always seem to spill over onto the ones who support me, witness Belos."

"You follow the Lord, Brother Paul," interrupted Silas. "We will follow you as you follow Christ! I was arrested with you in Philippi! But we prayed together and sang hymns. The Lord delivered us out of that prison and the jailer was saved! Even if we are not delivered, we will stand fast with you!"

"Yes! Hear! Amen!"

Paul's heart rejoiced to see so many who would risk their own necks for him and the message of the Gospel. Paul knew that by the power of the Lord, they would be victorious in Corinth. He felt a sudden inclination from the Spirit to pray for Sosthenes. He led the group in prayer for their arch enemy, Sosthenes.

"Forewarned is forearmed," Titius murmured to himself, determined to protect Paul from harm. He and others began carrying a gladius concealed under their clothing. Like Belos, there might come a time that they would give up their life for the gospel. But Titius did not believe that it was God's will to let some evil person murder anyone because of their faith. God's will or not, Titius determined not to let anyone of their group come to harm, especially Paul.

CHAPTER 15

SOSTHENES

But I say to you, love your enemies, and pray for the ones
who are persecuting you, so that you will become the sons of
your Father in heaven.

–Jesus Christ

"Lord, give me of your strength to minister these, Your precious people," Paul prayed quietly as he sat in the chair of honor next to Crispus and Aquila in the synagogue. Paul sat, head bowed in communion with the Lord. The Sabbath morning service proceeded the same as it had for centuries of Sabbaths. But there had never been seen the kind of Sabbath disturbances that had occurred since Paul had arrived in Corinth. Paul had only endured because Jesus had given him the victory of the conversion of Crispus, the Synagogue Leader. And he had the support of a number of influential Jews like Aquila, Pamphilos, and Andronicus. Now that

Timothy and Silas had arrived, Paul had been reinforced. Even so, conflict raged in the synagogue. Rabbi Philip had become the chief antagonist. But, Paul had to admit that he himself was the disturber of the peace. It was the Apostle of Jesus Christ that roiled up communities and disrupted centuries of tradition and religious authority. If Jesus had not smacked Paul down on the Damascus road, he would still be dogging the church, just like Sosthenes. Paul truly hated the turmoil that he brought to his fellow Jews. But, it was for the love of Jesus Christ and for the love of all people that Paul had brought the disturbing gospel message to Corinth. Sometimes, Paul thought that he would willing to be accursed, if that were possible, so that his fellow Jews could be saved. It was a comfort, however, when Paul considered that turmoil followed Jesus wherever He went. Paul had a good teacher.

Paul waited patiently for the inevitable crisis. The lurking form of Sosthenes seemed to be everywhere like some leopard ready to spring out of the shadows for an easy kill. And it was not just Paul that he was after. Sosthenes attacked those who protected Paul. When Paul was in Thessalonica, Jason hid him from the mob of Gentiles that Sosthenes had stirred up in the Agora. After they could not find Paul, Sosthenes and the mob dragged Jason into court and charged, "Those who have overturned the whole world are here also!" Paul had certainly overturned the world of the Synagogue of Corinth. Crispus and the others among the Jews who had believed had been baptized in the Synagogue mikveh, much to the chagrin of Philip. Paul had baptized Crispus and his family. Aquila had baptized the rest. Priscilla and Junia proved invaluable, assisting with the women. It was perfectly understandable that Paul would have drawn out some bitter opposition. Paul moved uneasily in his chair remembering that he had been far more harsh and violent with the church than Sosthenes.

Paul glanced up to where Castor sat with several other servants in the Godfearers' gallery along with Titius, Luke, Stephanas, Lilia, Fortunatus, and several other new believers. He looked across to the gallery of the women where Paul could hear the low sounds of Priscilla and Junia conducting a prayer meeting with the other believers. As he looked out in the congregation, he saw friendly and hostile faces among the men. The gospel had brought a disgraceful division to the synagogue. It bothered Paul to know that the message of grace, love, and peace would divide even the families of the congregation. The Holy Spirit brought to his remembrance the words of Jesus,

"Do not think that I came to cast peace upon the earth,
I came not to cast peace but a sword,
I came to divide a man from his father,
And a daughter from her mother,
A daughter-in-law against her mother-in-law,
The enemies of a man will be those of his own house."

Some people seemed to grasp the gospel immediately and with no effort throw off a closely held world view and assume new religious sensibilities. But others were so resistant to change that they simply would not entertain or even think about the possibility of another way of thinking or believing.

Paul knew that everyone's most cherished beliefs resided in an emotional and spiritual place. Jesus Christ could break through the barriers of prejudice and emotion. Leading people to a change of mind often required first receiving their anger and the bitter resistance of prejudice. But it was not just the Jewish community that was roiled by the gospel. The Pagans held to their idols and mysteries as ferociously as any Pharisee held to the Law and any scribe held to the Torah. But the power of the gospel resulted from the power of the Holy Spirit taking the message of the cross to the hearts of men and women, melting their resistance to change.

"Shame!" "Good for you!" "Apologize!" "Serves him well!" Many voices spoke up at once to bring Paul to attention to what was transpiring.

Rabbi Philip walked around the floor of the synagogue presenting the Torah Scroll to the people. Everyone touched it, and some kissed it. He had walked along the gallery of the women and they had reached through the lattice to touch the Word of God. But as Philip came by the front, he turned his back on the chairs and did not look at Paul, or Crispus, or Aquila. The young Rabbi who replaced Rabbi Benjamin followed Philip. He looked back at Crispus and gave him a look that said, "I do not know what to do!"

"Rabbi!" Crispus raised his voice, "We have not yet given our respects to the Torah."

Philip paid no attention to Crispus but walked across the platform to the ark and placed the scroll in its place. He descended on the opposite side and walked in front of Crispus and sat in his chair. Without looking at Crispus he said, "Do not ask me to assist at the ark."

Crispus leaned forward and looked down the row at the young man, "Rabbi?"

The young Rabbi gave a small worried shake of his head and whispered loudly, "I cannot!"

"Very well," Crispus arose and looked at Paul, "I will assist. Follow me, Brother Paul."

They both stepped up onto the platform. Paul asked Crispus for the First Book of Moses. Crispus smiled when Paul told him the text from which he was to give the homily. Crispus rolled the scroll out in the prescribed manner, and they found the passage.

Crispus said, "I want to say something to the people before you read." Paul stepped back and Crispus stood up to the pulpit.

"Beloved brothers and sisters." Crispus paused for a few seconds to let the words sink in. "Paul has not asked us to stop being Jews! He has asked us to consider that Jesus of Nazareth is the Messiah, the Christ of God. Whether we follow Jesus or not, we will always be the children of Abraham! We will always be true to Moses and the Ten Commandments of God. Solomon and David will still give us wisdom. The history of Israel and Judah will remain. Prophesy will not be broken, but rather fulfilled. The promise made to Abraham is the promise that is fulfilled in Messiah Jesus. We have debated this freely among us. No one can say that they have not had a chance to speak their mind in this matter. I have not forbidden anyone to speak. Rabbi Philip has given homilies and taught us from the chair, asking and answering questions. He has not been disrespected by any person. But now, he must apologize to Brother Paul."

"There will be no apology," Philip shot back. He spoke loudly toward the back of the synagogue, "This ends *today!*"

Paul saw a disturbance at the door of the synagogue as someone entered the building. Somehow, Paul knew who was coming through the door. The group of men at the back of the room parted as Sosthenes walked down to the front in tasseled, pharisaic splendor. He was accompanied by an acolyte and two young men with hard faces. The hilts of weapons were showing out of their Jewish clothing. Aquila rose quickly and stood before the platform, blocking the way of Sosthenes and his men. His hand was in his garment as though grasping a concealed weapon. Sosthenes and his men stopped before the hulking form of Aquila. Through the lattice work, Paul could see Titius and Stephanas moving swiftly out of the God-fearers' gallery and into the back of the synagogue. They did not care that their Gentile sandals were defiling the floor. The movement to their rear was not lost to the attention of the hard-faced men.

'Whatever we do," Crispus was speaking loudly, "let us have peace among us."

"There can be no peace with *blasphemers!*" Sosthenes replied sternly. "I am Sosthenes, a Pharisee and legate of the High Priest in Jerusalem. I also have credentials from the Synagogue of the Freedmen in Jerusalem." He looked up at Aquila. "Could you ask this ... *person* ... to move aside? I cannot see around him."

"My name is Aquila, a Jew in good standing and a citizen of Rome. Order your thugs outside. Then, I will move aside."

Sosthenes looked around and saw the men at the rear of the synagogue. He turned his head to his men and motioned toward the door. They turned and walked back to the rear of the synagogue. As they approached the door, Titius and Stephanas locked eyes with them. After they passed by, Titius and Stephanas followed the men out of the door into the street. When the door opened, the sound of a disturbance in the street entered the building and caused anxiety to rise in the stomach of Paul. When the door closed, they could only hear muffled loud talking.

"We want no blood shed on the floor of the synagogue." Sosthenes was smirking.

"If there is blood on the floor of the synagogue today, your blood will surely be mingled with it," Aquila said, bending down close to the face of Sosthenes.

"Enough of that talk," Paul exclaimed! "We will not repay evil with evil! Neither will we permit any of the believers to be murdered!"

"Please move aside, Aquila," Crispus spoke calmly. "Let me see your credentials, Sosthenes."

Warily, Sosthenes kept his eyes on Aquila and extended his hand toward his acolyte, who placed a scroll in his hand. Sosthenes then moved toward Crispus and gave him the document. Crispus rolled the scroll out on the pulpit and read.

"Yes," Crispus looked at Paul and then back at Sosthenes, "you have authority. What do you want?"

"*Want?*" Sosthenes laughed softly and gazed around at the assembly on the floor and in the gallery of the women and the God-fearers. "I want to *know*, are you, *Crispus*, a follower of Jesus the Nazarene, that dead Galilean blasphemer?"

"Yes," Crispus answered without hesitation. "I am a follower of Jesus the Messiah, whom you crucified, and God has raised from the dead!"

"I did not crucify him, but I wish I could have seen it. Next question. Will you recant your belief in the pretender, and curse Jesus in hell, which is where he is?" A gasp went throughout the building. Otherwise, there was complete silence from the assembly.

"No, I will *not* curse Jesus, neither will I recant," exclaimed Crispus. "I cannot ... I will not! He has given me eternal life!"

"I *told* you," exclaimed Rabbi Philip, "we have been enduring this for months!"

"Crispus," said Sosthenes, "you are *out* as leader of this synagogue. By the authority given to me, I am assuming the role of leader until new leadership can be found."

Sosthenes turned to face the congregation. He extended his hand and pointed at Paul, "THIS MAN!" Sosthenes paused for effect, "Saul of Tarsus, known as Paul! I have no question to ask of him! He is well known to be a blasphemer, a disturber of the peace of our synagogues wherever he has gone! Saul of Tarsus, you are no longer allowed to speak from the chair. You are excommunicated! OUT!"

Sosthenes turned to face Paul and Crispus. Calming his voice, he said, "Both of you, please, step down from the platform."

Crispus looked at Paul and nodded. Paul knew that they must respect the authority of the new leader of the synagogue, but only in the synagogue. As Crispus stepped down, he forgot to go down the opposite way that he went up.

"The *other* side, brother," Philip said snidely, still stinging from being humiliated months before on the same point. There was laughter from some.

"Oh, yes, of course." Crispus reversed course to the correct side. Philip seemed to be irritated that this did not seem to bother Crispus at all. Paul and Crispus stepped onto the floor and stood by Aquila, Timothy, Silas, Andronicus, and old Pamphilos who was leaning on his staff.

"Now," said Sosthenes as he mounted the platform and sat in the teacher's chair, "I want to speak to everyone before I make any more decrees."

Sosthenes carefully arranged his clothing, especially the beautiful mantle with its long dangling tassels. His chiton had some of the broadest purple vertical bands that Paul had ever seen. His prayer shawl and headpiece were fashioned beautifully. He exemplified a splendid, proud, and vain Pharisee. "Just like me, Lord," Paul whispered, "just like me."

"Careful investigation has been made into this imposter, Jesus," Sosthenes began speaking with his most pompous and pious voice. "His mother was a peasant girl in Nazareth, a no-account town in Galilee. She was raped by a Roman soldier and conceived. She was taken to Bethlehem where Jesus was born. They spent some time in Alexandria until the rumors and shame died down and then were brought back to Nazareth. Jesus was a mere tradesman, some say a worker in wood. He had no claim whatsoever to the throne of David. He was very charismatic, however, and attracted some followers. Like all false Messiahs, he was crucified by the Romans. He disciples connived to steal his body and claim that he was raised from the dead."

"*LIES!*" Pamphilos became so excited that he was no longer leaned on his staff but shook it at Sosthenes. "You are not a Pharisee! A Pharisee ought not to bear false witness! I saw Jesus! I saw Him work miracles and clean the crooks like you out of the temple!"

"I knew Jesus and his family personally," Silas was shouting, "Nothing of what you have said is true!"

The chaotic noise of shouts, angry words and rebuttal receded in Paul's consciousness. In the Spirit, the words of the Master came to him. *Sosthenes is as you were. I have been pursuing him as he has been pursuing you. It is hard to kick against the goads!*

"*YOU!*" Sosthenes pointed at Paul. "Yes, *you*! *You* have brought destruction upon this house. *You* are the enemy of God! *You* are persecuting the Children of Abraham!"

"And you, sir," Paul was waving his arms for silence. "You, Sosthenes, are dealing with a horrible thought! You must listen to the voice of Jesus, who is speaking to you!"

Sosthenes' face instantly turned crimson with rage, and his eyes bulged out as if they would fall upon his cheeks. "And you are OUT! And any other fool who holds to the blasphemer! OUT! Excommunicated, anathema, OUT!" Spittle flew out from his lips as he screamed his condemnation. Suddenly, he caught himself, and realized the spectacle that he was displaying to the people. They had been shocked into silence.

Consciously gathering himself together, Sosthenes began speaking more calmly. "I have something for you to think about." He snapped his fingers at his acolyte, who produced another document. The acolyte gave it to Paul. Paul unrolled it and read.

Sosthenes was gathering himself back into his pompous mode. "You are summoned to court. Tomorrow morning. I have been in Corinth for several days researching the damage that you are doing, so I entered these charges with the court. You are charged with disrupting the worship and practice of this Synagogue, an authorized religion of the Empire. You also are accused of sedition, having claimed that Jesus is the King, instead of Caesar. The charge is accompanied by an affidavit from the Legate of the High Priest that you are excommunicated and no longer under the protection of the edit. It petitions the court to ask you to give a pinch of incense to the Spirit of the Divine Caesar."

"You oppose blasphemy with blasphemy?" Crispus was incredulous.

"Call it what you will, Paul will have to answer in court. I understand that Gallio himself will hear this case!"

Sosthenes missed the slightly amused look on Paul's face. He continued, "Now, any who have proclaimed Jesus may curse him at once and be restored to fellowship. Those who will not, are permanently excommunicated and must leave immediately."

Tears flowed as the exodus began. Excommunication was, to the Jews, one of the worst things that could happen to them. It banished them from family and cut all cords of belonging. It ended their safety net if they were poor or disabled. The believers streamed out of the floor and the galleries and into the street. Not one of them recanted. But they possessed a new *koinonia*, a new fellowship, that bound them together in love by the Holy Spirit. The foundation of Western culture and a new social order was being formed and Paul would be its chief architect.

Paul was the last one to leave the synagogue. The street was full of people. They had gathered, as usual, outside of the synagogue on the Sabbath so that Paul and the other believers could minister to them. But there were more than usual. When Titius and Stephanas followed the two hard-faced men out of the door, they were confronted by two more of Sosthenes' associates. Titius called to his servant boy, Plato, and told him to run and raise up the church. Titius and Stephanas stayed by the door to guard it. The crowd built quickly and soon had the four hard-faced men pinned up against the outside wall of the synagogue, arms locked in an impenetrable barrier. The men's hard faces began to crack with fear, not daring to risk drawing their swords, and unable to move their arms in any case.

Paul walked several steps out of the synagogue door and turned to face Sosthenes, who stood in the doorway. Paul began, elaborately and slowly, shaking the dust out of his clothing and from his sandals and feet.

"Your blood is on your own head, Sosthenes, and the blood of all those whom you have dissuaded from the truth! I have declared the truth of Jesus Christ! I am innocent of the blood of all people! From now on, I am going to the Gentiles!"

Paul turned to the crowd, "Let those men of Sosthenes' return into the synagogue." He waited as the crowd released its grip on the men. The hard-faced men slithered along the wall and into the door.

Paul continued, "I am moving my residence to the home of Gaius Titius Justus, that door right over there. I will be outside of that door each Sabbath day to minister to the people of Corinth and to teach you about salvation in Jesus Christ. How many of you have received salvation by receiving Jesus Christ?" A host of hands went up. "If anyone has not received Jesus in faith, I urge you to talk to any one of these who are holding up their hands. If there are questions that cannot be answered, you can talk to the elders of the church."

Paul turned back to Sosthenes. "You have your synagogue back, pure and withered up. Jesus will have *all* of your God-fearers and proselytes!"

"See you in court, you accursed *hrupos*, filth!" Sosthenes turned back into the synagogue in a jealous rage, slamming the door behind him.

Paul and some others tried to comfort those Jews who had been expelled. It would be hard to measure the grief of a Jew being put out of the synagogue. It was an expulsion from a way of life and everything that made them secure in this world. But it was more than that. Some had left fathers and mothers behind, sisters and brothers who no longer considered them to be family. Employment was lost, and businesses ruined in the tight community of Judaism. And for what were they expelled? They did not reject the God of Abraham, Isaac, and Jacob. They simply accepted the promise of God, fulfilled in Jesus Christ. They did not mock the Prophets but received their word as revealed in the Savior of the World. They did not scoff at the commandments of God but obeyed them according to the Royal Law of love that Jesus taught them. They were banished because Jesus liberated them from the iron grip of religious traditions, regulations, and laws made by men and enforced as the commands of God. For this, they were even deemed worthy of death. If it was difficult to measure their grief at being expelled, it was harder to measure their joy and determination to follow Jesus Christ at every cost.

"It is just as Jesus said," Silas was talking to the council later that day at the home of Titius. "I was not one of the twelve, but I followed Him and was taught by Him. I had known Him from childhood. He always warned us that this was going to happen. I memorized His words,

> '*I have spoken so that you will not be trapped by these things. They will put you out of the synagogue. Furthermore, there comes an hour when everyone who kills you will reason that they are rendering an act of worship to God.*'"

Silence fell upon the group as they considered this. But not one of them was trying to think of a reason to wiggle their way out of their commitment to Jesus Christ. For a couple of minutes, the only sound heard was the scratching of Luke's pen as he took notes.

"So," said Titius, "What will be your defense tomorrow, Brother Paul? I know some excellent lawyers who can help you even at this late hour."

"No, thank you, Brother Titius," answered Paul. "I have a better advocate that will stand beside me. It is the *Parakletos*, the Holy Spirit. As to what I will say," Paul shrugged his shoulders, "It will be given me what to say. But we do need to make some preparations. Brother Castor?"

"Yes, sir?" Castor was always attentive to Paul's every request.

"Brother, I am sure that Titius has a razor and comb in the house. Would you be so kind as to cut my hair? I want it very short. I want a haircut like Brother Titius'."

"Begging your pardon, sir, but Brother Titius has a lot more hair than you."

Paul joined with the laughter of the group. "I look like a Jew with thinning hair. I want to look like a bald Roman."

"As you want, sir!"

"And, Brother Castor, I want you to cut off my beard. I want to be clean shaven." A collective gasp went up from the group.

"*Off?*" Castor exclaimed, "Clean off? I have never seen a Jew without his beard!"

"You would if you had seen one under a vow. I have made a vow unto the Lord."

"Sir, may I ask, what is the vow?"

"That is between me and the Lord. Now, Brother Castor, off with the beard and cut the hair!"

Castor started toward the door to get what he needed. But, the eavesdroppers had already fetched razor, comb, and a sheet, which they gave to Castor. Hair and beard rained down to the floor. The whole house and the group became audience to a transformation. They gave out many "*ahs*" and "*ohs.*" When Castor finished, he flourished a mirror of polished metal in front of Paul's face. Shocked by the sight of a stranger, Paul exclaimed, "I have worn a beard ever since I could grow one!"

Later, Paul got Titius aside for a private conversation. "I suppose, Brother Titius, that when you stand with me tomorrow at court, you will be wearing a toga, yes?"

"Yes, I wear it at ceremonial occasions and when at the courts. Why do you ask?"

"Do you have an extra one? I would like to borrow it."

"I do have another one, but they can only be worn by citizens of Rome."

"I *am* a citizen of Rome."

Titius was taken aback and just looked at Paul. Finally, he blinked three times and said, "*You* are a citizen of Rome?"

"Yes," answered Paul. "I have credential and certificate with me."

"I believe you!" Titius looked at Paul with amazement. "That had to cost you a fortune!"

"Not at all," Paul answered, "I am a natural-born Roman." Titius just looked at Paul, open-mouthed.

"So," Titius said, finally gathering his thoughts. "Tomorrow, Sosthenes will be standing before the Proconsul of a Roman colony bringing serious charges against a Roman citizen, claiming that you have offended Jewish religious sensibilities, and asking for severe punishment. And you will be standing there in your toga looking like an honorable citizen."

"That is the plan," Paul smiled. They both began laughing until tears came to their eyes.

"Why did you not tell us that you are a citizen?"

"I have found that it is wise to keep that fact secret until a propitious moment, such as we have now," Paul answered. "And I would ask you to keep it to yourself until we are in court tomorrow."

"Brother Paul," said Titius, "have you considered that Sosthenes could be crucified for bringing these charges? And, the people that stand with him could suffer the cross! I know that you would not want that to happen. His own people might kill him for risking their necks."

Paul answered, "Sosthenes will not be crucified, nor will he be killed. The Lord has assured me of that. None of the Jews will be harmed. I am confident of it."

"But Sosthenes will have a very bad morning."

"Yes," said Paul. "It is just as the Psalmist wrote,

'The sinner shall watch for the righteous,
And gnash his teeth upon him,
But the Lord shall laugh at him,
For he foresees that his day is coming,

Sinners have drawn their sword,

They have bent their bow,

To cast down the poor and needy one,

And to slay the upright in heart,

Let their sword enter into their own heart,

And their bows be broken.'

"Truly, it will be so," said Paul.

"Amen," said Titius.

"I want us to pray for Sosthenes, Brother Titius. Join me please for a while."

The two men joined together in earnest prayer for one of their worst enemies. Paul prayed that, through the trial that Sosthenes would endure on the following day, salvation would come to the man. They both pleaded for the life and soul of Sosthenes.

After the "amen," Titius asked, "Brother Paul, when you were getting ready to give the homily this morning, Brother Crispus smiled when you told him the passage. But we never heard it read. I am curious, what was the scripture?"

"It is the word of the Lord from Isaiah," Paul spoke softly. "We should all hold it fast in our hearts,

'And come, let us reason together, says the Lord,

Though your sins be as purple,

I will make them white as snow,

And though they be as scarlet,

I will make them white as wool,

And if you be willing, and harken to Me,

You shall eat of the good of the land,

But if you be not willing, nor harken to Me,

A sword shall devour you,

For the Word of the Lord has spoken it.'

"I have believed it for myself! Now, we must believe it for Sosthenes!"

CHAPTER 16

THE SHINING MAN

"The face of Jesus shone brilliantly like the sun, and his garments white as the light."

-Matthew the Apostle

When a man sails the ocean on a lonely journey for which he must make provision for water and supplies, there is a point of no return. Woe to the person who passes that point and then discovers that he has not enough provisions to sustain him to the destination and has traveled too far to return. There are many points like that in life. There are people who decided on a course of action that seemed right to them, but their decision took them into dangerous places beyond the point from which they were able to escape. Foresight and planning failed them because they were unfamiliar with the true challenges that were before them. There are people who pick fights with people they do not know. They make a judgment on outward appearance. But ignorance of the true skill, strength, and determination of their opponent can lead to their destruction. When the struggle begins, they are doomed because their arrogance and ignorance have taken them past the point of no return. Sosthenes was a man like that. He made an unwise decision when he entered an indictment against Paul. He assumed that he knew all he needed to know about Paul and the defense that the Apostle might be able to mount against him. When he stepped before the Bema to face Gallio, the Proconsul of Achaia and the Chief Magistrate of Corinth, Sosthenes stepped beyond the point of no return. He had not the slightest thought that he was doomed.

Paul was a man who also went beyond those points. But he did it knowingly and purposefully. Jesus constantly led him into unknown places and unforeseen events. When he stepped on board a ship bound for new fields of harvest, or entered city gates where unreasoning hostility greeted him, there was no return. Paul intentionally abandoned himself to the providence of God. Early on, after the Damascus Road, Paul did not seek God's will as much as being carried along by it. Paul yielded himself to the guidance of the Spirit and so found himself in the grip of God. It fashioned him into the powerful figure that he had become.

Paul and Titius stood in the Forum at the Bema while other cases were being heard by Gallio. They could see Sosthenes and several others standing on the other side. They seemed to be looking around for someone. Titius suddenly realized that they did not recognize Paul, beardless, hairless, and wrapped up in a toga. At that moment, someone tugged on Titius' clothing to get his attention. It was a Lector of the Court. "If you please, sir, The Magistrate wishes to talk to you at the Bema." Titius followed the Lector to the chair. Gallio motioned him to come close for a private conversation. Titius bent down close beside him so that he could hear.

Gallio whispered, "Is that Paul standing with you?"

"Yes, it is, Honored Sir."

"Is this some kind of a trick? He looks like a Roman!"

"Yes, Honored Sir, he *is* a citizen. Natural born. He has his credential and certificate with him. I have seen them."

"Why, by all the gods and Caesar's wife, did he keep it secret?"

"He told me, Honored Sir, that he always keeps it secret until the propitious moment comes."

Gallio looked over at the group where Sosthenes and the other complainants from the synagogue were looking around trying to see if Paul was somewhere near the court. "This ... Sosthenes," asked Gallio, "has no thought that Paul is a Roman citizen?"

"No, Honored Sir, he does not."

"So, the one who set a snare is about to be strangled in his own trap?"

"Apparently so, Honored Sir."

Gallio had to screw up his face to keep from laughing out loud. When he had regained control, he said, "Titius, you have always been a good friend to this court. I do not know enough of this controversy. You are a Christian, and a friend of the Jews, so you know more than me. How do you think I should rule? I can have Sosthenes crucified!"

"Honored Sir, Paul has no wish ... *we* have no wish to have Sosthenes crucified or harmed. But we do wish for peace that we may preach Jesus. This is a controversy about the Jewish religion. Jesus was a Jew and the churches' foundation is Jewish, although many non-Jews in Corinth are believers, witness Chloe, your daughter. Aquila the Tentmaker, you know him, is a Jewish refugee from Rome. He is also a citizen. He asks that no disturbance be allowed as happened in Rome between Christians and traditional Jews. Aquila said there was blame on both sides. Perhaps, a stern warning to all sides would be just, Honored Sir."

"Thank you, Titius, for your wisdom. You are too kind to your enemies. It is a good quality and a great weakness. You may rejoin Paul."

"Honored, Sir!" Titius walked back to where Paul and Aquila were standing. He noticed that Aquila had an anxious look on his face, but Paul looked as though he never had an anxious thought.

"I think all will be well," Titius said to Paul.

"Sosthenes will not be harmed?"

"I think Sosthenes will not be crucified. I recommended a warning. But the decision will be up to Gallio. He always knows more about things than he lets on. He has spies in all places. That is a good thing for us to remember. We should keep praying for Sosthenes."

They waited while another case was heard. Gallio did not allow elaborate, confusing arguments and so kept everyone to the point. Advocates in the court learned to be brief and succinct before Gallio. It was not long before Paul's case was called. When they stepped up to the Bema, Titius stood beside Paul, and Rabbi Philip stood beside Sosthenes. Sosthenes cast a nervous glance at Paul. An awful realization began to form on his face. A murmuring began to grow in the crowd and a few sounds of alarm as people began to see that Saul, the disturber, was Paul, the Roman.

The Amanuenses of the court announced, "A criminal complaint has been brought to this court by Sosthenes, the Leader of the Synagogue of the Jews, and on their behalf, against Saul of Tarsus, cognomen Paul. Is the complainant present?"

"Yes, but ..." Sosthenes' voice cracked.

"Is the defendant present?"

"Yes, Honored Sir," Paul's voice was calm and even.

Gallio said, "Let the complaint be read."

"Honored Sir," Sosthenes regained his voice with great effort, "we wish to withdraw the complaint, Honored Sir."

"Withdraw the complaint? Before it is read?" Gallio's face was hard as flint. "What kind of a fool's errand do you think you are on?" Sosthenes and Philip withered before the face of Gallio.

Some of those of the synagogue who had come with Sosthenes were turning away and trying to melt into the crowd of the Forum. Gallio saw them, and called out to the Lectors, pointing them out, "Bring them to the Bema, now!" The Lectors and the attending Politeia ran out and rounded them up quickly. They were all brought to stand with Sosthenes and Philip, where they gave Sosthenes a hateful look.

The Amanuenses began reading, "Sosthenes, The Leader of the Synagogue of the Jews and Legate of the High Priest of the Jews in Jerusalem, respectfully submits to the court an indictment charging Saul of Tarsus, also known as Paul, with being a disturber of the peace of Rome by disrupting the worship and practice of the Synagogue, an authorized religion of the Empire. He is accused of sedition, having claimed that one Jesus of Nazareth in Galilee is king instead of Caesar. The court is also petitioned to deny the people known as Christians protection under the Edit of Exemption. The court is also petitioned to order Paul to give a pinch of incense to the Spirit of Caesar."

"Sosthenes, you will begin your case against Paul." Gallio looked down at the group with Sosthenes. Several were quaking in their clothing.

"Honored Sir," said Sosthenes, "as I said, we wish to withdraw the charges." Everyone with him nodded their approval.

"Very well, they can be dropped." Gallio pierced them with his eyes. "But, before I quash the indictment, may I ask *why* you brought charges in the first place and wasted the time of this court? Do you realize that you have brought charges that could have cost this man his life? Perhaps *your* life is in danger."

"Well, uh," Sosthenes swallowed his fear and went on to make the best of it. "This man, Paul, came into our synagogue and convinced people to worship contrary to the Law, Sir ... Honored Sir."

"Tell me, Sosthenes, to my knowledge, Crispus is the Leader of the Synagogue of the Jews in Corinth. What happened to him?"

"He was deposed, and, uh, I am his replacement, Honored Sir."

"When did that happen?"

"Yesterday, Honored Sir."

"Yesterday?" Gallio turned to the Amanuenses and asked, "When was this complaint filed?"

"Four days ago, Honored Sir, and immediately put on today's docket."

Gallio turned back to face Sosthenes, "You presented yourself as the Leader of the Synagogue in this complaint. Even though Crispus was still the Leader! Explain that!"

"Well, Honored Sir, you see Paul came and really disrupted the—"

"If it were some vicious act or crime that you came with," Gallio's voice was gaining in volume, "perhaps you would not be wasting my time. But as it is, you must settle these questions of your own religion among yourselves. This is the same controversy that caused all the trouble in Rome and got all of you Jews kicked out of Rome. This WILL NOT

HAPPEN IN CORINTH! Get out of my court! If there is any more trouble, I will crucify the lot of you!"

Gallio looked at the Lectors and motioned with his head toward Sosthenes. The Lectors sprang upon Sosthenes like wolves on a sheep, knocking him to the ground, stripping off all his clothing. They began beating him with their rods. Some men of the synagogue began kicking Sosthenes in the ribs. One of the Lectors laughed, held out the rod in his hand to one of the men, and said, "Use this!" The Lectors often beat people who received a sentence of corporal punishment, but they inflicted a lot more pain than real damage, and it was never lethal. But the men who took over the beating of Sosthenes began raining blows on his face and head.

"You could have got us crucified! What have you done?" When Sosthenes tried to roll over and shield his face with his hands, they kicked him over on his back and began striking his hands, arms and elbows. "Break his teeth! Break his teeth, he won't cause no more trouble!" The Lector pursed his lips and winced as Sosthenes received blow after blow and the blood began to fly. He looked up at Gallio, to see if he should put an end to the beating, but Gallio seemed to be unconcerned.

Paul started to go over to Sosthenes, but Titius held him back. "You must not interfere!" Paul watched as Sosthenes became unable to shield his face with his hands. Paul was sickened as Sosthenes began coughing because the blood from his nose was running into his mouth. Teeth came out with the blood and lay on the paving stones of the forum. Sosthenes lapsed into unconsciousness and his chest stopped heaving. The men stopped beating him. One of the men spit on the body.

"Dear God," prayed Paul, "You promised that he would not die!"

Sosthenes is not dead.

"That's enough, he ain't breathin'. He's dead," said one of the Politeia, as he looked down on the lifeless body of Sosthenes. The Lectors began collecting the rods and started back to the Bema. Rabbi Philip, who had not participated in the beating, was standing nearby. He turned to leave.

"Where you goin'?" The officer grabbed Philip by the arm.

"I am going home."

"Take'm with ya. Ya came with'm. Ya hafta take'm home!"

"But he's dead!"

"Then take'm out n bury'm. Ya can't leav'm here."

"He is not dead! We will take him!" Paul had come running up with Titius, Aquila, and Luke. Stephanas went to retrieve Sosthenes' clothing. Crispus was trying to talk to some of the remaining members of the synagogue.

"You would desecrate the body of this man with the hands of Gentiles? You have done enough this day!" Phillip motioned for some of the men to come over. "Here," he said, "you get one foot and you, there, take the other, and we will drag him back to the synagogue."

"You are not preparing his body in the synagogue," said one. "No one wants that."

"And no one wants him in our homes, either," said the other.

"We can take him to my home," Aquila interrupted. "Paul and I know how to properly wash the defilement from his body and prepare him for burial. I will take care of all expenses."

"I am here to tell you that Sosthenes is not dead!" Paul was at the face of Philip. "Give him to me. He is going to be saved in the name of Jesus Christ!"

Philip glanced back and forth but could not decide.

"Give tha man tha body!" The officer was getting exasperated, "*You* don't want'm and yer *people* don't want'm. This man wants'm. A *moron* could figur' this out!"

Luke was kneeling beside Sosthenes. He looked up at Paul and shook his head, "It is not good."

The officer rolled his eyes and looked at Philip. "Either *you* say what ta do, or *I'm* saying."

Philip said nothing, but turned abruptly on his heel and walked away, taking his people with him. The officer threw up his hands and turned to Paul, "You got'm. Clean up tha blood when ya leave." He walked away from them, shaking his head and talking to himself.

"Brother Stephanas, bring Sosthenes' mantle over here and spread it out next to him." Paul helped him stretch the garment out like a large tablecloth on the pavement. "Now, let's lift him carefully over onto the cloth. It is very strong and will support his weight. He is not a large man." Paul called for Andronicus and Crispus. Fortunatus came with them, and together they lifted Sosthenes onto the cloth. Six men, three on each side, grasped the mantle and lifted him up. Paul said, "I picked up his teeth. He will need them to eat." No one dared to laugh or question Paul. They began to carry

Sosthenes across Corinth to the house of Aquila. Paul led the way, praying, with his eyes lifted to heaven. Luke followed, looking for the promised signs of life. The church trailed in a long procession. After about one hundred yards, Sosthenes coughed twice and began breathing.

Gallio watched as the procession wound its way out of the Forum. He watched as the women of the church began to clean up the blood from the pavement. They brought jars of water from the fountain and were washing the stains away. It would take the winter rain and many noonday suns to bleach the stains completely out. He saw people of the church talking to others in the Forum and the Agora about Jesus Christ. When he saw Chloe, his beloved daughter, among the evangelists, he closed his eyes and bowed his head in despair. He heard the distant sound of the church rejoicing and knew that some sign of life had been discovered in their enemy. "What will Rome do with these people," he said softly, "what *can* they do?"

When Paul and the procession got to the home of Aquila, Sosthenes moaned pitifully. They got him on a bed and began cleaning him up so that Luke could begin assessing his injuries. The worst injuries were to his head, face, and hands.

Sosthenes was regaining consciousness, but he could not see anything because of the swollen flesh over his eyes. He tried to sit up but fell back in pain. He held his mangled hands in the air as though he were trying to reach something. He lowered his hands and began what could have been sobbing.

"Sosthenes!" Paul was close down to his ear. "Sosthenes, this is Paul. Your eyes are swollen shut so you cannot see me. If you can hear me, nod your head. Don't try to speak, your teeth are broken, and your jaw may be broken also. If you can hear me, nod your head." Sosthenes nodded his head. "Good! You have received a severe beating with rods at the court today. Do you remember that?" Another nod. "The church of Jesus brought you to the home of Aquila the Tentmaker, a Jew. We have one of the best physicians in Corinth to attend to you. But our trust is not in physicians. We are going to pray to God in the name of *Jesus* for you to be restored." Several nods. "I want you to pray with us. I want you to pray to God in the name of Jesus. You don't have to say the words because our God knows the heart." More nods. "Very well, I am going to call the council of the church in here to pray for you."

There would be many controversies in the church about the role of women in ministry. But on this day, there would be no objections as both the men and the women of the church laid their hands upon the blood-stained body of Sosthenes and cried out to God as though the Almighty were hard of hearing. Paul anointed Sosthenes' head with oil, and it mixed with the blood and ran down the side of his face to stain the bedcover.

Luke cried out, "Look at his hands! His hands!"

The swelling in Sosthenes' hands was receding, revealing perfectly formed knuckles, joints, and bones. They watched as his eyes began to appear from behind swollen flesh and the broken sockets reformed. His nose bled no more but remained somewhat flattened. The cuts on his head, face and lips closed before their eyes, but left behind many scars.

"Here, Luke, I saved his teeth from the Forum pavement. I washed them off." Paul handed them to Luke. Many were just pieces and chips of teeth. "Luke, you know how they go. I do not. Sosthenes will need them to eat. Put them back in." Sosthenes looked at Luke and nodded vigorously.

Luke looked at the teeth in his hand and said, "Just like that?"

"Yes, just like that! Have you been observing what has happened? With God, all things are possible. Go!"

They got Sosthenes propped up so that Luke could work. Luke looked at his mouth and then looked at the teeth in his hand. "Oh, yes, this one looks like it goes here ..." Luke placed the piece of a tooth that matched a broken stump and then exclaimed, "It stayed!" He looked again and said, "It mended!"

Paul asked, "What did you expect, Luke, that it would fall out? Trust the Spirit, Luke! The Spirit will be strong in you!"

Like someone fitting together and gluing broken pot sherds, Luke began placing the teeth, and the Lord mended them all. Luke was saying, "Praise the *Lord*" with each restored piece of tooth. As the last one went in perfectly, he shouted, "Hallelujah, the Lord fixed them all!"

"Praise the Lord! Hallelujah!" Everyone clapped and cheered in the house, and Paul could hear rejoicing from outside.

They helped Sosthenes sit up on the side of the bed, although he really needed no help. He looked at his hands and made a fist and then extended his fingers out and looked at both sides of his hands. He felt his teeth and ran his tongue over the smooth surface of the enamel. Then, he looked up to the heavens and began shouting, "Thank you, *Jesus*! Thank you, *Jesus*! Thank you, *Jesus*!" Then he looked around at the church and began talking. Some say that he never stopped talking until the day of his death.

"Thank you, all," Sosthenes was just beginning to realize who was standing around him. "I am sorry that I have harmed you! Please forgive me!" Tears were running down his cheeks, "Everything that has happened is my fault!"

"We forgive you, Brother," answered Paul, "and Jesus forgives you also. He only asks that you forgive those who have harmed you."

"I think that I saw Him!" Sosthenes looked up at Paul, "When they began hitting me on the head, the stars flew, and I could see nothing! But I seemed to come out of my body and hover above it. Then, I could see *everything*! I saw those who I thought were my friends beating me with rods. Horrible! But I saw you, Paul, run up and tell them I was not dead. I heard the arguing over my body. I saw the ones who I thought were my enemies gently lifting me up in my own mantle. And I saw ... a man ... a *shining man*! His clothing was bright and radiant, whiter than anything I have ever seen! I could not see

His face. It was like trying to get a glimpse of the noonday sun! He helped you lift me up. Paul, did you see Him? Could that have been Jesus?"

"I do not know, Brother Sosthenes," Paul replied. "I did not see anyone besides the people of the church."

"I think it was Jesus," Sosthenes said with a far-off look. "He walked beside you, Paul, as you were praying and leading us here. After we had gone a short distance, the Shining Man turned and looked at me. The light of his face made everything go white, and I, sort of, fell back into my body. I knew nothing more until I heard your voice, Paul." He grasped Paul's hand, "Do you believe me?"

"I do believe you, brother," said Paul, "but, I believe God even more! I believe that He has forgiven your sins by the blood shed on the cross by Jesus, His Son. Do you believe that, Brother?"

"Yes, I do believe," Sosthenes was nodding his head, "I believe!"

"Do you believe that Jesus was raised from the dead, and that He sits by the right hand of the Throne of God?"

"Yes, yes!"

"Then it remains for you to receive the Holy Spirt and be baptized."

Sosthenes rose to his feet. "Yes! Now! At once!"

Paul gathered the church around Sosthenes once more, and once more, they laid hands on him. Paul anointed Sosthenes with oil, this time for receiving the Holy Spirit. There were many different reactions of people when they received the baptism of the Holy Spirit. Some were noisy, some were quiet, some had a great emotional rush, some were calm, sensing a great peace. Some spoke with languages they did not know, but all were cleansed by a wave of divine love that transformed their minds forever. Sosthenes was a one-man celebration. He danced, shouted, and sang songs of praise and thanksgiving to God. Paul finally had to bring him back to earth.

"Brother Crispus is going to baptize you!" Paul had his hands on Sosthenes' shoulders.

"He would do that for me?"

"Of course, he will. You are brothers now!"

Sosthenes became Paul's disciple and constant companion. The only one who stayed closer to Paul was Castor who insisted on remaining a servant to Paul. When Sosthenes later learned that Mother Lilia had touched him, and prayed for him, all he said was, "Hallelujah!"

Sosthenes would recount his conversion many times over in his life. He would get the most excited when he would say, "I could not see anything. But I heard my name *shouted* to the heavens as the saints were pleading for me, the chief of sinners!"

Paul would always say that the Lord healed him of all his wounds but left behind the scars to remind him of the One who healed him. "Besides," he would tell Sosthenes, "We were both ugly *before* we got all scarred up!" Together, they would laugh much in the coming years.

"We Pharisees become great followers of Jesus Christ," said Paul, "once the legalism and pride are beat out of us!"

Later that evening, Paul and Luke were discussing the events of the day. Luke said, "Do you think that he really saw Jesus, or was it just an illusion of a 'shining man'? Why did we not see?"

"I do not really know," Paul answered, "but I know what Jesus said to me when I asked Him why He blinded me on the Damascus Road. The Lord said, 'Because you believed that you could see, you had to be blinded so that you could see.' Luke, I was just like Sosthenes. I was a proud, third-generation Pharisee. My arrogance was unbounded, thinking that I knew the Scriptures, believing that I was perfect in the Law, favored of God because of my own righteousness, justifying murder because I was killing the enemies of God. Sosthenes' life mirrored my own. But when I was blinded, I began to see. When I was deafened by the voice from Heaven, I began to hear the voice of the Son of God. Then, I could see my awful depravity and the depth of my hypocrisy. I could then hear of Jesus' love and how much I was to suffer for His sake. With the first light that came to my eyes, I saw a servant of the Lord, Ananias of Damascus, laying hands on me, and calling me his brother. I then could see love.

"Some people say they admire me for all that I have given up to follow Jesus. Luke, I have given up *nothing*! I consider my former life without Christ to be garbage, filth, in comparison to knowing Christ and being found in Him, not having a righteousness of my own, but having the righteousness of God that comes though His grace in Christ Jesus."

"Well, I can see that the way is clear for us in Corinth." Luke paused for a moment, looking out of the western side of Aquila's home at a glorious sunset. "All of the enemies of Jesus have been defeated, or at least made of no effect."

"The greater challenge lies ahead." Paul looked out at the same view. "The church is more vulnerable to apathy, sin, and loveless actions between brothers than from its enemies. The saints are still people, needing to die daily to their own will."

"Amen."

"But, they are my joy and crown, Luke. The seal of my Apostleship. I love the saints with every part of my heart and soul." Paul stared out over Corinth, the wickedest city in the world, that some thought had no redemption. "God has blessed you, Corinth, with the gospel of salvation and peace. Amen."

Paul stayed in Corinth many more months. But after a year and half, Paul began feeling the need to move on to preach the gospel in areas where no Apostle had been. His itching feet won out over the comfortable life style that he enjoyed in Corinth. He took Timothy and Silas, Luke, Aquila and Priscilla, Castor, Sosthenes, and several others to Ephesus. There, Paul introduced them all to John the Apostle. He was living there secretly and quietly, protecting the Lord's mother, Mary. Luke was able to talk to her about the circumstances surrounding the birth of the Lord. Even though she was aged, she was very alert and animated. Mary would die before Paul and his group eventually got back to Ephesus later the next year. After consulting with John and paying his respects to Mary, Paul set sail for Caesarea, leaving Aquila and Priscilla in Ephesus to assist John. He took the group to Jerusalem and then up to Antioch to report to the church.

When Paul returned to Ephesus, a letter was awaiting him from Chloe informing him of many problems that had developed in the congregation at Corinth. Following his custom, Paul taught while he dictated a letter to the New Church in Corinth. Gathering the group together, Paul began his letter,

> *Paul, through the will of God a called Apostle, and the Brother Sosthenes, to the Church of God which is in Corinth, to the ones having been sanctified in Christ Jesus, called saints, with all the ones who are calling on the name of the Lord Jesus in every place, theirs and ours, grace to you and peace from God our Father and the Lord Jesus Christ.*

1 Corinthians 1:1-3

THE END

ABOUT THE AUTHOR

George Cargill is a fourth-generation pastor, preacher, church history teacher, and Bible instructor. He pastored at churches in Missouri, Iowa, and Oklahoma before retiring. During his career, he developed a great curiosity about the history and culture of Israel, the apostolic church and the first century Roman Empire in general. George's reading, research, and quest for answers, led to his first book, In the Grip of God. George found his author's voice after retiring from pastoring. He was born in Oklahoma, but put his roots down in Missouri near St Louis where he lives with Jo, his wife of fifty years. In 2011, he founded Following the Book Ministries, a non-profit international ministry for advancing biblical knowledge and the redeeming message of Jesus Christ.

BIBLIOGRAPHY

- Aland, Barbara, Kurt Aland, Johannes Karavidopoulos, Carlo M. Martini, Bruce M. Metzger, ed. *Greek New Testament* Reading, UK: United Bible Societies, 1975. WORD*search* CROSS e-book.

- Brenton, Sir Lancelot C. L. *The Septuagint with Apocrypha: Greek and English* London, UK: Samuel Bagster and Sons, Ltd., 1851

- Mounce, William D. *The Analytical Lexicon to the Greek New Testament* Grand Rapids, MI: Zondervan 1993.

- von Tischendorf, Constantin. *Tischendorf Interlinear Bible – Tischendorf Interlinear New Testament* Austin, TX: WORD*search* Corp., 2009. WORD*search* CROSS e-book.

49355692R00181

Made in the USA
Columbia, SC
20 January 2019